Paper Paulie

By

L.R. Claude

Paper Paulie

Paper Paulie

There is no weakness in seeking

Mental health help, in fact,

There is strength in obtaining it

For it betters you for the life

Ahead.

To the memory of a dear neighbor, compatriot, teacher,
and friend:

Bill Connor

01/03/25-06/15/16

Paper Paulie

Paper Paulie

4

Table of Contents

Paper Paulie

Paper Paulie

"Folks, we all know why we are all gathered her today, if everyone will have a seat I have a few things to say before we begin" a preacher that resembles Glynn Turman with a raspy solemn voice begins to speak over the group of people muttering in hush tones from his podium. "There is a tale that must be told because many of you don't know the whole story;I have to tell you about Paulie. There may not be many of you that know about Paulie and the few of you I have talked to have expressed your love so I will start from the beginning and tell all of you the harrowing journey that is his life story. Through three wars, through mud, rain, fire, gunfights, births and death, Paulie stood the time and today; he is still with us (the preacher leans back on his heels and shrugs his robe to better straighten out the shoulders as he takes in a deep breath).

Sometimes it's hard to see the big picture until you are far enough away that a picture actually develops before your eyes. Some pictures are so big you may not live long enough to see it while others you can't see until you have enough pieces, like a puzzle made out of life. I found the puzzle hidden before my eyes and I will help to reveal it to you if you'll bear with me. This puzzle has pieces that are over forty years old, this puzzle has pieces that have been around the world and this puzzle is one of the most touching and beautiful pictures that I have been witness to in my time. Sometimes the puzzle that someone is waiting on doesn't really make sense until a whole other puzzle finishes and then that puzzle might even begin, but enough about puzzles.

Our lives are what we make them to be, there are huge debates to each and every day and nobody really knows, is there a fate, does god exist, are things random or is there some little thread in the cosmos that if you bat at it like a kitten then maybe the wonders will be shown to you, we'll never know until long after our lives are gone so we should live, laugh, and love each and every day and embrace the wonderment around us, especially one another. Let us cast aside the shames, the guilts and the urges to turn away from being neighborly or caring, we all need someone to support us and accept us for who we are, who we are today, right now and right here on earth, worry about tomorrow tomorrow and live for today.

Let us begin.

In 1950 when Pee Wee Reese was still playing shortstop for the Dodgers; when they were still in Brooklyn I remind you, Ronetta and Eddie Venney were bringing their second son Isaiah into this world. Isaiah was an energetic baby that cooed and giggled at anyone that looked his way. Isaiah grew up with his father Eddie listening to Jackie Robinson on the crackling radio and he even recalls when the Dodgers took the Yanks in the fifty-five series, well he remembers his pa hooting and hollering while jumping around in the living room while Ronetta got on him about waking the babies(maybe not so much the game itself but the fuss) and he knew that he had love in his family.

Isaiah was familiar with the close streets like Flatbush and Kings and even though his parents warned him, he still ventured with his pals to watch some of the shiny new cars strolling the wider boulevards when he was coming up. Brooklyn was in a tough time, the later fifties gave way to harsh times like the Dodgers running away, jobs closing up and even when the dockyards began to dry up, the family remained strong together. Isaiah was unsure of the world around him in his youth, the area he grew up in reflected him and his family but traveling farther out of the neighborhood he learned that much of the world judged you based on the color of your skin and not much else.

Isaiah fought to remain a fair kid, his family worked hard and with three other brothers he also knew what it took to fight for what was yours. Near the end of the sixties many local neighborhoods had completely changed demographically and the streets grew tougher to grow up on. Playing stick-ball in the streets was much less safe than it was a few years prior and with turmoil in the world the news continued to broadcast both funerals and body counts of soldiers, but also some of the protesting going on about the war. Eddie educated his sons in the world, he had four boys to raise up to be good men and even though it was tough working long days and spending many tired hours riding to and from work on the train, he had pride in himself that he could provide for his family, like any good man would.

The first time Isaiah heard the n-word he was eight years old and had accompanied his father to his work in the dockyard to pick up his salary check a day before the summer holiday. Isaiah didn't understand why a man would shout a word and at first he thought it might have been someone's name, as strange as it was it might have been, but it wasn't. Eddie didn't even turn his head when the slanderous word rang out, he didn't respond and especially didn't cater to the idea that he fit into the category so he just kept walking while holding his second sons' hand. Looking back Isaiah was astounded that some men were so brazen to holler such things aloud; the problem is is that ignorance seems to have a higher podium to be preached from and it certainly has a higher following if anything.

"Just cause someone calls you a name son it doesn't mean that you have to prove them right" Eddie told Isaiah on the return trip home after there were many questions about the close conflict on the work grounds. Isaiah understood that names and labels were what others

saw you as, not necessarily what you should be or what you had in your heart. Eddie explained that *N* word was a term that to him meant dumb, ignorant, uneducated, lazy, and described someone who didn't commit to their community; none of which applied to him so he didn't pay it any attention. Isaiah was still bothered that a stranger would holler such a word to his father and he didn't like it, in fact he lost sleep over the ordeal over the next few days.

War broke out for good in Vietnam and the news was nonstop broadcasting political debates, tension, and movements that were popping up around the country and it was all overwhelming to follow. Isaiah tried to get good jobs around the area but many of the good paying manufacturing jobs packed up and were headed to nicer towns that paid lower wages and all that seemed to be left were mediocre jobs that you couldn't start a family with. Isaiah wanted to be able to help his parents and at the same time he also wanted to set himself up with a good job to buy himself a house one day and have a family. Isaiah's older brother Clarence moved to a bigger city in New York to work at a mill while his younger two brothers Ronnie and Saul scattered around for small jobs like slinging newspapers or stocking sodas.

Isaiah enlisted into the United States Army (a big **Hooah** bellows out from the crowd) even though Eddie and Ronetta were concerned against it for their son. Isaiah Dante Venny enlisted to the infantry and after his initial training in boot camp he boarded a large plane and was headed to a fight in a jungle that is still a hot topic among thousands today. Isaiah was full of young angst when he boarded his plane, he said his goodbyes to his brothers and his parents and with plenty of tears being shed at the airport, he and dozens of other soldiers were headed far from home.

It was 1968 when Isaiah had first stepped foot onto foreign soil. The flight was long and broken up but among all of the fresh green soldiers there was plenty of speculation about what to expect. Each solider that Isaiah ran into had come from somewhere new, Detroit Michigan, Sarasota Florida, St. Paul Minnesota, Ribbitsville Washington and many places he had never heard of. The long flight put the size of the world into better perspective for Isaiah, he realized that the speed he was flying and the distance he was traveling meant that his big neighborhood back home was "smaller that an ant's eyelash" (friendly laughter erupts) when it came to its' relativity to the world.

The first steps Isaiah took down onto a land that he had never heard of until the Army was shipping him there, was new, there were men covering the entire black top and officers shouting orders in many directions. Isaiah followed his directions and joined up with his platoon and spent the first few hours acclimating to the new world around him, receiving instructions and getting breakdowns as to what was expected from him. Vietnam was a brutal change compared to anything Isaiah had ever known, the mass amounts of men his age, the pushing elbows between races and the sheer volume of soldiers was all new and an eye opener to the world outside of the tall Brooklyn buildings back home, there was also more foliage than all of the city parks he'd ever seen put together.

Most of Isaiah's first days were filled with stockpiling supply sheds and getting to know where everything was located, as general infantry they were in charge of filling trucks with supplies to go and refill the forward lines until the next platoon arrived from the States and then it was their turn to move forward in engaging with the enemy deep in the thick. Isaiah's platoon was a mix of men, some ready for action while others skeptical and full of dread over what they'd heard about their enemy.

The Vietcong were a vast group of soldiers that had adapted to the thick jungles and harsh terrain all while having dug deep networks of tunnels beneath the jungle floor in order to pop up behind the US soldiers, it was an unfair advantage and Isaiah was nervous about it. Commotion around the base was nonstop, even in the dark hours helicopters were dropping off and picking up around the clock and nobody seemed to walk, everyone was in a jog or hurried pace anywhere they had to go. Convoys moved all about, trucks loaded with men or supplies all day and all night, it was scary that the war was so involved and it was unlike anything Isaiah had ever imagined in his life.

"Mail call" interrupted the last morning meal before Isaiah and his platoon were to load up onto a personnel carrier and drive north for the entire day to begin their fighting. Isaiah wrote to his family, especially his mother Ronetta who he knew worried terribly for him so he made sure he had all of his outgoing letters ready to deliver and stood in line to hand them off to the mail carrier. There were nearly two-dozen fellow soldiers standing in front of Isaiah, everyone was hurrying to pack their bags and clear their racks before heading out for who knows how long to fight in the jungle and many men were mailing handfuls of letters not knowing if it would be their last. Isaiah waited his turn and watched as one man in his green fatigues pulled a brown cardboard box out from under a table.

One mail carrier was calling out men by their last names that received mail, they had only been in the camp a week so incoming mail was still being held or in transit so there were only a few men that received letters from back home and each one smiled or clapped their hands when they frantically ripped open letters or small care package boxes from loved ones. Isaiah knew that he wouldn't have a letter from home for some time still and he could have surely used some comforting words being so far from home. The man standing next to the cardboard box was handing out envelopes to men who didn't receive any other letters from home, it was peculiar but anyone dropping off letters to the carrier was being handed one envelope from a box marked:

Paper Paulie

Ch.2

Soldiers

A-Company

Vietnam

Isaiah reached out and took his letter and inspected it, the outside was simply addressed to "*Soldier*" written nearly illegibly in a child's handwriting. Isaiah folded the letter in half and shoved it crudely into his cargo pocket until later so he could return to clearing his bunk, A-Company was supposed to clear out for the next incoming platoon for the one week infiltration before being shipped around the country to support their fellow soldiers in the fight and time was waning. The bunk area was a mess of men shoving clothes into their big green duffle bags and hurrying about to check off that they turned in their bedrolls. Isaiah bumped into plenty of other soldiers as did most, there was very little time because their bus north was due to leave just minutes after mail call and everyone was in a huff.

Isaiah bounced and jostled in the back of a loaded bus cram packed with soldiers all holding their duffle bags and headed to an unknown destination. The ride was long and dreary in the hot humid weather of the jungle; each man had heavy eyes and drenched sweaty green shirts as the bus driver made sharp turns down long overgrown roads. The scenery to the sides at first was of a long brown river, vast rice fields with small dots of people walking around and military trucks here and there. The longer drive grew more scenic, more trees in the distance and large leaves slapped against the windshield as they navigated deeper and deeper into the thick brush. Isaiah was worried about where they were going, each face he saw as he looked around was heavy with tired weariness from the ride but each soldier knew that they had their gun on their back and a pack on their lap, the rest was unknown.

The sun wore down as the bus neared their destination, the anxiety began to climb as they rode in past mounds of sandbags piled high against the road and fellow soldiers standing guard with stern looks and a large machine mounted weapon to defend their forward base they nicknamed "Chicago". Isaiah was filled with worry, against the fading afternoon sky large fireballs zipped across like shooting stars and with all of his heart he wanted to wish himself back home with his brothers, but those weren't stars overhead, they were rockets will ill intentions and no matter what; he wasn't wishing himself anywhere. The constant snapping of gunfire in the distance was met with the booms of rockets being fired into the farther distance and it hit Isaiah like a truck, his knees felt weak, his stomach began to lurch and his head began to feel heavy.

Isaiah struggled to haul his pack to the designated tent that was set up for incoming soldiers and it was all blurring together into a haze of fading daylight and illuminated spot lights. There were small pit fires around the area that men had different foods cooking at, either on stick or pit there were different foods being cooked all around, the smell of smoke from fires was also mixing with a burning smell coming from near the base, either the explosions or rocket fire wafted smoke across the high walls and into the noses of everyone within. The smells all mixed together, there was the hot chemical smell, the smoldering brush, the charring meats and the burning material that was mixed with the latrines to sanitize them all, after a week you become nose blind but the first few days are dizzying and painful, and his stomach began to churn.

The bunks in the large dark green tents were barely lit with a few measly flickering light bulbs and all that mattered was that there was a dry flat surface to lie down on that wasn't on the muddy ground. Most of the soldiers on the bus hurried to toss their gear onto a bed and then run out for chow, the long ride on the bus was hot, dreadful, filled with the smell of stank body odor and without much more than a few chew bars for food, the idea of a hot meal was tempting but Isaiah found a bunk that had minimal mud on it and he laid out. The smells of chopper fumes and gunpowder smoke resonated in his head; even breathing through his mouth left a taste on his tongue and caused his belly to remain a little tight.A lot had happened, he had traveled a long way in a short time and it was all catching up to him in flashbacks that were progressing in speed and making his head spin as he struggled to keep his boot from flopping sideways off his cot.

The sounds of men running and hustling all around droned together as Isaiah felt his eyelids fall close.Everything was dark until sometime in the night,remembering that he was in war Isaiah jumped from his bed and nearly hit his head as he rushed to pull his jacket on and grab his gun to go in his panic. Isaiah wasn't sure where he was going but his feet nearly carried him to the door flap of the tent before he realized it was still dark out in the sky. Isaiah held onto the door for a moment of bodily swaying as he paused, trying to decide if he was going to faint or go and get something to eat. Isaiah was completely wet from sweating; his shirt reminded him of a time Eddie took him and Clarence to the docks where he worked in order to jump into the water for some midday splashing in the heat. Back then they weren't allowed in many of the pools and he didn't really understand why but Eddie was good at hiding the ugliness of people from his young sons.

"The world can be full of ugliness if you let yourself see it" Eddie once told his sons. Isaiah didn't really understand but he came to when he began to hear what people had to say to him based solely on his exterior without getting to know his interior. Eddie worked hard, he took the time to pick up random garbage on the streets as he walked because he liked having a clean community to raise his sons into and he had pride in a good days work. Isaiah admired his father for having a strong work ethic, when he was coming up there were always men trying to hustle for money or spending their days on a stoop smoking or gambling with dice, he never understood why they did that when his father worked so much but he figured it out later on;*sheer laziness.*

The lights were scant overnight in *Chicago* where they rallied to refuel trucks and restock soldiers. Isaiah leaned forward on his last sway and rather than fight it he followed his momentum out towards the small pit fires in hopes of finding a burger or hot-dog cooking. Even in the dark hours there were still men hustling and running around, some men were jogging for fitness while others scurried about checking on different piles of incoming or outgoing boxes or supplies. After stumbling for a few minutes through some of the grounds of Chicago Isaiah found a small group of guys sitting around a small pit fire with something roasting on it, the area smelled of chemicals and burning rubber but underneath it all there was a hint of grilling meat and it made Isaiah hungry.

"Whatcha all got cooking" Isaiah made a half attempt to introduce himself when one man slapped a small folding chair, "sit" he suggested.Isaiah fiddled with a small chair for a moment trying to get it on even enough ground to not tip him into the fire before he got a hunk of food into his mouth. "I'm Venney, from Brooklyn, what about you guys, been here long?" Isaiah began to try and converse but another man poking the fire with a long stick piped up; "it doesn't matter, we're body bag fillers here, just bodies to shoot at Vietcong until one gets us then we get to go home." The man was dreary sounding, in the darkness of the night Isaiah felt alone in the world.

One man swung a long metal pipe with hunks of meat skewered onto it towards Isaiah; "pull your knife and cut you a bit, that's about as five-star as you'll get Brooklyn" the man instructed. Isaiah cut off a healthy wad of meat and tried to smell it, he couldn't place the scent as he tried to blow on it enough to keep from burning his mouth as he ripped pieces off like an animal just to put food in his stomach. "Two rules Brooklyn; keep eating so you don't die with an empty stomach cause there wouldn't be any worse way to go and don't get nobody kilt" the man began sharing his war worthy advice with the new fresh soldier. "If you get a man killed and you survive you have to live with that, plus if you get a man killed then he might not be there to protect someone else so then you got more than that man killed," it made plenty of sense to Isaiah, sort of.

A handful of men sat around and chewed on wads of charred meat near the fire, the air was warm and humid sitting around the fire but sitting close was comforting and was even hot enough to dry Isaiah's shirt by the end of his jungle meal. "What am I eating, anybody know?"

Isaiah wasn't complaining but half way through it was cool enough to actually taste and it wasn't familiar. "I ain't never had it before is all but I'm thankful for the bite." One man muttered "zebra" while another man cleared his throat and replied; "don't know, someone shot something outside in the woods and put it on the spit yesterday, it ain't human so who cares, keep food in your belly remember?" Isaiah thought about the texture and size of the meat and nodded that he was ready for a smaller second bit to top himself off with before returning to his rack for some more sleep.

Early the next morning Isaiah was woken up to someone hollering, it was his new platoon leader "Ruckus" and he was gathering his new crew to go out and storm into the jungle for a few days until he found the enemy base he was out to take down. Isaiah felt ill about his mission after Ruckus shouted out what his mission was so he sat down quickly and scribbled out a last goodbye letter to his family. One man with the last name "Yoot" stenciled on his shirt nearly climbed down onto Isaiah as he was scribbling; "sorry pal, hurry up or you'll miss the war" he said in passing. Yoot was a light skinned guy with skinny shoulders and a long torso; he was excited to go where he was going, except he didn't really seem know where that was. Kerch was a white guy that leaned over as Isaiah was lick sealing his envelope and handed him a stamp without saying a word before returning to shove more clothes into his field pack.

Paper Paulie

Everyone was gearing up for a long walk out into the jungle, many knew that some men never returned but nobody ever talked about it, the truth hung heavier than the moisture in the air, they just did what they were instructed and prayed to whoever they believed in that they would return. There were too many men scrambling in the large tent to keep track of who all of them were, some were familiar faces from the bus others spilled in from another bus and joined in later with everything going on in *Chicago*. The tent was like a beehive that someone had kicked around; everyone was stirred up and buzzing about and until Ruckus left through the flap while still shouting, nobody even knew it was still dark outside until many of them spilled on out through the door flap.

Everyone loaded up their gear and extra magazine pouches; it was due to be a long walk into the dark forest and into the unknown. Isaiah couldn't keep his mind from returning to back home, he wondered what his brother's might have been up to, perhaps still looking for good jobs or his father going back to the Docks that were slowly closing up because bigger boats needed deeper water ways. It was chaos trying to make sure you had all of your assigned gear as well as extra of things you might need, along with thirty other soldiers. None of the soldiers Isaiah was heading out with had ever been in combat, they were all as green as their uniforms and aligning to march out into the war.

Isaiah stood in a row of three; he was towards the back so it was hard to hear when Ruckus gave orders so he just followed when his platoon began to walk. Isaiah thought he was supposed to march and was parade ready when men began to lightly jog to head out passed the safety of the metal gates that faced north. Ten yards out of the big clanging metal gates riddled with divots from bullets trying to penetrate the thick metal were rows of sandbags that were meant to add reinforcements against barraging shells from the far distance. The ground was still pitch black but it was beginning to lighten up in the eastern sky above as the men shuffled along.

In the breaks of all the men chattering and talking to one another the sounds of retching and vomiting could be heard ahead, there was no way to know if you stepped in it unless you felt your boots slip in the wet ground or the person in front of you kicked some up and you got a strong whiff of stomach acid in the air; battle made many men queasy. The men scurried along a worn dirt path that headed north towards a river that kept their base separated from a dense patch of enemy filled jungle to the northeast. Isaiah felt uneasy as he trudged further and further into enemy territory, he followed his fellow soldiers and tried to keep watch for the small spark that came when someone was shooting at you, that was about all the knowledge he had in the world at that point. Some men seemed to sleep as they walked, some would start to veer until you gave them a guiding hand back into formation while others just wobbled on the soft dirt below their boots.

Ruckus hollered in the base that there was enemy spotted during the night and that that was who they were going to engage with to keep them from killing innocent soldiers at the Chicago base. The men gripped their guns and ran towards an enemy that they didn't know existed. Ruckus waved his hand over top as the men went along, he wanted some of the front running men to spread out to the sides and protect their route back to the base and twenty men still charged towards the river. As the sun rose to expose the men to the morning land around them the first sure sign that they were at war sounded off, a rocket blew up on the bank of the river sending mud into the air and the soldiers to the ground. Ruckus crouched down while everyone else took up their guns and began popping of rounds into a patch of trees at the base of a hill from lying positions.

Ruckus waved his hands for a ceasefire and turned to shout more orders. Ruckus knew that the trajectory of the rocket was from pretty far away and it was a waste of ammo shooting towards the enemy line without being able to see your target, there could also have been American soldiers in between and "we'd sure hate to help the enemy here folks" he explained. Isaiah and two other men were ordered to spread along the bank and take up safe positions that could keep watch over to the other side while trying to spot the origin of another rocket if one fired while he took fifteen men and swam across to the other side to try to engage the enemy closer to their own territory.

Isaiah did as he was told and slid along the river bank for about thirty yards and sunk down in a small muddy crater that had been left days before from another such explosive round. As Isaiah got comfortable in his small sunken in spot in the hard dirt he slowly eased some of the nearby foliage over top of him to keep any of his shiny metal from reflecting off the rising sun above him and giving him away under enemy fire. As Isaiah slid back onto his rear in the small crater another explosion alerted him to a problem. From the northeast there was another explosion and it rattled him to his bones. Isaiah took up his gun and panned around looking across the river for a source of the firefight coming towards him.

Looking down the water a little Isaiah could count sixteen boonie hat covered heads bobbing along in the water, treading to get to the other side. Isaiah couched real low to do as he was taught in training and to aim over the sight rail of his firearm and cover his mates crossing the river. As Ruckus lead his men towards the far bank a long patch of grass began to move a few yards in front of them, the tall grass wriggled side to side and then it began to fall backwards away from the water's edge as enemy fighters sprung upwards to begin shooting at the men in the water. The three other men that bunkered down on the river's edge on the same side of Isaiah began to open fire, slowly picking off men that stood to fire into the water as the water sprayed upwards from bullet fire.

Isaiah froze for a moment as he couldn't believe his eyes for the two to three seconds it took for everything to erupt. Isaiah had a clear view from deep under his brush as he watched his riverbank defenders jump to action and begin rattling off bullets into the enemies that were shooting at the men trying to swim across and from the same side of the river bank, six Vietnamese soldiers popped up from the ground like springs and began firing on the riverbank defenders. Isaiah watched as his fellow soldier's sprayed blood into the air as bullets slowly tore apart their bodies and sent them shaking in ricochet with each shot. The ground sent lumps of grass and dirt into the air to meet the falling soldiers and then training kicked in.

Isaiah was frightened and in his moment of hesitation he watched as a second wave of enemy soldiers sprung up from the near bank to riddle his pals with deadly shots. Isaiah snapped and unknown to the men that were firing on the American soldiers, he began to fire back. Alone and outnumbers all Isaiah thought about was squeezing his trigger as fast as he could and hoping that with the random swiveling of his rifle barrel that he hit enough of his targets to make it back to Chicago alive. Each small flash of fire that erupted from the barrel of his rifle made him more and more angry and from a hunkered down position in a small dent in the ground bullets began to rip up the ground right near his body.

It was six on the far shore that were killing his platoon leader Ruckus and the fifteen men that followed him into the river and nearly as many that ambushed the men defending the river bank. The three men lay dead on the ground, their olive drab uniforms soaked in blood, the five enemy soldiers that jumped to kill the defenders were slumped over one another and there was Isaiah; afraid and alone and already half buried. Isaiah waited a moment after pulling the trigger a few times without the muzzle flash, it didn't register that his magazine was empty so he just sat there and shook for a moment still trying to shoot.

A moment later Isaiah felt the sprinkle of falling dirt land on his face and as reality came back to the scared man from Brooklyn, it didn't make sense, how did half of his platoon nearly crawl over top of the Vietcong crouched along the river bank until most of the men were sitting ducks in the water. Isaiah wasn't sure how many men he shot but he knew he was the one pulling the trigger as the men made agonizing faces while falling to the ground dead. Another moment of raining dirt alerted Isaiah that some of the men on the other side of the bank were in fact still shooting at him so he rolled slowly to stay mostly hidden to see where the bullets were coming from and he reached for another magazine to reload.

Reaching down into his cargo pocket to grab another ammo magazine Isaiah clenched down onto a piece of paper in his pocket that shouldn't have been there, the letter he received at mail call. "I'll live long enough to read it" Isaiah promised himself as he pulled a magazine from his pouch and reloaded his rifle. Isaiah took aim and opened fire to the few enemy men still standing across the riverbank, they were pointing into the water at Ruckus and the rest of the men they killed that were floating in the shallow shore nearest to them when Isaiah took their lives.

Isaiah waited till almost midday before removing the brush that covered over him in the wet hole in the ground, he kept his ears tuned and eyes wide open to any sight or sound that might be near him. With cramped legs and numb arms Isaiah waited until the sun was high overhead before he eased himself back out onto the riverbank. The bodies of his fellow bank defenders were slunk down and already attracting flies as they warmed in the day's sun and humidity. The sight was terrible, over a dozen soldiers floating and bobbing in the water and half a dozen men shot and killed right on the riverbank just feet from where Isaiah lucked into a bit of a crater that sheltered him from enemy fire.

Isaiah stockpiled all the ammo he could and made sure that the enemies were all face up and free from booby traps as well as dead. Isaiah checked all of his men that he could without much movement, hoping to come across someone he could save, but there wasn't. Handling the dead bodies was scary, at any moment Isaiah felt that the eyes would pop open and then he would have to fight hand to hand for his life and it was very creepy all alone out in the exposed area of the jungle. Isaiah dragged up the American soldiers that hadn't floated down stream and out of reach. With each face Isaiah uncovered the images flashed through his mind of having seen that man earlier in the morning, some of them were at mail call while others just moved about in the tent gearing up for their excursion, their last moments of life before being extinguished right in front of him.

It was heart wrenching that just hours ago these young men were alive and healthy and fresh to Vietnam and now just moments later they were dead and just lying on the ground in a foreign country. Isaiah wondered if each man had someone back home, a wife, kids, parents or best friends, it was a loss to look at each man and wonder what his short life was like. Would the news stations report the deaths as numbers or actually report on each man that gave his life? Perhaps each town each fallen man was from would hold an honorary memorial for their own town resident that fell in a conflict that they never should have been at.

The bodies were limp, they were much heavier than you'd expect a grown man to weigh and they were just like rag-dolls. Isaiah just waited for any moment that one of the men would gasp for breath or for an arm to twitch but as he slowly dragged each man into a position to be recovered by their fellow soldiers there was nothing but silence as he worked from a belly crawl. Isaiah felt that white envelope crunch in his cargo pocket as he crawled, he worried for a moment that somebody might hear the paper crinkle as he tried to be stealthy and quiet while he worked and he told himself that if he made it back to Chicago, he'd read the letter with the child's handwriting on it and then he kept working.

Arranging the bodies of the deceased Vietcong was a different experience; it was hard to tell what the much smaller men had done in their lives. One man had more gray hair than black hair, a man of his age surely wasn't a soldier but maybe was threatened into fighting or even scared into fighting by the propaganda that we were at war to rape their women or something. Isaiah tried to be respectful to the bodies of the fallen soldiers as he laid them out all side to side, the Vietnamese in one group and the Americans in another, all while belly crawling to make sure he didn't get shot while trying to honor his fallen brothers. Isaiah felt the tinge of hatred in his heart, he hated the men he didn't know for trying to kill him, for killing his fellow soldiers and for an instance, for merely being Vietnamese, Eddie's words came back to Isaiah about judging someone based solely on what you can see, and he cared for those deceased as well.

Ruckus gave the orders to march towards the river, he also gave orders to stay at the riverbank and defend it against any enemies but then everyone was killed except a few soldiers that were left to cover the return route to the base nicknamed Chicago, and then there was Isaiah. With half a day gone and no idea what the original mark was supposed to be for the men that walked out into the thick foliage Isaiah decided to work his way back to the men guarding the road in hopes that someone would know what to do next. Isaiah was cutoff and unsure of what he was supposed to do so in order to stay hidden enough he crawled alongside the road to get back to the forward base Chicago.

Along the crawl Isaiah took painfully slow sweeps with his arms to reach out and then pull himself closer and closer to his base, it was a few hours' walk in the morning so it was probably even longer crawling but he wanted to stay low and keep from getting shot. Along the crawl Isaiah found a long sliver of wire that shouldn't have been where it was, not far from the riverbank he discovered a trip wire. With a snip of the wire Isaiah could have disabled the booby trap but the problem at hand was that there was still a live explosive waiting for some other platoon to walk passed and he couldn't just let it sit in wait. Isaiah crawled to follow the wire to discover it was linked to more than one grenade, this was an intricate trap.

Had the platoon spread out wider than the road the booby trap would have tripped and triggered in a V-patter than would have inflicted serious injuries to a maximum amount of soldiers so it had to be dismantled. The crude trap had one long wire linked to a spring loaded piece of metal that looked like a mouse trap. Tripping the wire even a little would have set off the coiled metal like spring which would have then set off a total of six explosives that were covered with rocks, which would have shattered and fired towards marching troops leaving the Chicago base.

Isaiah made it half way back to the base when he found the trip wire in the late afternoon, it was scary to find since there were supposed to be mine clearers having gone out before them, it told Isaiah that the trap was set just after the clearers swept through, meaning the enemy was stealthy to be in and out undetected. The enemy was skilled at silently moving about in the dark and it was a danger to all the Americans that fought in the war and now Isaiah was in the heat of the mix also. It was getting late and from what he could tell the men assigned to guard the road had moved along either back to the base or forward to the river after hearing the gunfight, leaving the roadways empty. Isaiah was still worried he would trip in a wire so he eased along more on his knees and elbows while dragging along the few explosives and wire that he took apart, he figured it was safer to keep it with him rather than leave it behind to be reconfigured and deadly.

As it grew dark Isaiah placed the found explosives in a half circle that they would explode outwards with just the tug of the wire, the idea was to guard against an oncoming rush of enemies while he laid down in the grass and tried his best to pretend being dead in order to sleep a little. Isaiah tried to pop his head up a little now and then to look for anybody, the hope was that there were patrols of fellow soldiers that would find him and join him but each time he noticed the help never came. With a crescent shape of explosive charges and his rifle tucked down along his leg Isaiah took some refuge for the night and curled up along a ball of tall grass root that helped to hide him away in the dark.

With rockets still firing overhead occasionally Isaiah knew it was too dangerous to wander around in the dark, he didn't want one of his own men to fire on him thinking he was an enemy rushing the base, he was also terrified to keep laying still in the grass just waiting for any number of things to find him, a snake sensing the body heat, a rat that was finding bodies to eat on, any other wild animal or even worse, an enemy soldier creeping around in the grass too. With the fear of anything near him and the lights zipping overhead all night Isaiah had no ability to sleep, straining to hear any strange sound kept him high on alert and reviewing the entire day's events.

"*Crsshh*" a strange leaf crunching sound came out of nowhere to break the silence. It was hard to tell what the noise was but Isaiah's heart nearly beat out of his chest. With a heart that was beating too loudly to let Isaiah hear the rest of the noises all that he could do while lying in the grass was let his eyes dart around and around while fighting to remain as still as the dead. There was a subtle series of tongue clicks and whisps that seemed to become more and more frequent and moving towards him. Some of the grass crunching sounds were faint, Isaiah convinced himself at first that maybe it was an animal but as slow as the pace was, the sense of sickening dread filled him that he was being approached. With a dry mouth and eyes bulging out of his face trying to recognize anything in the dark Isaiah was on the cusp of jerking his trip wire and hopping up to start shooting and running for his life, but he held it and waited.

Isaiah clenched his weapon that lay along his right leg and the wire to trip his self-defense explosive setup he readied himself for his final moments, and to break the promise that he made to himself to read the envelope when he made it back to the base safely. "*Thdon*" was a sound that came out, someone was near him and if they took one more step they would have stepped right on him in the grass. The strange slight whisper wasn't English and Isaiah had to be certain before he risked killing any of his own men so he slowly began to lift his head. "Thump thump" his heart beat in his ears as he strained his neck muscles to lift his head a little, he had to see what was going on and he decided that if he was going to die it was going to be fighting and not just lying there already pretending to be dead.

Looking just above the black grass line Isaiah could make out nearly ten small framed silhouettes against the light of an overhead rocket tail. Straining to keep from shaking Isaiah tried to look for telltale signs they were American, deeply hoping that he could see the shadow of an ammo belt or canteen or even a helmet but against the dark background all that he could see were short and small framed guys carrying guns that resembled those of the enemy. Isaiah was already pinned to the ground and a ways from any help so he decided to wrap the wire around his finger to make sure that when he yanked it that it was good enough to trigger the small explosives and give him enough time to rise up firing and make it a ways away towards the base.

Isaiah took a deep breath to steady his hands and followed up with another one to ready himself before he convinced himself it was time. As soon as Isaiah convinced himself to jerk the wire running to the few small bombs he set up to guard himself he raised his machine gun and all at once he began pulling. The area close to him lit up when the explosives blew up, some of the men creeping towards him fell with the explosion and in the light Isaiah began snapping off round after round in the direction he remembered seeing an enemy as the explosion lit up the night. Isaiah tried to fire as many rounds as he could before he hurled himself to his knees to stand up and begin running towards Chicago and he held his breath to do it.

Isaiah made it to his feet after his initial defensive run and tried to keep from turning around to fire in order to get away before falling back to the ground to hide again until morning when a large ball of fire rose up from the ground a few yards in front of him. Isaiah watched as the ball of fire shot straight up from the ground to illuminate the ground all around him. Isaiah turned to begin firing on the invading hoard of enemy soldiers when two dozen fellow US soldiers jumped up from the ground and joined him in his firefight. Isaiah fired until his magazine pouch was empty and he began to shout that he was a friendly soldier, luckily he was close enough that some of the guarding fighters could tell he was American rather than an enemy still charging in at them.

Isaiah dropped down flat to fumble a new magazine into his weapon, each time he felt himself no longer shooting he dropped flat to be a hard target against the ground. When the new magazine snapped into place Isaiah pivoted on his belly and rose back up to be sure of his target before returning fire on the approaching enemies in the dark. The adrenaline that fueled Isaiah in the dark was the same that fueled everyone, each whizzing bullet that skimmed past his head kept him grounded and mortal but the fury that spat fire in his hands filled his chest with anger and intensity and he fought. The small group of men moved in and out around each other, one man protecting the flank of another and each time one man dropped down to reload or shot, the men regrouped over and over to ensure that the enemy stayed at bay.

The guarding soldiers took Isaiah back to Chicago and looked him over to make sure that he was in healthy fighting shape when some of the men began to ask what happed to Ruckus and his platoon. Isaiah sat in a tent with half a dozen officers taking notes and asking a barrage of questions in which Isaiah had to recount in detail to each of the men he could remember from the day. The men guarding the road back from the river were found by scouting troops that were patrolling to make sure that enemy soldiers weren't sneaking in near the camp, which they did and killed the six men guarding the return route for Ruckus, their bodies were already recovered and sent to the black tent for processing before returning home.

1968 was the deadliest year for Americans in Vietnam and the Army suffered the most losses of all the branches so the odds were greatly stacked against Isaiah but he was the sole survivor of A-company that went out patrolling with squad leader Ruckus that day, he was the only one to make it back and it was just his first day in the battle.

Paper Paulie

Ch.3

When Isaiah made it back to his bunk he was exhausted from such a long day but even after visiting the small pit fire that had a new hunk of meat slow roasting on it he still couldn't quiet his mind enough to sleep. It had only been one day but walking back into Chicago with an armed guard felt like years had gone by. Isaiah felt different, weathered and aged all at the same time and he didn't know how to feel being the only man left alive of the thirty or so that followed Ruckus out the same gates so early in the morning. Everything was ominous and shrouded in illusion; as if the smoky haze was a hint that it was all a bad dream or something. Days ran long and hot, hot days run together and even if you get a break from the hot days, you really just think about the heat.

Isaiah made his way back into his tent to lie down for a few hours, he was certain he'd be recruited into another platoon or battalion and headed back out into the killing zones of the jungle again and again until finally one day he wouldn't come back. Most of the tent was silent with some men snoring and others just dead still. Isaiah felt the chills run up him seeing soldiers lying completely still and it reminded him of the dead soldiers he lined up earlier in the day, men he fought beside for mere minutes in the ambush that didn't make it back alive. All the faces, those young but now lifeless faces seem to become shadows in the back of your mind.

Lying back in his rack Isaiah heard the crinkle that he had heard several times during the day, the envelope in his pocket. Isaiah debated not opening it since he promised himself he would when he made it back to the base alive and in fact he did. The luck of the letter kept Isaiah alive and the hope of getting to read it kept him motivated enough to make it back to his bunk so he owed it to whoever penned the letter a response and a thanks so he pulled out his side knife and eased it into the folded flap of the envelope to begin to slowly saw it open. Tucked inside a tri-folded piece of paper was a small thick paper doll. The letter read:

"Dear Soldier,

My name is George Ernest Harwell, my family calls me Georgie. I am eight years old and in Mrs. Benson's third grade class in Roosevelt elementary school. I like recess and skip-ball. I have a pet dog names Rex and I have red hair. This is Paper Paulie, he is a friend for you while you fight for us in Vietnam and I hope he keeps you safe until you get back home to your family. Mrs. Benson said we should each write a thank you letter to a soldier; my grandfather was a soldier so they are very special so I wanted to make you a friend. You can write back if you like I am in North Dakota.

Your Pen Pal,

Georgie Harwell."

The letter was nicely written for a third grader and in a woman's nice hand writing was an address to the school in Iroquois Falls so he thought about writing back. Isaiah unfolded a small wad of waxy feeling paper to investigate this "Paper Paulie" and see what this new friend was all about. A small piece of paper unfolded to be the size of his hand, it had blue pants, black shoes and a red shirt, all colored with crayon and then sealed in paraffin to make it water proof. Paper Paulie had a big reddish brown smile and scraggly red hair drawn across the top with two unevenly spaced Blue eyes. "Paper Paulie" Isaiah said to himself with a smirk as he folded the piece of paper back over itself to tuck it into his shirt for further safe keeping and good luck before retiring to sleep.

The next morning Isaiah learned he had time before his next patrol and some of his bunk mates heard he was the only survivor of Ruckus' patrol so they wanted to hear his tale over and over about his firefight and engagement and also about his close call in the field overnight, all stories that the wide eyed soldiers wanted to hear for encouragement that they weren't just being sent out to their deaths like so many others. Isaiah was leery about all the attention, his father had raised him to be humble because nobody like a cocky pompous person that is loud and rudely intruding into the lives of others but he felt validated in his choice to join the Army to fight for a country he believed in.

The young recruits were only a day or two behind his own arrival in the country but they already looked to the man they saw as the lucky chance soldier that made it back, the *rough tough* that could tell them all how he escaped his encounter and kept his life, and his cool the whole time. Isaiah was brunt about how terrified he was, even to the end when he yanked his line of explosives hoping to take out enemies before they got to him, nothing was guaranteed, not the day, not the night, not the next morning or even a last breath. Isaiah lamented telling them about Paulie and his childish promise to a folded envelope, that was just for him.

Isaiah wrote his first letter to his mother and father, he wanted to tell them that during his first day in combat he was the only person of thirty-three to come back and that he was wishing he was back in Brooklyn already. Isaiah wanted to tell his parents more but he didn't want his dear mother to have a heart attack from worry so he decided to talk about some of the fellas he was meeting and new foods he was trying, like that unknown animal leg over a fire in the dark night. Isaiah wished his brothers all well and hoped to hear from them soon and signed off.

The next letter was for Georgie to thank him for Paper Paulie, he concentrated really hard to form each letter and in his best handwriting he wrote:

"Dear Georgie,

I want to thank you dearly for Paper Paulie; from the first day he became my friend he kept me safe from within my pocket. Vietnam is a very dangerous place and I am glad to have him on my side until I safely return to my home in Brooklyn. I have never been to North Dakota what is it like? I hope my letter finds you in good health and with good marks in school.

To your teacher Mrs. Benson; myself and some of my platoon members that didn't fall, your classroom letters were received with the utmost thoughts, thank you.

Sincerely, Isaiah Dante Venney

A-company, 171st platoon Vietnam"

Isaiah wrote his letter and sent it to the address written on the back of Paper Paulie before he folded it back up and tucked it back into his pocket. Isaiah wasn't the most superstitious of men but his new friend certainly seemed to be a good luck charm to him so he kept it close. Isaiah wanted to chat with the young lad that wrote him at first, being in combat can be lonely and he had to remember he was writing to an eight year old so telling him of his dead friends or killing enemy soldiers was a topic best left to his letters to his brothers. Writing to

45

Georgie helped Isaiah to keep his mind on the good, to block out the ugliness his father Eddie warned him of and that was a good thing out there.

Georgie took a while to write back and the time in between letters dragged on for Isaiah. Patrols were often embedded with conflict but none as severe or in-depth as that during the first day but after surviving skirmish after skirmish Isaiah began to thank Paper Paulie more and more each time. Some of the men of the newly formed platoons that caught eye of the folded up wax paper asked Isaiah plenty of questions about it, each time he made his explanation and talked about Georgie back in Iroquois Falls. Some of the men that were closest to Isaiah and Paper Paulie seemed to also be survivors of heated battles with the enemy, after enough close calls with death and the maiming that came from gunfights with automatic weapons several of the men that knew of Paulie also joined in singing his praise and thanking Isaiah for his little paper pal.

"Dear Soldier Isaiah Venney,

I am happy that Paper Paulie is keeping you safe. My mom says that I have to wash my ears better or I'll get potatoes, I like potatoes but not washing. My dog Rex is sick, I think it's because he eats some of my mom's clothes, I think eating clothes would make me sick too. I am sorry some of your friends fell, I hope they are ok, I fell once and hurt my knee, there was blood on my nice pants. It's time for recess now.

Goodbye, from

Georgie"

Hearing from Georgie was fun, Isaiah commented
in his next letter that potatoes were very good and he
preferred his mashed with a pinch of salt but washing was
very important. Telling Georgie that it was good manners
to wash was up to his parents; Isaiah suggested that
Georgie do as he is told because he does as his mother
told him and it has helped him to be a good soldier. After
the amounts of marching and the constantly being wet
Isaiah favored new socks, more than anything else, more
than grilled food or the thought of getting a working dog
to take out on patrols, clean dry socks were the hottest
commodity in *Chicago*.

The innocence that came with writing the third
grader kept a peaceful corner of Isaiah's mind swept clean
of the names, the attitudes, the sights, sounds, and smells
of the war. The clean slate that Isaiah started with in his
mind took him back to before the war and before he was
subjected to the horrors he now lived each and every day.
Many men united across the racial barriers that were first
prevalent, men saving each other's lives broke down
walls and assumptions left and right but there were still
many undertones that had to be dealt with now and then.
Georgie was a saving grace in all honestly, if Isaiah had a
niece or nephew to write to he'd had to cast aside the

ugliness and write about things he'd found to be touching in the area so he had to look hard each day but he tried to find something worth being grateful each day.

Cases of Jungle rot were plaguing soldiers, large chunks of flesh peeled from soldiers feet that were several layers deep and painful were sidelining or inhibiting soldiers left and right and the best way Isaiah could relay that to his eight year old writing buddy was that the feeling of new or clean socks was far better than warm sand or cool grass in the summer and it was his most favorite thing, Georgie still liked recess and his dog Rex. Isaiah counted the days until he heard from his family or his Pen-pal to get through, it was hard to look down and think of a year or two when you weren't certain you would see the end of the day each time you woke up.

A fellow soldier got a service dog trained to help locate people in the tunnels that ran for miles underground that the enemy used to surprise the soldiers, the dog was name Newton. A month after Newton joined the ranks Georgie spoke about his dog Rex passing away and how sad he was, understandably of course so he hoped that Rex became a dog angel and helped Newton do his job as a dog soldier. Rumor was spreading around the camp that there was going to be a large scale offensive in a place everyone called "The grinder". The Grinder was a hill that had a sunken valley that surrounded it; you had to drop almost fifty feet down a steep gorge before you could try to climb up the other side while taking heavy gun fire. The odds of taking the Grinder were on the same scale as Normandy or Omaha beach but it had to be done.

The Vietcong heavily fortified The Grinder with trees and the dirt dug from the gorge around the Grinder and from the top they had the ability to propel rockets outward towards planes and helicopters that were flying along the valley looking for trails of Vietnamese moving to or from locations at night. The Grinder was going to have heavy fire from the air while soldiers and gun mounted helicopters took to barraging large caliber weapons at the hill until it fell to the American soldiers, Isaiah was nervous about it all, in fact everybody was. There was never any confirmation to casualties, it just wasn't good for morale but there was ample rumors everyday about hundreds of bodies being shipped here or there to go home for proper burials, the daily tallies of body counts spread like wild fire and the upcoming assault made everyone feel like it was a certain death sentence.

Newton was an ideal name for the dog, one of Newton's laws of physics are than an object will stay at rest until acted upon, Newton's handler Kamine was a strong man that had to often pick Newton up by scooping under him to clear him from his bunk. Newton would run from anywhere on the base to scamper into a bunk and lay out before Kamine could get close, Newton would then whimper and growl a little when Kamine tried to remove the stubborn dog from his bunk, there was always a struggle between them two over a bed. When Newton had his service vest on he was the best taught dog you could imagine, but once on base he'd wriggle out of the vest and then find the best way to avoid being evicted from a bunk. Newton would spread his legs out and then muzzle your hands away from him to keep you from snatching him by his collar and sending him to the floor, he liked a padded bed better than any of the other soldiers in the Army.

Georgie liked to hear about Newton because he missed his own dog Rex but his parents said that Rex was in heaven and it was all ok. Newton was a young German Shepherd like most other working dogs and when he had his vest on he was a hard working dog, when Kamine took his vest off he was nearly as rambunctious as a puppy and caused some mischief also. Newton didn't like to sit or stay as he was commanded and often times on the base he was running through tents or snagging stray food off of an unwatched plate to run off and eat on Kamine's bunk, which often left a drool covered pile somewhere on the blanket much to his displeasure.

Gearing up for The Grinder was a large coordinated event, the enemy was nestled in tightly and the taking of the hill meant many less shot down helicopters, which were the true angels in the skies overhead. Helicopters ran night and day and all of the pilots that flew were skilled operators that saved more lives than could be counted. Isaiah and his new platoon were going to be charging up the east hill of The Grinder, their job was to make the faster ascent up the steep gorge walls and take out many of the gun turrets, Newton was supposed to go up the wall and also do his part to take out the gunners in order for the human soldiers to get a foothold and take out gunners as fast as they could while slowly making progress up the fortified hill.

Isaiah was slowly growing hardened to the war around him, he didn't feel as saddened when he passed bodies of soldiers getting ready to be shipped home and often found himself mumbling that they were the lucky ones to be leaving Vietnam. One of the hard parts about war isn't knowing you are going to die but the wait was what sucked the life out of you; the endless hours and the slowing down of time while engaged in combat, the waiting to find out was dreadful and each time you think that you might be done for but somehow you survive really takes a toll on you. Isaiah thanked the folded square that was Paper Paulie each night, men fell around him, behind him and in front of him but each night he fell asleep and each morning he woke up he owed to his small paper pal.

Paper Paulie

Ch.4

The attack on The Grinder was a full-fledged brutal assault. Over three-hundred men in three waves stormed the fortified hill and less than ten percent survived to take the strong hold. Isaiah lined up behind sandbag stacked walls along with Kamine and Newton, there were men shouting all around and everyone was preparing for a full charge down the steep embankment walls only to run right into a tall rock wall to have to stand on each others shoulders to climb up enough to attack. From the air the hovering angels unleashed a barrage of bullet fire mixed with rockets to precede the attack to force the opposition deep into their tunnels to cause enough of a cease fire to give the ground soldiers a foothold.

Less than an hour into the taking of the Grinder mud ran down the sides of the slopes, red with blood in small streams that began to fill the small valley that surrounded the hill. Helicopter after helicopter swarmed in to open fire and launch rockets to take out many of the concrete enforced pill-boxes but being dug in so far the Vietcong still held the advantage. Planes from above couldn't drop bombs out of concern for hitting their own men so the helicopters pivoted with heavy gunfire while the men dropped down into the carved out muddy moat around the hill.

Once the whistle charged it was the sign to attack and everyone hurled themselves into the battle. The edges of the ravine were worn down from foot traffic and slippery from the constant raining or morning dew, making it dangerous to hurry and risk falling onto sharpened spears and sticks down at the bottom. Newton charged ahead and tried to find his way up the steep wall along with many other attack dogs that were recruited for the charge. Waves of men stood up to charge, a sea of green fatigues followed dozens of charging dogs down into the ravine to begin assembling ladders and stairs to get up the sharp embankment on the other side. The eruption of gunfire was deafening, the hill covered in smoke as the helicopters fired rockets at the bunkers towards the top and left, streams of fire erupt from hidden inlets within the small mountain while spent shell casings rained down from above as the helicopters spat fury into the hill.

Handfuls of men managed to make it up the steep rock face only to fall just up the other side; Isaiah sprinted and dodged left and right while trying not to lose his footing in the bloody mud that was slushing down towards him. Just ahead Isaiah watched as Newton charged up further and then into a small divot in the foliage so he readied, it was a sure sign of a dug in enemy. The war dogs were trained to seek out men; the small Vietnamese tunneled and dug like prairie dogs into everywhere and having the agile dogs chase them out saved many lives, but this time, Newton never returned.

Isaiah continued to charge up the hill; the higher defenses were lobbing grenades down the hill and also sending long logs to simply roll down against the incoming assault, rolling right over men and dogs on the way down the hill, injuring many in their paths.

There was no sight of Kamine anywhere. Newton made it up the rock wall but his trainer did not. Any hole in the mountain got a grenade tossed into it for the safety of the upcoming soldiers and Isaiah watched a soldier lob a grenade into the same hole that Newton went into just minutes before, ensuring that he'd never return. The ground was slippery with blood, the ground was wet from the night before and many of the small plants that kept the mud from succumbing to gravity had been long cleared leaving hard packed slippery runs in the ground so you had to keep your feet moving to keep from getting tripped up or sliding down the hill.

Isaiah thought back to watching the great Muhammad Ali box with his father and brothers. There was a television in a store front that was replaying a fight they had listened to on the radio so they stopped what they were doing and stood around to watch for a while. The boxer kept his feet moving, his quick stepping carried his bulkier upper body around the ring and supported him while he delivered jab after jab to his opponent. Isaiah thought back to that boxing match and tried to picture that his feet were carrying him further and further up the hill to deliver deadly punch after deadly punch, except it felt like they were cemented into that wet sticky mud on the hillside.

The helicopters still continued to swarm from above but they had to keep their distance to avoid being shot out of the sky and crashing on battalions of their own men below. Isaiah aimed his rifle into each small hole he could find and pulled his trigger several times before moving further up the hill, there were men sprawled out dead all around and all he could do was step over them and keep moving towards his imagined area of safety at the very top. Magazine after magazine traded out for spent clips and dug-in hole after dug-in hole was cleared as he raced to the top along with many other steadfast soldiers, Isaiah continued to charge upwards.

The Grinder must have resembled an ant colony overtaking an ice-cream cone, scurrying everywhere while men exchanged gunfire and shell casings flung through the smoke filled air. Each time a cloud of smoke cleared there was another person shooting, some towards men coming up the hill, some were men shooting at those men. Isaiah thought back to North Dakota, he thought back to Iroquois Falls and how simple life must have been for his young pen-pal Georgie.

In Brooklyn the buildings were tall and the streets were crowded, in Vietnam everyone was out to kill someone and everything was in a fast rush, but from the nicely addressed letters from Georgie, it sounded like North Dakota was a slow paced tranquil place to raise a family or simply enjoy walking your dog through a flowery meadow, not chasing a dog trained to kill up a mountain with an automatic rifle snapping off round after round at little Asian men shooting back at you from small dugouts in the side of a mountain while your fellow countrymen fall dead or wounded all around you.

Isaiah never knew much of North Dakota when he was coming up, in school geography classes barely browsed over some of the Midwest states and focused more on their close region, automotive production in Detroit, immigration in New York, coal mining in Virginia or Kentucky and train routes to ship it all that transverse all over the country or ship around the world. The thought of North Dakota seemed like a dream, a quiet place that wasn't filled with bright lights, loud cars, or angry people moving about like cluttered garbage on a shore; that was the place Isaiah thought about going if he made it out of Vietnam alive.

With the exchange of a few letters Isaiah got to know Georgie a little, he missed his dog Rex and still liked recess but his teacher Mrs. Benson was very nice and even when it wasn't recess she was helpful to learn their lesson plans. Isaiah held onto the letters, he kept them folded and tucked into his left breast pocket while Paper Paulie remained folded in half and tucked inside,also for safe keeping. Each mission that Isaiah survived he wondered if it was in fact Paper Paulie watching over him, the small paper cutout with blue pants, a red shirt and scruffy red hair with a little boys address written on the back. Georgie told Isaiah about his friends and liking to play hide and seek with them in his daddy's barn, it was a big red barn with ducks and sheep that made noises all day long.

Most of the animals Isaiah had ever seen were at the zoo once or in his books until he landed in Vietnam. Many of the villagers had cows or chickens just wandering around when they marched through villages. The reddish brown dirt made for reddish brown mud which never really washed out of his uniform. Within a week of landing in the country Isaiah and many of the men strayed from the strict uniform codes and took to removing the hot shirt sleeves to keep from sweating to death in the heat. Each village they marched through was a new experience; many of them had simple farming lives and were stricken with fear when soldiers with guns marched in, it was understandingly scary so he tried to smile at the citizens as if to assure them that he meant them no harm, it wasn't a peace keeping mission but it made him feel just a little better about himself, perhaps remind him of his own humanity.

Isaiah felt for the citizens that were caught up in battle, some were subjected to the chemicals that were sprayed from large planes to strip the trees of the dense foliage, others were shot at or shot from helicopter gunners far above, others had their simple huts burned down for simply being there and it was all inhumane. War is the epitome of hell, each moment is unknown and the thought of a future is paralyzing, all the while you have to be on edge to take someone's life while putting your own at risk. Each time Isaiah had to pack up or fill his pockets with ammo clips he heard the slight rustle of the paper in his pockets and he immediately thought back to his little pal in North Dakota and it helped to clear his head.

In a land of murders and animosity, cut off from a family that loved you but a home that despised you and your fellow soldiers that were just following orders Paper Paulie reminded Isaiah of exactly what he was doing:he was doing his best. The political unrest was tiresome and the constant marches and rally's laden with terms such as; "baby killers" and "village rapers" made it hard to keep believing in what you were fighting for: your country.

Paper Paulie had become a small square that was blue on one side and faded red on the other after time but just looking at it reminded Isaiah that that simple innocent gesture to a complete stranger by a young kid that was being raised right by his parents was proof that what he was doing was right. There was no tension of race, no subtle hints or agendas in the letters from Georgie to Isaiah or vice versa, they were friendly letters passed between two strangers trying to make friends, a small thread that would mean ever so much for a long time.

Isaiah continued to write to his mom and learned that his younger brother Ronnie was drafted. Ronnie was also sent into infantry and was already in Vietnam by the time he received the letter. Isaiah never wanted to hear that any of his brothers were in the same country he was, he held back on telling his folks about most of the horrors he crossed with the burned bodies or atrocities he had to endure but he hoped that his parents knew enough to keep the rest of their boys from signing up. Isaiah held in a lot of pain, any soldier has their own hell to carry around inside of them, especially if they've felt the heat of battle but writing to Georgie once in a while felt like his heart still had care and love in it so he held it dear, writing his parents felt like a lie sometimes but he knew it was for the better.

Corresponding with a young boy that was ignorant to the real monsters in the world gave Isaiah hope for the future, there were still bright eyed youngsters that existed away from the newsreels and media reports about a war that seemed endless. The war felt like a killing machine in itself, you put soldiers and civilians in and you get numbers of dead bodies out. Isaiah was worn out, war weary and each day he woke up in one piece was a day he spent just trying to get to have one more night of rest. Hope was a dangerous thing in the war, the harder men hoped to get back to their wives or children the faster they were being zipped up and then shipped home in a bag it seemed so there was a weary consciousness to how you had to think.

There was something to the small paper square that had sealed itself closed with the paraffin wax it came sealed in for water protection. The small square of paper contained the hopes that Isaiah had so that he could just focus on getting through his day. Georgie had the innocence of youth on his side and that was enough to fill Isaiah with enough hope in himself to carry him through his two years of duty in Vietnam. Isaiah and Georgie wrote a few times and by the time Isaiah was charging up the hill named The Grinder he was close to going home and the little paper figurine had sealed over on itself for good.

Isaiah was afraid to hope, each day was long and after enough of them he could hardly remember when he arrived in the war. Day marches lasted weeks, rains storms seemed to turn into monsoons and a small little rustle in the leave often revealed a poisonous snake or a trip wire linked to several booby traps that nearly killed him each time. Day in and day out Isaiah kept Paper Paulie in his helmet or his shirt pocket and together they made it through each day. It was hard to make friends during the battles, you chat with a few guys one day and the next they could be shipped out, moved around or simply dead so sitting around a pit fire was a constant changing of faces. Isaiah grew out of the title of "Ruckus' one remaining" after two days and two more marches into the jungle, men were moved in just as fast as they fell and like that; memories of somebody were snuffed out just as quickly as the life it represented.

Paper Paulie

Still charging up The Grinder there were grenades exploding all around, the smoke burned in his lungs and his legs were on fire from the steep incline he continued to struggle against. With men behind him Isaiah pushed on towards the top. There was gunfire coming at him from the front and from behind him but he kept pushing upwards to keep taking out bunker after bunker. Suddenly there was a sharp sound and stings of something burning on his arm as he continued to swing his rifle left and right to keep going. Isaiah couldn't help but to keep yelling, there were so many explosions that it was impossible to even hear himself but he yelled and shouted to keep himself going anyway.

Explosion after explosion rang out from his sides but he still charged; it was near the top that Isaiah realized that he was still alive and fighting when he came face to face with a small bunker and began shooting into it. Not knowing what was inside but afraid to find out Isaiah kept shooting, to the right in the smoke and debris flying into the air from grenade explosions Isaiah caught a glimpse of a man rising up from the ground and he froze. The silhouette of a small man rose up and pointed his gun right at Isaiah, everything but the sight at the end of the gun blurred into the background. The small man was only a few yards away and climbed up from his small foxhole that was hidden beneath some shrubbery, it was hidden very well actually and was hard to distinguish from the ground itself. Isaiah tried to turn to get a look at the man but he couldn't swivel his gun fast enough to save his own life.

A fellow soldier appeared between Isaiah and the enemy holding the machine gun that sent fire flashing from the front. The soldier unleashed his rifle and sent several rounds into the enemy that was firing at them as his body jerked and riddled with bullets from the enemy. The soldier took the bullets that were meant for Isaiah and it saved his life. More American soldiers swarmed in and continued to secure the mountain by shooting into the tunnels and sending in remaining dogs to attack any enemies they might find. Wave after wave climbed the embankments and scurried upwards to overpower the enemy strong hold and the longer you stood in one place the more you were shouldered by men racing passed you and into the battle.

Soldiers didn't stop fighting until the gunfire had stopped so Isaiah dropped to the ground for a few minutes entangled with the soldier that saved his life. The stranger had stepped into the gunfire that was meant to kill him and he was still alive because of it. It took a moment to move the lifeless body off of him in the bloody mud near the top of The Grinder while angry charging men swarmed all around. Once the top of the Grinder was taken from one side Men covered around the sides to take the entire hill in the rest of the afternoon. Taking The Grinder was hard and almost ninety-percent of the men that stormed it were killed in action but it was a vital win at the time for the war efforts.

Isaiah squirmed and worked to get the deceased man that saved his life off of him, between the weight of the body and the vacuum below him from the mud it took some wrangling. There was so much blood and the air was thick with smoke as small flames still licked out of the bunkers nearest him that your eyes couldn't stop watering. The strange man was covered in blood; he had bits of small black facial hair and a thin mustache dripping in blood from his nose still wet and glistening. In all the blood stained uniform it was hard to find one of the many stenciled names to identify the soldier that died so that Isaiah could live, who was this man?

Isaiah got to his feet and set the soldier to lay completely still in the mud he died in while he tried to make sense of the last few minutes. With bullets whizzing by his head and grenades exploding nearby it was hard to see everything that was going on and then when he turned to face an enemy soldier that was about to fire on him, this stranger popped up in the middle and spared Isaiah's life, and for that he needed to know that man's name. Isaiah knelt down to feel around the man's neck to find his dog tags; he had to know this man's name before he could return back to battle.

Isaiah was stained in the man's blood and as he pulled out the slippery metal tags he cleared away some of the blood to find the identity he needed. Isaiah felt like he was shot in the stomach from it knotting so badly, he found the name on the dog tag and felt like he was looking at a ghost. "Venney" was the first name he read on the dog tag that was covered in blood. It couldn't be, it was impossible, in all the soldiers in all of Vietnam that were charging forth to fight the enemy, his own brother died in his arms on The Grinder. Isaiah lifted Ronnie up and held him close for a few minutes, he hadn't spoken to or even seen his brother in years and didn't even recognize his lifeless face anymore and just a moment before; he was a complete stranger.

Ronnie didn't seem to know who he was risking his life for when he saw a fellow soldier getting ready to be ambushed and stepped in. Ronnie was in the country several months and had fought gallantly for the army much like his older brother and in the name of being a soldier he put his life on the line for someone else. Isaiah still had that spark deep inside that meant he was human, he didn't want to laugh and cheer at the death of an enemy like many others but freezing at a time when he should have been fighting didn't help to save many others on the riverbank that first day out with Ruckus in the water either. Ronnie was a slender man and back home he was a bit of a prankster until the army straightened him out and made him behave, but Isaiah didn't know this man, he remembered back to the one he knew.

Isaiah looked at a man that was wearing his own brother's name tags but he still didn't recognize him. The man in his arms didn't have the same kind brown eyes he looked into when they were young brothers building blanket tents in their living room back in Brooklyn, they were different, perhaps hardened by war and the things he had seen, or maybe time had changed them both. Isaiah had become a stranger to his brother while he was away, to all of his brothers really; and he was finally ready to find hope and fight to get back home. Isaiah fought most days to get through another day and he also fought for his country but the one thing he realized he had not done yet was fight to go home.

Isaiah pulled Paper Paulie out of his pocket, the small square of folded paper covered in wax was now unrecognizable but he still remembered what it looked like since day one and now he was ready to go home. The view from the top of The Grinder was disheartening; the long jungle that stretched out below could have been a grand sight if it wasn't littered with smoke trails from fires or patches of brown that had been poisoned away with the foliage spray that killed the green shrubbery. The view was a collage of smoke trails, machine gun equipped helicopters that were sending lightning bolt looking sprays of gunfire and rockets down into the brush to kill enemy soldiers and patches of cancerous looking opening and it was so shameful.

As soldiers Isaiah lived by doing as he was ordered to do, but by doing so others' died. Looking one last time into the face of his fallen brother he felt the heart ache that he knew would befell his own mother and it assured him that he was ready to go home. Being atop of The Grinder was something that would have amazed the four Venney brothers back home, a small mountain or large hill that would have towered over any of the tallest buildings they had ever seen back in Brooklyn but it was covered in sadness. Isaiah sat for a moment with his own brother passed away in his lap and all he could think to do was cry. Isaiah's eyes burned, not only from the smoke but from the tears, the emotions he hid from for a long time that never went away, now it was ok to find them.

When a soldier cries it isn't out of weakness, it isn't out of being hurt, it's because they are so full of so many emotions that there aren't any words or there aren't any actions to express how they feel, there are only tears. Isaiah couldn't figure out how he was feeling, he walled himself up to survive each day and with Paper Paulie tucked into his pocked he somehow made it. When thousands of soldiers were killed in action in the war, Isaiah was one of the lucky ones to live, even his own flesh and blood brother died right next to him. Isaiah grabbed his brother by the jacket collar as he stood up and hoisted him up onto his shoulders and began to head back down the mountain, uneasy with each step.

Medics tried to save soldiers that could be saved, they would roughly patch them up then evac them to a med station before they would be stabilized and then forwarded on to a medical hospital. Ronnie was passed on and there was no helping him, it was long too late. Landing zones were all marked by poofing smoke in areas that were safe enough for choppers to land in so Isaiah had his destination. The walk down The Grinder was rough and rocky and with the body of his fallen brother strewn across his shoulders he was struggling to keep from falling with each slippery step. Isaiah knew there was no bringing his brother back but he couldn't bear the thought of leaving his body behind to attract flies or to be crudely loaded up onto a wagon and carted off like most of the other deceased soldiers. Ronnie deserved better than that, he deserved to die late in his life surrounded by his wife and kids and grand kids and maybe even great grand kids, not in a mud puddle of blood with lungs full of burning smoke in a foreign land full of unfriendly people.

Isaiah marched and charged at sun up with hundreds of other soldiers and at the end of the day he was carrying his own brother back down for the mortuary trucks to take his body away for the last time he'd ever see him in his life, it had been a long day, the longest and most terrible in his whole life in fact. Isaiah made it a point to write to his mother Ronetta and father Eddie and describe in detail what had happened and that they should be proud of their third child in that he acted heroically as they had raised him to do. Growing up the Venney brothers all fought, all boys do, but the Venney brothers all stood up for each other when anyone else tried to mess with them also. The older brother Clarence wasn't much bigger but being the oldest of the four boys it was his job to protect them no matter what. Isaiah picked on Ronnie a bit more as a boy because everyone was scolded if they picked on the baby Saul.

Clarence once fought a boy on the playground for slinging slurs at both Isaiah and Ronnie when they were smaller. The older boy wore a small white cotton shirt and his blue jeans had a roll to the bottom when he called out and blamed the Venney boys for being part of the reason the jobs were going away and that was why his own daddy was out of work. Isaiah remembered back to what Eddie once told him that if someone calls you a name and you know it's not to be true than it doesn't make no never mind as long as you know it's not true, so he ignored it. Ronnie was upset hearing an older boy say such things so big Clarence had to step in and bloody a lip in honor of his family name.

Isaiah thought back to many of those memories of growing up and in each one Ronnie was always the more quiet, but cunning little brother, now he was a grown man that would never know what it was like to be a good husband to a good women and raise children that would call him dad, he was just gone. There was a large green personnel carrier with a wagon on the back that was loaded with the bodies of fallen soldiers, the sight of the truck and the thought of handing over Ronnie's dead body made him weep even more with each exhausted step. Isaiah would miss getting to know his brother as a man and the things that made him a man rather than the younger brother he once knew,nearing the truck he knew it was time to let go of all of that. You don't really learn to cope very well in war, you learn to push things to the side and convince yourself that you'll deal with it later but even when later comes, you push it aside again, and again.

The days after the taking of The Grinder were all chaotic, the war was still raging on but Isaiah wrote his parents and told them of Ronnie and his passing. Offloading Ronnie's body gave way to the notice that all of Isaiah's muscles were tense and tight from the long walk down hill and some stumbles along the way. It took half a day and then some to get back to Chicago after the hill was taken from enemy control and it was then that Isaiah realized that the blood that once gave life to his younger brother Ronnie had completely ruined the letters he kept close in his pocket from Georgie.

The wax sealant on Paper Paulie kept him from being ruined but the plain paper letters were ruined with the blood that soaked him. Paper Paulie once had the full name of Georgie and his address in Iroquois Falls but he had been folded over on himself to prevent ripping or tearing and his wax coating sealed in his address from then on out; refusing to reveal his secret ever again. Isaiah felt the great loss, he was friendly with Georgie and his simple gift had meant ever so much more because he began to believe that maybe Paper Paulie was in deed a good luck charm and that Paulie might actually get him home safely. Now Isaiah had no way to write to Georgie or to thank him again for his friendship once he stepped back onto American soil, the addresses were all gone with the blood soaked paper. Isaiah remembered Iroquois Falls North Dakota but not the address to write him.

The end of Isaiah's tour of duty was bittersweet, he felt that the bloodshed he left behind hadn't warranted the lives lost but he was certainly glad to be lucky enough to go home. Isaiah lost a brother and a friend so leaving Vietnam behind knowing the losses of his country was hard to accept. Isaiah knew that Georgie lived in Iroquois Falls North Dakota but he couldn't remember the rest of the address since he had only written him a few times over the span of several months. Isaiah was busy as he was processed out of the war and of the Army after his tour was finished and even though he didn't get to thank Georgie for sending Paper Paulie to him to keep him safe, he still kept the small paper square with him for luck.

Isaiah hoped that maybe once he was home and had the ability to find some silence for himself that somewhere in all the commotion of war he might be able to recall the memory of the address, one he had only written a few times in responses to Georgie. Isaiah wanted to thank the young lad for helping him to remember the peaceful times; the youth filled memories of growing up with his brothers, the times long before the color of your skin mattered and before you learned the hard truth of what death really was. Georgie was a young boy from somewhere on the other side of the country, he was given a writing assignment by his teacher and without knowing how deep he could impact a stranger, he gave Isaiah a small sliver of something to hold onto while in the deepest reaches of depravity: fighting in a war. Isaiah thought long and hard about the men that fell around him, the men being loaded up onto helicopters and flown away to some hospital to be ignored by the news and the government and no matter how hard he wanted to scream and shout about all of his feelings, he wrote softly to the boy that was naïve to the outside world.

The men flying in combat were the real angels if there ever was such a thing, not bedsheet clad fellows with wings to sing in a high pitch and protect you from harm, none of which ever made themselves apparent on a field of battle when they were needed the most but the men that flew mission after mission taking bullet after bullet and risking their lives in order to evacuate their own men. "Combat pilots are nothing short of true angels" Isaiah muttered to himself as the plane home took off. In the distance helicopters could still be seen floating through the air and risking a barrage of gunfire from the ground, it didn't matter how many pilots heard about the losses other aircrafts suffered they still landed in the hottest of LZ's and pulled as many men out of the thicket as possible, day and night. Both sides of the war were full of men, scared, frightened, unsure, brave, and willing men, there can never be a winner in war when there is death, sometimes it's just a matter of who loses the least.

The farther Isaiah flew from the war the lighter the hardened cloak of war felt, when in war you keep your head down and do what you have to do, it's an old adage but that is all there is to do. Isaiah had to carry his younger brother's body down a mountain, once the body was down he also helped to gather a few more men in order to help get them to transport and get them out of the fighting zones, he did it because it doesn't take sharing the same parents, last name or even skin color to be a brother, everybody was a brother in arms and that was how it was supposed to be.

The pilots saw every soldier as a brother and many pilots went down with planes or choppers working to do their job out of honor for their military brothers and knowing that there might be one solider that might not make it home was painful, every serving man deserves to be returned home, especially the pilots that took on such huge risks over and over and over.

Paper Paulie

Ch. 5

Stepping off the final flight home Isaiah expected to find a different world below his feet. Walking out onto the tarmac was different than before, instead of leaving home to go to war he was leaving war to return home, except it wasn't really home. Years had gone by, hard years of eating scraps or carving hunks of meat off a skewer slung over a fire to keep it crackling, years of eating the mud that men died in and was soiled with their blood. The air was missing the burning jet fuel smell or the smell of bombed forestry in the distance, it still smelled of vehicle exhaust but it was still different. In the jungles Isaiah realized that he was smelling the earth when he was face down in shrubs or the riverbank, it didn't smell like he knew the air to smell like growing up in the big city. The earth smelled dirty when there was a clearing in the billows of smoke and there was fresh foliage nearby, dirty, but somehow cleaner than the streets he knew.

The city smelled of thousands of cars, the dirty black exhaust that penetrated the millions of tons of concrete that made his home city and gave it the distinct smell he knew growing up. The war had a subtle undertone of burning tires but there was still more earthen air than vehicle exhaust and it was foreign. Isaiah felt out of place again, he was the foreigner when he went to a

75

different country and he knew it but he kept it in his mind that once he made it back home that everything would be ok, except it wasn't. Isaiah felt like a stranger again, he had only been gone a few years and even though not much had changed around his home, he had become the stranger because he himself had made the changes. The news shows playing in store front televisions showed brawls among people protesting, police using water hoses and dogs on groups of students and it made his heart sink when he realized he hadn't in fact escaped the animosity of mankind when he flew far away from the war.

The ugliness of society had only grown worse in his absence, growing up Isaiah never knew what the n-word was nor its' inflections but once his eyes were opened to it there was no turning back. Isaiah did his best to keep his ears closed to such words and hoped to take away some of the power that using such a word could wield but in his absence his own country had embraced such ugliness among its' own citizens. Everything seemed like it was a bad version of a good dream, being home was emotional and rewarding for Isaiah once he stepped foot down onto familiar ground but the world he once knew, the world he left behind to go and fight a war, had been shrouded in a smokey haze, as if a blanket of hatred and violence had been laid down on his city streets.

Being back home was a hard transition for Isaiah, he had planned to look for work near the docks just like his father had and perhaps spend a year or so saving some money up along with his military money he had sent back home and then maybe open a small radio store or something. One of the men Isaiah met in the war was a man named Childress, he was a radio repairman and seemed to know everything there was to know about radios. Isaiah was intrigued that Childress knew so much about electronics and told himself that he would find some manuals or maybe even buy a few radios to learn everything he could about them and look for work. Childress was a diligent worker and Isaiah took plenty of notes when he could look into some of the radios that were damaged during the fighting, wires and magnets and small little capsule looking things, Childress took the time and had the patience to explain each step to troubleshoot and begin to repair damages, he even showed Isaiah how to coil thin copper wire around a toilet paper tube to make a small makeshift radio receiver to listen to the radio for some music if there was any being broadcasted nearby.

The city hustled and bustled but even faster, cars roared by and didn't even bother to honk in a friendly manner, they blew on their horns if you were in the way at all and then they hurried off. People used to stand in the street and catch up with one another as old friends are supposed to but now there were guys standing around asking any passerby for spare change. The streets seemed dirtier, the people more unfriendly and even the shop owners that used to wave as kids walked by were shooing them away if they didn't have any money. Shopkeepers were vigilant against thieves and looters, no longer were the days of strangers smiling to one another but now walking with your hand on your billfold for fear of being robbed or pick pocketed. Isaiah continued to wander the once familiar streets of his past, hoping to find comfort in the city he once loved dearly. Turning corner after corner on his way home was more and more depressing, images of some of the bombed cities flashed back to him and with each one he froze in his steps for a moment.

A man in a brown leather coat with sharp lapels rounded a corner nearly the same time as Isaiah and the two men gently collided. "Excuse me" Isaiah politely began their conversation. "Ain't no excuse man, you be watching where you going" the other man stood promptly and ready to defend that he hadn't done anything in the wrong. Isaiah was already tired of the heavy attitude around him and was on the verge of sidestepping before he recognized the dark black mole at the corner of the mans' mouth; "Rocket Ricky?"Isaiah questioned. The man was once known as Rocket Ricky when he was a boy because there wasn't anybody that could out run him; it was like his legs were rockets when it came to racing down the long stretches of pavement. The man drew an arm up in aggression and Isaiah lifted both of his hands out of defense, Isaiah felt his blood boil and for a moment he couldn't see the man he was squaring off with; fire was his only vision. In the white hot flash of a battle hardened man Isaiah felt his hands grip in preparation to fight to the death out of instinct and it took a moment to swallow it down.

"It's just Ricky, who wants to know" the man asked before deciding whether or not to throw a punch. "Isaiah Venney" Isaiah answered as he slowly let his arms drop and his shoulders droop. Ricky opened his clenched hand and apologized that he didn't recognize the boy from his youth, after all it had been man years and time changes everyone. The two men exchanged quick "how-do's" and as the pleasantries stretched out Isaiah asked Ricky what he had been doing for work since it was scarce in the area. Isaiah hoped that his childhood friend could give him a lead on a job or even a good mention to a boss but even more heartache came out. "Man I just been doing me things you know?" Ricky began to explain that since his father was into grass that he ended up being just like him, mostly just grass but sometimes depending on who was wanting what, he could do some more.

Isaiah tried to explain that he came from a hard-working man and that was a good thing but his old-man Eddie was a dock-man and it didn't mean that he had to be a dock-man also. Ricky argued that he liked the grass and smoked when he could, nothing much else bothered him and he liked things the way they was. Isaiah was saddened that things were so glum and he was beginning to become sullen to the once proud city and then Ricky piped up again: "Hey you got any cash?" Isaiah pulled a few singles out of his pocket, the only money he had with him and it only came to about three dollars, while still looking down at his pocket "*THWACK*" a closed right fist connected with his left temple at the hairline; knocking him to the ground.

Isaiah remained conscious as he laid on that sidewalk, the cold from the pavement numbed his backside as he watched the sky continue to cloud over. "Has love gone for good?" he asked himself out loud. Isaiah had love growing up, he and his three brothers were shown what love was; Eddie and Ronetta loved each other and their sons. Isaiah knew that there was no love in Vietnam as everyone was trying to kill one another and even among soldiers; there was only a profound love of killing and it was sad. The innocent words written by Georgie had left Isaiah with hope that when he left the war behind that he could return to the city he once loved but it appeared that even in such a large city, there was no love left. "It was three dollars" Isaiah shouted out to no one as he laid on the ground befuddled, there was no response to his shout, just throbbing in his head.

Even with heroes such as Lt Frank Petersen that flew in Korea and Vietnam and proved that black men were just as capable there were still people out there standing up against treating men like men. The flashes of small segregated groups in battle still showed how little mankind has come to being kind men and Isaiah was laid out on the ground with a pounding headache because a man would rather steal three whole dollars than work for it. News stations covered Hanoi Jane and her endless shame she brought to America and the war showed more and more casualties but injured men never graced the screens because it would have brought shame on the government that allowed crippled injured men to remain crippled. The pulsing headache only added to Isaiah's awareness that the other war wasn't one being fought with guns but with signs, dogs, water hoses and rallies.

The fight to be simply treated as an equal was a hard one in the area because everything was unequal, businesses were laying off people with any seniority in order to bring in cheaper labor and hordes of fine fit men were simply being traded in for cheaper bodies, the downturn was in a snowball and the more people getting pink slips meant that more people were doing shameful things out of necessity and desperation, even to the point that a childhood friend needed to rob him for three measly dollars. Isaiah wasn't in a hurry to stand up, there were people walking around him and after the twentieth person stepped over him he was disgusted that not a single person made any attempt to help the fallen man, and a war solider at that, to his feet.

Isaiah spent years watching fellow soldiers fight for his countrymen and not a single one of them bothered to extend a hand to help him up. The cold dirty ground was the epitome of what had become of his community, once upon a time his father Eddie explained that people of the same neighborhood need to watch out for one another, get your neighbors good jobs and encourage them to raise up good kids.

Paper Paulie

The sense of community had gone, Isaiah had no idea how much had changed in the time he was away but coming back he looked forward to being able to idly chit chat with men along the streets like his father used to when he was a boy. Sitting around some of the small fires on base back during the war brought him back to his days watching his father put on his nicer clothes and go and shake hands on the way to the market and back. "You can't know everybody, but you can know a great many people if you just start by shaking hands" Eddie once told Isaiah. It would be hard to know everybody but as a manner of speaking if you knew enough people then the people they knew might know you also Isaiah remembered figuring out when he was trying to make introductions while at basic training before going to war.

Getting up wasn't the hard part when Isaiah rose up, it was getting going again. Isaiah had been shown strength time and time again when Eddie worked, he often worked long days or long weeks and even when he got home late most nights he took a moment to kiss each of his sons on the forehead as a reminder of why he pushed himself to work as hard as he did before nearly collapsing for a short night of rest before returning the next day and doing it all over again. Isaiah knew how to be relentless and as hard working as an ox; his father showed him how,the hardest part of getting going now was finding a purpose and following it.

After some hearty rubbing Isaiah decided that the city he once knew and loved was no longer familiar to him and that meant that if any city was strange that he could start over in any city and feel the same. Isaiah had a hard time coming up with a game plan at first but he had some money he saved up from the army (at a rate of $58 per month hazard pay it wasn't much) and he decided that he could indeed follow his dream. Ronetta was sad to think that her last son would be moving away and Isaiah had a hard time realizing that she already lost Ronnie but that his death was for a purpose and he wanted to uphold that purpose by moving on with his own life. Eddie supported his sons, when each one moved out or moved on they did so knowing that both of their parents wished the best for them. Isaiah played with a map to look into cities that might have more to offer before settling on a new destination.

Scranton was where Isaiah moved to, he found an ad in a newspaper that the large train yard there was hiring men to work overnight to keep many drifters away from their cargo, there were many positions opening up and with a phone call, he had a job to look forward to. Riding the bus helped Isaiah to meet some new people; he met a boy carrying a guitar and heading west to be a performer,he met two ladies that heard that Detroit was putting out new music and a jumping place to live. Isaiah even met a man that had been down south and marched in a peace movement that left him with broken bones and scars across his face, "some peace movement" Isaiah thought to himself as he listened on.Each person had their own life and purpose; it was different riding that bus compared to any of the ones in Vietnam.

The bus ride was long and drawn out in order for Isaiah to get to where he needed to go but he made it. Scranton wasn't nearly the size of Brooklyn nor was it on the water like he was used to but he was determined to make it his home. The foreman at the train yard was a tall Irish fellow, he had a large upper body from years of shoveling coal or whatever else and he spoke with a hefty grumble. Kerby Willoughby was an army man that served in Korea and even though he was as tough as any Irishman could be, he stuck up for fellow servicemen no matter who they was. Kerby caught some heat for hiring the wrong kind of man and he told Isaiah that he had better be as hard a worker as any of the others coming back from the war because there were many of them that wanted his job; basically,he'd have to work hard to keep the job in not so many words.

Working the Scranton locomotive rail yard was not an easy job at first, there was plenty of equipment to learn in order to load gear or goods from the rail cars, Isaiah didn't like the plumes of coal ash that rose up into the air and settled down on him most days, he was often put on the tinder cars because it was a hard hot filthy job that nobody else wanted to do, but it was a job. Each time Isaiah wanted to quit he thought about where his life might be had his own father quit, he might have ended up like that cat Rocket Ricky and that only made him work harder. Isaiah drank a little in Nam and knew that it wasn't for him, he didn't like how tired it made him or the stomach effects it had on him the next day but the first time Kerby suggested he go to a local pub with him he was quick to accept. Isaiah had seen plenty of men give up good things for a drink, or lose good things over drinking and he had too much to do in his life so he didn't take to it much.

The two men went to a small pub and immediately there was heat, a large scowling man standing with his arms crossed shoved his hand out and told Isaiah "move along boy."Kerby seemed to have a smile on his face when the doorman blocked Isaiah from going into *The Piston*." Isaiah wasn't bothered that he couldn't have a beer, he wouldn't miss it, but he found himself getting hot under the collar about the lack of respect to himself as a person, especially from Kerby as the inviter. "Hundred and seventy-first platoon, A-company" Isaiah began to ramble out his credentials as the bouncer guy held up his hand again and pressed it against his chest. Isaiah flashed for a moment that all he had to do was reach up and grab onto the man's thumb and twist it counterclockwise and the man would not only lose the use of that thumb but he would also drop to his knees in pain and no longer be in the way. Instead Isaiah thought that maybe offering the man ten dollars would be good enough to get him through the door, he still had no interest in drinking but he didn't appreciate the disrespect.

As Isaiah pried his wallet open to offer some money for entrance, there it was, the small folded square had been sealed and now hardened with time but it was still Paper Paulie. Isaiah thought back to his first impression of the boy that made Paulie, an innocent young man just trying to help a stranger have a better day. Staring into the wallet fold Isaiah began to smile, his smirk caused the bouncer to lower his hand and outstretch his head a little trying to pry into Isaiah's view, "What are you laughing at boy" the man demanded to know with an even more aggressive tone in his voice. Isaiah took in a deep breath before he began to talk.

"I once had a boy write me a letter and wish for my safety, the letter sat with me through an ambush and while I watched half of my platoon cut down under enemy fire I kept relying on that letter to keep me alive, and it did, it would be a shame if my promise to stay alive through an ugly war was tarnished because some ignorant fool wanted to huff and puff and I happened to beat the snot out of him and leave him bleeding; have a good night." Isaiah closed up his wallet and tucked it back into his pocket and about faced and walked back for the night. Walking away from "The Piston" pub Isaiah took in a deep breath, his adrenaline pumped a bit from the near brush with the larger older man but he was proud of himself, he was still a young man and more than equipped to physically handle anyone he needed to and the military trained him to be able to do so but more than being in physical control of someone else, he was empowered because he was mentally in control of himself.

The next day Kerby actually apologized and didn't mean for the confrontation, he thought Isaiah was right on his boot heels and didn't realize he wasn't until Isaiah had already gone. Isaiah wanted to spit in his face but he thought back to the innocent letters that Georgie from North Dakota had written and he told himself that community can't be entirely gone unless he himself gives up on it too.Kerby unofficially put Isaiah in a supervisor position for how well he handled everything so his forward momentum began.Isaiah worked the overnight shift and found places around the train yard to sleep until he found a good enough place that he could put a bed, it was tough living out of a duffle bag for a few weeks and it was hard not having an address to receive letters from his mother Ronetta but it was much easier than sleeping in the mud so he made the best from what he could.

With enough money saved up and a good job Isaiah began looking for a small storefront to begin his radio store, he liked music and he liked the idea of working for himself so he got started on building his dream rather than helping someone else build theirs. Isaiah found a small inlet shop for rent on Bass street, it looked like it used to be a newspaper stand or small five and dime but the price was good and it would do. Isaiah found places to order radios and in the back of the small store there was enough room for a bunk bed, the top to sleep in and the bottom to tuck away a dresser for clothes and a work table for repairs. Isaiah had his own store within two weeks; he rushed to open because the longer it took the more money it cost so Ronnie's Radio's was open for business in no time. The small strip of stores was welcoming to the new business; they all shared in the common goal of bringing shoppers and consumers so more businesses meant more business.

Isaiah kept working his overnight job and then went straight to open his store, in the evenings he would close up and sleep for a couple few hours in order to be rested enough to work overnight for Kerby and keep up on his promise to be a hard worker. Next to Ronnie's Radio's was a small butchery run by a Greek man named Agepatos, or Augie as he was known. Augie had thick black hair on the sides of his head but very thinned on the top, the corners of his eyes wrinkled when he smiled and he was genuine when he tried to help his customers, including Isaiah. Isaiah would sometimes stand out front with Augie and discuss goings on around the neighborhood trying to slowly learn the city better and better each day. Augie had thick hands and forearms from years of working large hunks of meats and carving knives, he also has a thundering laugh when he'd get carried away with a story from his past.

Down from Augie and the meat market was a bakery that was run by a Romanian couple; the Vasillas and a younger girl that worked for them. The girl was a beautiful lighter skinned girl named Delores, she was a few years younger than Isaiah and she had a bright toothy smile. Isaiah liked Delores from the start, except that he worked two hard jobs to keep his store open and profitable and he was often too tired to talk much. Delores worked hard for the Vasillas and even though she hardly got much of a break, she would sometimes run a small loaf of extra bread down to Isaiah or casually stroll down the sidewalk passed the stores just to get to glance at him toiling away in his shop under the excuse of getting some fresh air. Delores worked from very early to around midday, by the time Isaiah was closing his store to sleep Delores would sometimes have walked by and waved on her way home, Isaiah would usually make sure he was close to the front window around the early afternoon when she was on her way home in order to make good eye contact and exchange smiles.

Delores respected that Isaiah was such a hard worker, she worked for the small bakery long enough to know the struggles of running a business and she was afraid of being a distraction so she held back on spending too much time getting to know Isaiah for the first while. Isaiah was distraught working all the time but seeing the girls' bright smile helped him to find reason to keep working both jobs. It was hard living out of the back of his own store and still maintaining his own business but Isaiah told himself, and Paper Paulie, that he would work hard enough to earn the right to ask the girl on a proper date. Isaiah also had ideology that he wanted to be able to deserve such a girl and only such a girl would date a man with real substance, not one of those cats like Rocket Ricky that just pilfers or swindles day to day.

Isaiah had a small box of his belongings when he moved from his store into a home with Delores, in it contained his boots from the army, his dog-tags and also a small wax square that was once Paper Paulie. Isaiah felt comfortable leaving Paulie behind when he began dating Delores, the woman was vibrant, smart, and diligent in her ways which made her an exemplary employee at the bakery. When he was starting out Isaiah kept his store open as many hours as he physically could in order to attract business and show that he was a reputable shop owner, it was slow to build a clientele base but living at the store meant his wages from the train yard could be spent to keep his store open while the slow process of building a reputation commenced. Delores didn't mind spending time with Isaiah listening to the radio playing Otis Redding or Diana Ross through a speaker in the small shop, they also danced when no one else was around; the main floor of his shop was also their own private dance floor.

Isaiah couldn't afford much but he knew almost immediately that he felt towards her the way his father felt towards his mother and that was that. One night shortly after slowly moving into their small home together Delores asked about the closed box, it was heavier than it looked and things inside thunked around which spiked her curiosity. Isaiah explained the contents but pulled out the small wax square and held it up; "this is very dear to me, only when I met you did I feel safe enough to put my friend in a special place, this is Paper Paulie" he began. Delores smiled thinking that Isaiah was clowning around until his voice took a different tone. Isaiah spoke about the ambush on the riverbank and watching the men get cut down by enemy machine gun fire and his promises to a mere envelope in his pocket if he were to survive the onslaught.

Delores sat bent with her forearms pressed against their kitchen counter as Isaiah acted out crouching down in the small pit, hidden under brush and praying to anything that could hear him that he wanted to survive. Isaiah knew that it may have been silly to promise a piece of paper that he would read it if he survived but he did in fact survive. "In all the men in my platoon I was the one with this little paper doll coated in wax tucked into my pocket and I was the only one to make out of that day alive." Skirmish after skirmish and fight after fight Isaiah was entangled in; fights that he should have perished in, especially on the hill they called "The Grinder," and each time he knew that Paper Paulie was keeping him alive and safe. Delores welled up a little when Isaiah reached the point that he spoke about Ronnie, turning an injured man over and looking into the bloodied face of his younger brother; thousands of miles from home and dying, scared.

Delores understood the strong desire to hold onto something pure and innocent, that was Paper Paulie and with a small kiss of thanks for keeping Isaiah safe, Delores tucked Paper Paulie back into the box where he belonged. Isaiah didn't like to talk about the war, not many people did, it was easier for many people to blame one thing or another and then turn their backs on their very brothers that tried to protect them in a foreign land and that made for harsh times to live in. Isaiah focused on his job and his business and when Delores was done at the bakery she often helped to work in the radio store so that Isaiah could sleep a bit more. Together Isaiah and Delores both worked hard, Delores was a wonderful cook and many of her meals included bread bowls or biscuits that came from recipes she picked up in the bakery, Isaiah couldn't have been happier.

The business corridor where *Ronnie's Radio's* was located was a cultural mixture of owners, each trying to make their way to success and the ability to amply provide for their own families. Augie worked hard to provide for a wife and three daughters while the bakers had their own children they often went to go and see. The small mixture of people made for a small but comfortable secondary family.There was a small family of Asians that worked the pharmacy on the far corner and each time any of them went out they were very polite and waved to everyone. It was hard to keep working both jobs but the radio store wasn't sufficient enough to let go of working for Kerby at the train yard even when Delores pleaded a few times for Isaiah to not work as hard and to see her more he knew he needed the money and like his father, he was willing to work for it.

The wedding was small and with much misfortune, nobody from Isaiah's family made the long bus ride but it didn't stop them from sharing a small gifted cake from the bakery and some upbeat songs to dance to on a newer model radio he borrowed from his own store, the only day that month he closed the store and it was a right good Sunday for it. Isaiah and Delores made the ride back to Brooklyn shortly after the wedding and like a proud father; Eddie was quick to shake his sons hand in congratulations. Ronetta bypassed her second son with open arms and misty eyes to welcome her daughter-in-law to the family; she had raised four sons so having another girl around for a bit was a great relief for her.

Delores wore her favorite yellow dress with white polka dots on it and white gloves; she was always an elegant lady and dressed to reflect how she felt about herself. Ronetta knew that it had only been a few weeks from the wedding but once the hug was in place and the two ladies were cheek to cheek, she knew. "Girl you're pregnant" Ronetta began hollering out. At that point Delores only had a slight suspicion because she had felt a bit warmer on their trip to Brooklyn but with a slight embrace, Ronetta was all but certain. Delores let her cheeks flush and she dipped her chin down, she wanted to be the first to find out and share it with her husband but his mother exposed their secret. Isaiah couldn't have been happier even though deep down he knew it would take more hard work, he wanted a family with Delores and it was coming quickly.

Isaiah was on top of the world to find out that his family was blooming, he was delighted to meet with his parents and introduce them to his new wife but to find out he was going to be a father was more than enough to ensure him that Delores was his good luck charm in life. Nineteen seventy-one came with a wedding and ended with the birth of a baby boy, Sidney Hendrix Venney, to honor Eddie's long time hero Sidney Poitier and Delores' idol Jimi Hendrix. The radio store picked up through the summer and it was enough that once Sidney was born Delores could drop down to part time or less with the bakery. Isaiah trudged on working, it was crucial that he kept working in order to have the best for his son and he juggled the two jobs for a long time. Isaiah had Eddie to look up to and each time he felt like he was wearing down he thought back to his father working endless hours for weeks on end so that Ronetta could watch over him and his brothers to ensure that they each knew that they had loving parents, so he carried on.

Sidney was a healthy boy, he crawled early and was quick to pick up his shapes and colors; all tasks his mother Delores encouraged him to learn. Delores and Isaiah struggled but they struggled together, the long nights without Isaiah were sometimes hard on Delores and through some of them she learned to talk to her husband and he also learned to just listen. Once Sidney was big enough to crawl or move around and no longer dependent Delores for feedings he was toted with Isaiah to the radio store to show off to his business friends such as Augie and the Vassilles. Augie loved the little lad and made joking references that little Sidney looked just like him (Augie). Sidney would crawl all around the radio store while Delores worked two doors down at the bakery and in the midst of crawls to explore near the windows, certain songs would stop him mid-crawl.

Sidney liked the Supremes or Stevie Wonder and he would sway side to side while on his hands and knees. As Sidney grew he watched out the front window of the radio store, times changed and Isaiah adapted to selling newer equipment and record players but it didn't matter, his taste in music still kept his young son dancing. Isaiah and Delores kept their love for one another and even though it only resulted in Sidney, he was a happy healthy young boy and the Venney's were a close happy family on Bass street.

Paper Paulie

Ch. 6

As kids grow their curiosity does as well, Sidney was a typical boy that liked to play army with his friends, even against the insistence of his mother and father. Sidney followed in his fathers' footsteps, he kept his hair cut short and kept his shoulders back in good form as he walked, he even emulated the sharp snaps that still remained in some of Isaiah's cadent walking. Sidney liked mathematics; he even had a teacher named Harvey Rene that encouraged him in elementary school to play with numbers and find patterns or to exercise different practices when playing with numbers. Sidney was talented at manipulating numbers to get different outcomes, it came in handy when he was playing with resistors at the shop with his father Isaiah and he was also an astute pupil when it came time to learn about electronics and circuits.

Around the time Sidney was thirteen or so he took more of an interest in his father's time in the military, while other boys at his school were taking to skateboarding he was hearing of the increasing tension in Granada, a Caribbean island that was growing in political tension. Sidney loved his parents both but the more they encouraged him to enjoy being a young man and not to worry so much about the possible outbreak of any war, the more he was sitting with friends and watching the news coverage of military troops gearing up for a possible invasion. Stories of Vietnam were scarce in the Venney home, Delores cooked and hummed along to Tina Turner on the radio and Isaiah kept working hard to load and off load train cars for the locomotive yard as well as keep up on his still thriving radio store, neither wanted to sit down and talk brass tacks about such an ugly war that happened during even uglier times for the united states.

Sidney learned plenty from his friends and during the time he was in junior high school, many of his playmates and teammates shared their takes on the history that came with being black. His history was a tarnished one and it was hard to grasp the reality of it all, men doing atrocious things to other men and the degree of it all was sickening. Isaiah and Delores had ample friends that spanned the spectrum of people, Delores adored the Romanians that taught her endless baking skills and Sidney looked up to them as adopted grandparents when he got to go to the bakery for sweets and deserts, they made Turkish delights as well as sugared Hungarian pastries (Augie was always window bound for them). Isaiah and Delores both wanted their son to know a world where love wasn't just present but a precedent, one that may have been born from a tattered history but one that was vibrant and beautiful anyways with a flourishing future.

Sidney loved having the mixed stores nearby, the Chinese couple that ran the pharmacy were the Yans and they adored Sidney when he came around to help them load up the newspaper bins, the bundles were heavy and he took it upon himself to go and help out of his father's dream of a blooming community. The Yans were always willing to offer Sidney a candy bar for his trouble but the truth was it was no trouble at all. Sidney was raised to take pride in himself and his surroundings, he felt at home among the clean shops and stores and each of the owners knew him by name and it made him feel good. Sidney held his head up high when he palled around with his friends and all the shop owners waved to him or called out to him by name, there was a pride that elated the boy and Sidney had it from many people in his life.

Sidney had many friends, he liked to play baseball with boys from school, he enjoyed playing Augie in checkers out front of the stores and of course his Romanian adopted grandparents the Vassilles (their names were always hard to pronounce so he referred to them as Nan and Pap) often had small wooden brain teaser puzzles to stump him with but he liked the challenges. Sidney was an ambitious child, once he saved up his candy bar credits with the Yans to bribe some of his teammates to come down and help him hose off and then scrub the sidewalks around the stores to help keep things clean for his parents at the radio store as well as his friends the Vassilles and Augie, everyone was extremely appreciative and impressed at the creativity to get a good job done.

Sidney had many friends that were like him, friends that had parents that were in the war but hardly spoke about it or friends that also took pride in their home town. All young boys feel patriotic with morning pledges of allegiance and recesses full of mock war games and Sidney loved each dirt crawling moment of it, even if his parents did not. Isaiah knew all too well the horrors that came from battle and he did his best to put it all behind him until one day when Sidney was a young teen and the one small memory box of military origin was pried open by his curious son. "Dad, is this your army stuff?" Sidney tilted the box to reveal a worn pair of boots and listen to the *clink* of the metal dog-tags sliding inside. Isaiah gave a brief nod to his son while reaching to close the lid and once again hide away all of the memories, he had hoped that his own son would never know the hardships faced on foreign soil and that his own battles would pave a brighter future for his son.

Something slid inside the boot as it tilted while Isaiah was closing the box, "wait" Sidney hurried to reach into the box and pull out a small wad of hardened matter from the boot, it almost looked like a lump of coal but he had to know what it was. As Isaiah was closing the lid Sidney made the fastest hand dash known to man and stabbed his straight hand deep down into the boot like an eagle snatching a fish from the water and retrieved the small object. Sidney rolled and turned the small object around while investigating the random hairs or fabric strings embedded into the coating, it was once folded neatly but after tumbling around in an old boot for many years the corners had worn down and the once smooth outer coating of wax had divots and random dirt pressed in.

"Hey pappy" Sidney held up the waxy briquette looking curiosity with a raised eyebrow. Watching Sidney turn the small object over and over with his fingers Isaiah paused for a moment and let the corners of his mouth rise up; "that is my pal" he began. Sidney looked over the object in focus and let his eyes fixate on his father that was now seated near his feet and staring at him intently. It was hard for Sidney to understand what his father was talking about and he had hardly remembered some of the stories his father made up to tell him when he was a boy, stories about a boy named Paulie traveling far far away to make friends and keep people safe. Isaiah made up the stories to sooth a crying child fending off ear infections or a fever like some children do at times, but as he aged the stories faded away from both presence and memory.

Isaiah did his best to leave out many of the details that Sidney didn't need exposure to but he told his son of how Paper Paulie helped to save him in the war across the world. Paper Paulie showed up at a hard time; shortly after he arrived in a foreign land, Paulie became his friend because he had someone with him even when there was nobody else. Paper Paulie was just a cut out and colored paper creation sent to him from a boy in the Midwest but in the overall that small paper man spent years at war with him. Paper Paulie outlasted platoons and even when he was hunkered down avoiding enemy fire, he could still whisper to Paulie and ask him to help him find a way out of the tight spot he was in. Paulie didn't come to life or any fairy-tale sort of thing but the moment of silence and calmness that came from talking to Paulie often gave him that moment to clear his mind and plan a course of action.

Sidney snarked a little thinking about his tough worldly father consulting with a small paper doll while enemy gunfire zipped by overhead or rockets exploded nearby, he thought for a moment that his father was joking until Isaiah reached over to remove his war friend from the clutches of Sidney and return it to the relative safety of the boot bottom before placing the lid back over the box and returning it to storage. Sidney couldn't just let Paulie go, he vaguely recalled hearing mention of it a time or two when he was younger but he always thought it was actually a man Isaiah fought beside or perhaps even knew when he himself was a young man, he never guessed or had any notion that Paper Paulie was in fact a small paper cut out, it baffled him and since his father was quick to dissuade him from prodding even further, there was only one other source to turn to.

Delores was fixing fresh biscuits in the kitchen when Sidney came strolling in a few days after his strange discovery, he had a bounce in his step as he moved along on his tippy toes. Sidney kept his hands shoved into his pockets and moved with high steps like Frank Sinatra as he tried to glide across the kitchen floor. Trying to high-step dance is a tricky thing to do and it can be dangerous on a slippery floor, it's also highly recommended that you don't do it with your hands wedged deep into the pockets of your slacks either. Sidney made it halfway into the kitchen when his feet got out from underneath him. Sidney began to call for his mother when both of his feet rose up higher than his rear-end, sending him flying backwards to the ground.

Delores threw a handful of flour into the air as she used her hands to sling herself towards her falling son in an attempt to catch him before he hit the floor. Sidney slowly fell backwards, his eyes opened as wide as they could go and the whites gleaned out from his fear. Delores pulled as hard against the counter as she could while watching her son slowly tumble to the ground, her heart seized with dread. There was nothing Delores could do as she fumbled through the hard oak chairs while rushing to her son, he continued to fall while his body curled and contorted in motion.

Sidney landed with a hard thud on the ground; his body curled slightly but on his way down the back of his head caught the sharp edge of a chair, splitting it open. Delores watched as a red pool began to form beneath the still settling body of her son as his body fell motionless to the floor, her chest suddenly felt heavy and she was unable to move. Delores hit her knees as she tumbled to Sidney's side, his body falling limp as it collapsed to the ground. Sidney was always a well-dressed kid, both Delores and Isaiah took pride in themselves and they raised a young boy that liked to wear dress shirts and bow-ties when he was much younger but resorted back to collared shirts as a teen. Sidney laid on the floor, his eyes closed and his red and blue striped polo shirt beginning to wick blood along the collar of the shirt, there was no movement in the young man.

Delores let out a glass shattering shriek in horror and then her heart and her head began to argue. Her motherly instincts wanted to coddle her son and begin to pray that he'd be alright but her head told her to call for an ambulance to get him medical help as fast as possible but her body seized in panic. Sidney laid still; there was almost no motion in his body now so her urgency was dire. With tear filled eyes Delores hurried to her feet and began to frantically reach out for the telephone. The operator promised to dispatch an ambulance in a hurry and she let the phone fall in order to race back to be by her son's side to begin trying to stop the bleeding. Delores knew to try and hold the wound closed to slow the bleeding and as she raised her sons head to her body the pool of blood was even larger. Delores couldn't contain her crying; her tears poured down her face and began to soak the chest of Sidney's shirt.

The lump on the back of Sidney's head was as large as Delores' fist; she held on as tightly as she could and continued to pray that her son would be alright. The wait seemed to take not hours but days before there was a knock at the door, the paramedics announced their arrival and were told to enter the home. The main door was open but out of safety Delores always locked the front screen door and the larger of the two men had to brace one foot and break the handle on the door to enter. The men strapped Sidney to a board and hurried them both out the door. Delores was trembling with fear through the whole ride in the back of the ambulance, her fear froze her but her eyes continued to stream tears down her face as she watched her motionless son bobble and jostle lightly on the gurney while the vehicle sped through town and hit small bumps in the road.

The hospital staff were very quick and diligent in assessing Sidney while rushing him to surgery for a head trauma. Delores was so overwhelmed with trying to make sure that her son would be safe that she hadn't found the moment to phone her husband Isaiah and inform him of what had happened. Isaiah was still at the radio store when the phone rang, the couple had worked out an ideal work schedule that Delores would go and work at the bakery very early in the morning and Isaiah would handle the early mornings of getting Sidney up and ready for school and then he would go and open the radio store and then Delores would be home in the afternoons to welcome Sidney home and help to coordinate getting homework done and so on. The morning routine between Isaiah and Sidney had the military cadence Isaiah liked in his life, sometimes he would put on his Sam Cooke record and let the rhythm of *Chain Gang* put both men into motion while dressing and readying for their day together.

The tone of Delores' voice immediately sent Isaiah into a panic, his wife always kept a soothing tone when she spoke and to hear her in tears as she forced out mumbled words made his forehead instantly turn hot and begin to perspire. Isaiah closed early and headed to the hospital to join his wife in hoping for their son's recovery and positive outcome from his freak accident. Isaiah was rife with dread the entire ride, it seemed to take days before finally being able to step into the hospital and locate his shaken wife. Delores was wearing a pretty pink blouse that was splattered with the blood of their child, a terrible sight for any parent. Isaiah was already amped up with adrenaline mixed with anticipation from not knowing much about everything, he was given the news about his son over the phone and then had to deal with a long ride to the hospital and the entire time he was riddled with anxiety and worry from not knowing anything.

Delores couldn't squeeze Isaiah any tighter in her hug when they found each other, all of the rest of her emotions and concerns were pent up and finally seeing her strong husband gave her some reassurance and she unleashed her sobs and crying into the crick of his neck as she held him tightly. The long wait was dreadful, it was grueling to have to wait, the lobby of the hospital was frightfully sterile, everything was sanitary white and without any calming adornments to comfort the worried couple. Every parent has a moment of sheer terror, that moment when their young child wasn't directly where they were supposed to be or they make that motion like they might turn out and run into the path of an oncoming car but to watch your child have to be strapped into a stretcher or to have to pace the long hours while they sit in surgery without any idea of how things are going is a miserably long time to have to wait.

The clock on the wall had two long black hands that hardly moved, minutes, hours and days filled in between the small shuttered movements of the minute hand and time nearly went in reverse as Isaiah and Delores waited for anyone to come to them with information about their son. Everything went through the minds of the worried parents, could they afford a funeral, they didn't have the fortune of more children other than Sidney so would it be too late to be blessed with another child if Sidney does in fact pass away or would it be just the two of them growing old together without the love of grandchildren? The worry continued, people came and went in and out of the lobby and the couple tried their best to be strong for their son but the long hours wore heavy.

After a third or fourth cup of coffee a man in a long white coat finally came out of the double doors and walked straight towards the Venney's. Isaiah took a deep breath, having been through battle he knew that squeezing his leg muscles and filling his lungs with breath before moving helped to prevent blacking out or getting light

headed or riddled with adrenaline and then he stood up.
"Sir" the man in the white coat began to speak. "Sidney is
waiting for you, I'll escort you both back." Isaiah was
rendered mute for a moment, he tried to speak and ask
how he was waiting but his voice was not there. Delores
was still weeping and couldn't ask in what sorts her son
was in. The Venney's were both scared of what they were
about to find, no one had told them what to expect and
with the lapse in time they were both certain that the news
would be terrible.

Isaiah and Delores followed the man closely, the
tails from his coat flowed behind him from his fast
walking pace but Delores and Isaiah were both in a rush
to get to their son and they nearly trampled the man.
Rounding the first corner all Isaiah could see were pulled
curtains and some nurses standing in the hallway, of all
the people that were standing around surely someone
could have taken the minute to come and give him and his
terrified wife some reassurance or an update on Sidney's
condition, but they had to sit in worry. A moment of
anger crept into the mind of Isaiah, he had been in high
adrenaline situations plenty but this was over the life of
his one and only son and the shear lack of respect was one
that wasn't going to be forgotten quickly.

Turning around one last corner Delores saw her
son; the sight nearly stopped her heart. Sidney was lying
on a hospital bed; bed sheet pulled up to his armpits and
tucked in tightly. Sidney's toes were still, his legs did not

move and as she scanned upwards he was lying there, sucking on a blue popsicle with a smile on his face. "Hey, they have red too" he said as he waved his popsicle to his parents while they rushed towards him, nearly bowling over the man that came to guide them back to their son. Isaiah flipped from angry to shakenly relieved to angry to happy at least a dozen times in the time it took him to walk the three last large square tiles on the floor. Delores began crying again as she reached out to hug her son.

"Hey boss, what the heck here?" Isaiah had to ask the man in the flowy coat before he scampered off. The man explained that Sidney knocked himself pretty good and they had to buzz a small patch of his hair out to put in eight stitches. The hospital staff wanted to monitor him for a short while to make sure there was no brain injury and that there appeared to be no problems other than the small bald spot in the back of his head, which would grow back soon enough. Isaiah was greatly relieved but he inquired why he and his wife had been left without answers for hours, it was downright rude after all. The man apologized about the mix up, there was a heavy set redhead nurse that was in charge of relaying information to patient families and she must have messed up and told the wrong family, she was infamous around the ward for mistakes and screw ups, some of the other nurses were glad she wasn't in charge or making work schedules or doing anything of dire importance, due to the frequent failures to do her job but that was how it goes sometimes.

"Can you hand me something" Sidney piped up as he hugged his mother back and raised his free hand to shake his father's hand. Isaiah was holding his sons hand and looking his son over to make sure that he was indeed ok and then he nodded in response. Sidney pointed to his plastic belongings bag and motioned that he needed to have something in it. "I'm sorry for getting blood on the floor, and my shirt, and on those nice men that helped to carry me; if we see them can I apologize to them?" Sidney asked as he began to rummage through his bag to find his pants. Sidney handed his mother his popsicle to hold while he pulled and pried at an item inside the bag before he removed his head and closed his eyes. "Sorry dad" he muttered as he pulled out the small folded beaten square of wax. "I was going to ask mom more about it before you got home because you didn't really want to talk about much" Sidney mentioned as he handed Paper Paulie back to his father.

"Boy, I will tell you what I need to tell you when the time comes, how's that?" Delores began swiping her left arm behind her to catch Isaiah's attention as he reached to take back his small paper pal. "Isaiah, don't you realize that Paulie protected your son." Isaiah looked at the small wad of paper and gave it a sincere "thanks pal" before tucking it into his shirt pocket, "I sure do, I sure do" Isaiah repeated in amazement.It was time to get out of the hospital and with great relief. Sidney dealt with a headache when moving a whole lot but his parents both looped their arms with his and they looked like they were ready to march down the yellow brick road while helping to hold him up just in case his dizziness overtook him on their way out.

The small shaved patch in the back of Sidney's hair did grow back, he still found the small spots where hair no longer grew from the scar whenever he took his hair down really short in the back but like many other things in life, it was behind him. Sidney graduated high school and continued to strive in the community that his parents helped to maintain. When it came to the business family Augie and the Vassilles were all there to witness their collectively adopted son Sidney don his cap and gown and get his diploma. Augie had grown gray and his bushy mustache had slowly inched down over his mouth, making it harder to understand him with his thick accent but he was proud of the once very young boy he taught chess to. During the summers Sidney learned carving and curing processes from Augie, as well as rolling and shaping from the bakers. Sidney learned all sorts of life skills from the neighbor businesses that needed the extra set of hands on busy days and he was always willing to pick up shifts to help out anyone that needed him too, he also managed to pocket good money from his hard work.

With an uncertainty of where to go next and high-school behind him Sidney did exactly what Isaiah and Delores had hoped he wouldn't do, he enlisted. The military was a much more accepting place for a young man than it was when Isaiah joined, it had been almost twenty years since Isaiah finally made it home but there were still thousands of soldiers that hadn't and that was still a hard truth to accept. Sidney wanted to serve his country as well as his parents. To honor his father Sidney wanted to follow in his footsteps and if it meant putting his life on the line than he was going to do it proudly. Delores was supportive of Sidney but she also knew things that he didn't, she knew the long term risks if he were to be deployed as she had been married to Isaiah for two decades now and there were still nights he would jolt awake, scaring the tar out of her in the midst of a bad dream and she didn't want that for her son.

Things were calm around the world when Sidney first joined up, there had been tension among imbeciles in the Middle East ever since there was a Middle East and Isaiah monitored it frequently as his son aged from the televisions in his store but once Sidney signed the papers, he was much more vigilant and concerned about his son. Isaiah encouraged his son to find a safer role to play, he suggested communications and pointed out how prepared he had been for that job his entire life but Sidney was determined to be a fighting man just like his father. Isaiah still had a hard time talking about the things he crossed while he was at war and with all of his might he hoped that Sidney's military enlistment would be short and peaceful, much to the opposite of his tour of duty.

Sidney said farewell to his parent's shortly after high school and spent his time in basic training. Sidney excelled at math from working with electronics growing up and even though he didn't want to be fully involved with communications, he was tasked with assisting in troop logistics. The job was fun for Sidney; it was a challenge keeping track of men, supplies, and armory, much like a large chess game, but with many more pieces. Sidney remained stateside through his additional schooling for his job but then he was to be relocated to a base in Germany. Isaiah was concerned for Sidney and knew that he would miss his son but this was a chance for him to stamp his boot print somewhere else in the world as he did and become a man. Delores didn't like the idea of her son being so far away but she also knew that she and Isaiah raised a fine young man, and now it was time to let him prove how well he was raised up.

The times between letters were a bit of a struggle for Delores and Isaiah. The unknown silence often times went for weeks between letters or phone calls. The calls were so crackled and hard to hear that it was just as frustrating as the silence. Delores had become part owner of the bakery while Sidney was in basic training, the Vasilles wanted to leave it to their daughter that went away for school and never returned to live but she didn't have any interest in following in her parents' traditions, she went into banking instead. Delores wanted to do her best to keep the business open and running like everyone knew it to and she was already well equipped to run a business due to practice with Isaiah and the radio store.

Paper Paulie

Things around the Venney home were much quieter without a little boy running around and being a boy. Many times both Isaiah and Delores had wished that they had been blessed with a second child but they also looked forward to time to be adults and then get to be grandparents. Isaiah had stopped working brutal hours of midnights and days while Sidney was in junior high, he still picked up a shift here and there when Kerby had called and begged but once Kerby passed away, the new yard manager had very little use for a man that only worked when he was called to. Isaiah didn't mind no longer getting calls from the yard, it was strange to teach himself how to sleep at night rather than when it was light out but he slowly adjusted and then began to feel spoiled over it.

Sidney and Delores attended Kerby's funeral, the man died of liver failure and left behind a little girl named Mindy and an ex-wife that did seem to miss him once he was gone. Kerby spent most of his life in the train yard or the pub and there were more pub patrons attending his funeral than family members but Isaiah worked for him for nearly fifteen full years, he owed the man the respect and appreciation for keeping him employed so long. The Venney's left Sidney behind at school rather than take him with them. Isaiah recalled being taken with Eddie to the shipyard and docks when he was a child, it was a blast to get to see the giant ships and watch the men conduct business but back then there wasn't much else in ways of getting to know your father, Sidney spend many afternoons learning or working with his father so he and his wife thought better of it when it came to taking their young teen to a funeral.

The times were growing faster, televisions got smaller, radio's changed from record players and 8-tracks to cassettes and rumors on the market were that some new laser disc sort of radio was going to be the next big thing and Isaiah was trying to keep up with the trends. It took work for Isaiah and Delores to raise their son with their hard working schedules but the boy learned that hard work is the best way to make anything of yourself and he in fact did. As a military logistic engineer Sidney was having a grand adventure in Germany, he sure missed his parents and his home but he was learning a new language and new culture as well as making friends with guys that he knew he'd be friends with for the rest of his life. Sidney would sometimes mail flyers home about some of the newer radios and electronics coming from Japan or China to his father, many of the military bases did exceptionally well at staying up to speed with some of the newer technology and Sidney did his part to help make sure his father kept up as well.

The first half of Isaiah's life was spent under the care of Eddie and Ronetta; his parents,when he shipped out to Vietnam he had to find out real quickly who he was and what sort of man he wanted to be and by the end it hadn't really worked. Each day in the jungle was spent trying to stay alive so in reality the only sort of thing

Isaiah learned about himself was that he was a survivor and tough enough to survive many things. When Isaiah returned everything was different, like a strange haze had rolled in and taken over a familiar setting and once Rocket Ricky had clocked him for three dollars and left him lying there on the pavement that cloudy afternoon, he was certain that he didn't know anything for sure anymore. Moving to Scranton and relying on himself to a point where Isaiah was sure he was going to figure out who he was, he met Delores then he learned what sort of husband he wanted to be, then thanks to Sidney he became the sort of father he never dreamed he could be; now it was his sons turn.

Keeping in mind how well things worked out for Isaiah and how far he had come from hard diligent work Isaiah was comforted that his son was grown and taking the steps to also become a good man on his own. Delores knew that Isaiah was proud of his son, she was also but she also kept in the back of her mind what happened to Isaiah's younger brother Ronnie. Isaiah's electronic store was still called "Ronnie's Radio's" to honor his late brother and the thought of possibly losing her son still kept her riddled with anxiety more often than not when there were long weeks without any word from Sidney. The electronic store still kept Isaiah busy, he retained the small shop he started in and just moved around counters and shelving to accommodate the larger boom-boxes that were very popular while Sidney was coming up. Isaiah did his best to keep up with the times and also to take the time to fix the small pocket radios for the young kids or old timers for free because he believed so strongly in the sense of community.

Sidney had a great time learning many of the skills he needed at various bases around the country before going abroad. Sidney wrote a letter about a girl named Shayla he met in Florida. Shayla was a linguistics operator that caught his attention immediately. Isaiah wasn't ready to tell Delores that their boy was eyeing a young girl he met; both parents had hoped that he would be out of the military like he was before he found a girl he really liked but Isaiah understood how strongly you feel about having a special someone to speak with while you are away. Delores would have given him the riot act so he held onto the news for a day before he found the best way to tell his wife. Shayla was half Puerto Rican and half Jamaican. Sidney fell in love with the girl at a small restaurant where she ordered her Cuban meal in Spanish and then returned to speaking German to her company. With some on base tutoring Shayla helped Sidney to begin to learn some German before he shipped over there. Shayla was born and raised right in Florida so English was her native tongue but Spanish was equally as important. Shayla loved the appeal of other languages and was learning sensual languages like Gaelic but also some Kurdish due to some of the heavier presence in the Middle East.

Paper Paulie

Sidney and Shayla seemed to be a sweet couple as Sidney described in his letters or calls. Sidney was worried about leaving Shayla behind when he was stationed in Germany, he knew that he would surely miss the girl but they had only been dating a short while and it was way too soon to pop the question. Isaiah consulted on the marriage topic and suggested that Sidney wait for a while, not for that long but let the distance be the weight that drives them together or apart, if they can make it through several months of being apart then it will be that much sweeter when they make it official. Sidney was unsure he was getting the best council but his father had never lead him astray so he decided to wait before purchasing an engagement ring, besides he was still pretty broke and would want to afford a much better one.

Once Sidney moved to Germany the Venney's knew it was time to accept that their son was a man and to consider packing up his remaining things, things that were fond memories to them. Sidney and Shayla didn't like it but they agreed to make the long distance work out, they spoke as often as they could and they would mail sweets and fun items to one another on the side. Sidney liked to send her exorbitant treats like Swedish candies while she would send him college university t-shirts that he liked. Sidney did care for Shayla and was always impressed at her intellect and passion for many things, including him and he often hoped he was showing her his gratitude enough. The move was fairly effortless, what Sidney couldn't take he sent back to his folks to hold onto and the rest fit into a duffle bag to take to Germany with him, except the blossoming love of his life.

Isaiah and Delores did their best to keep tabs on where they packed things when they decided it was time to consolidate Sidney's room, their boy was a man and with hope if he came back it would be to visit or bring news of a wedding. Packing things up was hard for the Venney's, each item carried a memory, each baseball card or jersey that adorned the wall, every ball cap of favorite players or shoe box containing memories from his childhood only cemented that their only son was now grown. The tears dripped over the floor as they marked each box meant for storage and playfully volleyed ideas of what to turn the spare room into, a knitting room or a library. Isaiah and Delores were coming to a new phase in their life and it was an expected one, the unexpected part was how quickly it arrived.

Paper Paulie

Ch. 7

The phone rang one Thursday afternoon at the Venney's home, it was late in the day and Delores was still putting away the dishes after their afternoon supper when Isaiah popped the phone off the receiver base; "Yellow" Isaiah answered. "I'm shipping out" a solemn and serious Sidney broke through the silence. Isaiah let his smile turn into a heavy frown as he began to snap his fingers to get Delores' attention. Sidney had been helping to monitor rising tension in Iraq and many of the leaders finally decided to begin to load up troops to begin to make forward bases in the desert to anticipate an actual outbreak of military action. The news shocked Isaiah and his heart sank, being in personnel logistics Isaiah hoped that Sidney would steer clear of the combat, but that was a far-fetched hope.

Delores pleaded and begged Sidney to find a way to get out of going, she was frightened for her son and dreaded any injury he might sustain; as any parent would, except she knew he'd strap up and go like a strong Venney man. Sidney knew he was well trained and like his father, he was willing to go to war and prove his devotion to his country. Isaiah tried his best to keep his conversation a listening one but he did ask Sidney to call him at the shop later on the following day, what Isaiah had to say he didn't want his dear wife to overhear and further worry herself. Isaiah knew first hand that if there was a hell, it wouldn't be as messy or horrible as war. Delores began thinking of things she could send him, she already made cookies to send to him in Germany and Sidney was often boasting about the treats Shayla would also send him but now he was going to war and there was no telling how long mail delays would be, and besides, chocolate chips melt in the hot desert sun.

Delores and Isaiah spent the rest of the afternoon trying to come up with a list of supplies that their son would need.Both parents expected Sidney to get a leave to come home and be with his family for a short time, maybe even bring Shayla so they could all meet but he was kept in Germany until he flew to Saudi Arabia. Sidney thought back to needing socks by the bundle when he was in the jungle, the needs of a soldier can vary from shaving supplies to candy to impress the local kids to even soccer balls to play around with, a soldier is always on the clock when they are war and playing cards or volley balls can be very useful to help relieve tension, all of these things came in handy when Isaiah was in Vietnam and he suspected that Sidney will be in the same boat in Saudi Arabia.

The call came in as anticipated while Isaiah was at the radio store; he wasn't sure what time it was over in Germany so he wanted to make sure he had the chance to talk for a few minutes without Delores nearby. "I was your age when I stepped foot onto foreign soil, armed and tasked to kill enemies that were different than me" Isaiah began. "The chaos of battle can strip you away from yourself like stripping the meat from a barbecued rib bone, you need to find the one reason to stay human, the men you might have to fight are just that; men, the men you fight beside need to remain men because if they don't they may become animals." Isaiah warned Sidney about the dangers of blood lust and how easy it is to get angry and stay angry and then you don't know how to get back. Isaiah had been briefed about what to expect from his commanders but it was different, they spat out orders and protocols that were read from a textbook written by some butter-bar (officer) that graduated with a high rank from officer school, not someone that shared blood or mud with actual fighting soldiers, this was coming from the heart of his dear father.

The tone on a battlefield is nothing like you can ever imagine, fear is not only present it takes over every cell in your body and rips through you like a wildfire. Not freezing is impossible but getting out of it is part of the key to survival. You need to get into a few brawls to begin to hone your skills as a fighter but wading out during a battle or firefight is a sure way to get yourself killed. Isaiah didn't recommend hiding but remaining a small target when possible and not just standing up into a stream of bullets and dying because you did something stupid. Sidney listened as Isaiah continued to inform him

123

that shooting an enemy is mere survival but becoming an animal and getting into the mentality of brutality or torture because you are amped up like you've never known before was something that you would regret, you have to stay human, sensible, and reasoning.

Isaiah assured Sidney that he never went into the full animal mode but he felt the buzzing in his veins as the rest of him went cold during battles. Sitting in the muddy crater while his platoon was being cut down by an enemy ambush, he wanted to fling up and begin spitting lead but the quiet crinkle of an envelope in his pocket made a sound that didn't belong there. The crinkle seemed like a slap in the brain for Isaiah and once he realized that he had the unopened letter jammed deep down into his pocket he waited long enough to realize that his men on his own side of the riverbank were being annihilated too. Had Isaiah sprung up to attack the men across the river he would have died with his platoon members when the enemy soldiers popped up on his side of the riverbank also, it was the waiting that gave him the moment to gather his thoughts before surprising the ambushers and getting the jump on them. Isaiah finally admitted for the first time in over half his life that he killed more than half a dozen men there on that riverbank, he lost three times as many but *he* made it back alive.

Sidney finally understood why his father hadn't spoken much about his time in the jungle for his whole life and that was just the first few days of the war for him.

Isaiah spoke about slowly crawling his way back toward *Chicago* and how each time he was a trigger pull from death, he kept promising the letter in his pocket that he would get back to the base safely and read it. Isaiah admitted that it was silly to put any stock in a paper cut out doll some kid made up but there was still a comfort, even if only a superstitious one, in hoping that an object had any effect on whether or not you live through the day. Sidney admitted that Delores told him when he was younger that Isaiah discovered the dying Ronnie on the ground on the hill they called *The Grinder* and that they called it that because that was how people left that mountain, looking like they had been through a meat grinder but he didn't get to hear more of it.

Isaiah didn't want to dig deep down and bring up the long buried memories of the war but if they might save the life of his son then he would shed the tears and fight being choked up and tell him everything. The battle on the grinder was one that took a long time to heal from, watching the service dogs run into tunnels and never return weren't the hard images to erase, the hard ones were those of men fully engulfed in flames running at you hoping that you would put a bullet in their brains to end their pain while your commanding officer tells you not to waste the ammo. The images of friends clasping their severed limbs or holding their guts in while crying like scared children are sights and sounds that you can't escape from.

Isaiah found some comfort in working at nights because the deeper sleep that came at night was heavier with the memories of battle, some nights he still sprung awake with the smell of burning human flesh still filling his nose and he watched many men at the VA or VFW halls try to drink away their pain. Eddie was a hardworking man and Isaiah learned his work ethic from his father so he worked and worked to escape from his own memories, even though it hardly worked. Isaiah found comfort with Delores; her voice soothed him and being with her made him feel normal again. Isaiah told Sidney that if Shayla made him feel safe in this world than that was something special.

Sidney knew that his being shipped out wasn't going to be some lunch on the lawn, he was told that he was going to be in a command center on the ground but far enough away that they could monitor and move around troops and artillery but anywhere inside foreign land could still mean trouble. Isaiah still held back from telling Sidney about every detail of his time at war, it was war and war is worse than any hell anyone could concoct to sell someone something. Isaiah worried for Sidney and he was already across the world so there was no last chance to hug his son just in case it was the last time he might ever see him alive. The tears began to well up at the fear of having to bury his son, all he could do was sniffle hard and hope that the fine young man that he raised would also be a good soldier and come home safely.

"I still want to marry her" Sidney interjected to change the subject. "Well you're a smart man, so do it" Isaiah responded, "But call your mother first." Sidney chuckled because he knew that his father would take some heat for not sharing the news with his mother so he agreed to make the call as soon as they hung up. Sidney wanted to fly Shayla out to Germany for several days before he was scheduled to fly to the desert to begin engaging in combat. Isaiah was impressed that his son was making plenty of good decisions but he was afraid that the young lady would marry his son and then become a young widow quickly if something bad were to happen, he also worried she'd be a distraction but he kept that fear to himself.

Isaiah closed the shop a little early after speaking with Sidney, he wanted to get to his wife Delores and begin to talk about the possible shotgun nuptials for Sidney, even though it might be a fast to-do all the way away. Isaiah knew that Delores wouldn't take the fast wedding very well, she dreamt of sitting in the front pew while her only child waited to take a bride but with the pending circumstances there might be some heat of the moment wedding things to just leave as a daydream. Sure enough Delores was sitting on the front stoop waiting for Isaiah; the look on her face was full of disappointment as she waited for her husband, he felt the heat from her glare as he rounded the corner and it slowed him in his pace. Isaiah knew not to dillydally too long getting home but he also wanted to make sure he had enough time to go over any other options in his head before he had to confront an upset Delores.

Men know that it's worth tiptoeing around many subjects to keep a wife happy; most men grow weary of arguing while some women seem to have the *marathon-argument* gene in them and Isaiah knew the dread that was welling up in the back of this throat was his preparation for her argument gene to emerge. Delores was in a navy blue blouse, her hands rubbing up and down on her bare arms as the days' temperature had begun to drop a bit with the sun while she waited for the return of her husband. The angle of the shadow that Delores sat in made it hard to clearly see her facial expression as Isaiah neared, there was a deep down part of him that knew running wouldn't solve anything but he wondered if he could dart around to the back, get in and jump into bed then pretend to be asleep before she caught on, but he knew that was silly and she wasn't going to be in a laughing mood. Isaiah took in a long drawn breath and as his nostrils searched the air for signs of food but all he could catch was the normal grassy earthen smell that surrounded his front steps.

"Sai" Delores muttered her husband's nickname; her voice didn't crack or tremble so she couldn't have been all that upset. "Honey, I'm sorry" Isaiah defensively apologized to his wife about Sidney's decision to marry quickly. Delores wasn't upset about the marriage or even that her husband and son conspired but having to miss the wedding all together was what broke her heart. Isaiah knew his wife was hurt, it hurt his heart that she might miss out on such an important dream but she understood the rush before Sidney shipped out as well as the pressure that can come down on someone about to go to war, but just because she understood it didn't mean she had to like it. Isaiah stepped to Delores and knelt down to embrace her, his touch gave her permission to have a moment to let out the tears of disappointment, she was endlessly proud of herself and her husband for the amazing man they raised but since he arrived she envisioned a grand white wedding with an organ in the background and a large gathering of family to join in the celebration of commending him, but that was gone now.

Isaiah just sat and held his wife, they needed each other for more than just having to miss the wedding but because the risks of going to a war were never good and they were both very afraid for their son. In the best of times and the worst of times Delores held tightly onto Isaiah and he firmly held right back, the realization that their son was going off to war was the worst moment the two had ever feared together and there was nothing they could do and because he was in Germany they couldn't even get to see him before he flew out, all they had left were memories and hopes.

Isaiah was mid weep when his whole body shot upwards. Isaiah stood up and bolted into the house leaving Delores dumbfounded on the steps behind him.

The screen door slammed shut just as Delores turned to try and ask what had startled him so badly but her inquisition had been silenced by the aluminum door slamming against the frame. Delores stood up and brushed herself off from the cold cement steps and then hustled in right behind her husband to find out what was the matter. Isaiah was already out of sight, the man seemed to have vanished into the thin air and Delores began to worry for a moment as to what was going on. "Sweetheart" bellowed to Delores as she turned her head to find the origin of the beckon. Delores located Isaiah up the stairs, he was dug in so deep into the closet that the top half of him wasn't visible when she reached him at the top of the stairs.

"Sidney proved there was no secret door in there" Delores joked to Isaiah referring back to a young Sidney and his penchant for exploring and pretending as Isaiah's feet twitched while he rummaged. "I have it, I found it, I needed it" Isaiah grunted while still jarring his elbows (and who knows what else) inside the small linen closet. Isaiah jerked his feet backwards to get his body enough momentum to wriggle his way out, the bags of winter coats hanging above him swayed and jostled as he fought his way out to show his wife what he had that would make many things much better. Delores helped to straighten out the garment storage bags that Isaiah had made a mess in when he jumped into the closet like it were a lake, she huffed and puffed to clear her nose from sobbing and was brushing the bags straight to keep them

130

from wrinkling while in storage when Isaiah spun to her with his arm outstretched and a wild "A-HA."

Isaiah whipped around to show Delores that he found the small square sealed in wax that was left in a closest for half a decade. "Paper Paulie" Delores wondered if this was her husband's way of trying to make her laugh or if perhaps maybe he might have been serious for some unknown reason, she hoped it was just to make her smile but it didn't work anyways. "Remember when Sid hit his head and Paulie was in his pocket? I am not saying this small square is divine or any other sort of voodoo magic like that but in terms of good-luck charms he has been a good one, I want him with my boy when he goes into combat and if he makes it by the wedding, would that make you feel better at all?" Delores chewed her bottom lip, she knew that the small ragged paper square had been long overdue to be thrown out but it was one of those things that her husband held onto and it served as a place marker in his mind for good memories during a time when a good memory meant life or death for soldiers, but she couldn't even fake a half smile for him.

Isaiah tucked Paper Paulie into his shirt pocket and reached forward to return to comforting his wife after remembering where he left off. Delores wasn't entirely enthused with Isaiah's idea, she hoped that maybe he had an idea about trying to fly them both to Germany to get to see their son or some sort of something like that but when the small black square came into the overhead light, she felt her heart sink into her stomach and her chest grow tight with frustration at the situation. Isaiah and Delores hugged for the remainder of the night. Sidney always called when it was late in the day for him and about midday for his parents, he couldn't call in the morning because it would have still been the middle of the night so Isaiah and Delores had to wait until better time the next day before they could call and talk to Sidney more, like always, when unsure about something they held onto each other a little tighter.

The long distance charges were expensive for the Venney's, Sidney was spending money calling Shayla often and time was beginning to run out before he was due to ship out to the desert for the latest US conflict. Because Shayla was also employed by the military she was able to finagle a flight to Germany to spend the last week with Sidney before he went out, she requested the urgent time off and secured a flight even though it was with three hundred other soldiers heading over to the base, she made the arrival in the middle of the night to be with Sidney for his last few days. Shayla felt a little guilty that his parents couldn't visit him but she was glad to mostly have Sidney all to herself, well except for his duties of course. Shayla was lucky her boss Tom helped her to switch shifts in order to get the vacation time, it was of an urgent matter and even though there were several dozen gals worrying about loved ones shipping out, with luck and good graces she let the tumblers fall into place so that she could take eight days off, even though almost two full days were meant to be spent jumping through airports.

Shayla was a mix of Jamaican and Puerto Rican, with beautiful light skin and ample bounce to her hair when it wasn't tied up in military standards she was one heck of a cook. Shayla knew recipes from both sides of her family and even though red beans and rice was a staple of her diet in her youth, she was adventurous with her cuisine. Shayla promised Sidney that she would make his favorite version, with Andouille sausage, large chunks of sweet peppers and minced jalapeno's for heat. Sidney couldn't handle the heat in his food like Shayla could and often times she had a bottle of hot sauce beside her at each meal just so that she could taste it, meanwhile most others' that were eating her food were sweating through a t-shirt, (Sidney was no different) she was still a master at her passion. Shayla loved to sample foods from all over and the many ways one dish could be cooked, Sidney loved her knowledge and awareness to flavors in both food, and life.

In the small barracks Sidney had bribed his bunk-mates to scatter for the evening that he intended to propose, he knew Shayla would be surprised and even though it was all a hurry, they were smart enough to have discussed getting married sometime in the future when their tour in the military was over and they could be together and never have to separate again. Sidney had everything Shayla would need to cook for him, he was glad to avoid the mess hall for at least one meal and even though the pending deployment weighed heavily on his mind, as soon as he saw the night's glint in her eyes he was at peace. Shayla and Sidney cooked together, she would slice and dice and allow him to stir. Sidney liked that Shayla was independent, he wanted to be wanted and not always needed and she was raised that a strong girl can and will do everything for herself, together they saw the rewards in each other's company.

The meal went well and even though it was late they both fought to stay awake and savor each moment they had left. Sidney didn't want to admit his fears or frights and Shayla refused to let herself get emotional, she knew that she needed to stay positive and supporting for Sidney. Shayla loved Sidney's deep dimples, his hard work ethic and the love in his heart for his parents, he was a good man and she knew she was lucky to have found him. Both Shayla and Sidney fought off sleep as long as they could, they survived until late into the wee hours before the comfort of his thick arms under her head finally caused her eyelids to droop and then it was lights out. Sidney watched as the muscles in Shayla's face relaxed, her thin eyebrows twitched a little as she slid into dreams and her breath became shallow. Sidney knew that his arm would be asleep in no time and the pins and needles pain of paresthesia would soon kick in but lying with her was worth it, she was worth everything to him.

Sidney loved that Shayla clasped her hands between their chests as she slept on his narrow cot, it was easy to tilt his head down to kiss her crossed fingers and then up a little to kiss her on her nose and it all felt right. Sidney stared at the girls' folded hands, it was confusing for a moment in the dim lights to figure out which fingers belonged to which hands but once he did he reached down into his side pocket slowly and as stealthily as possible to retrieve the engagement ring he bought at the PX. Sidney worked and wedged her nimble finger so that when she woke up, she would discover the small engagement ring and hopefully be surprised. Both Sidney and Shayla had come a long way, they were quick to get to know each other in Florida but despite many odds they held on tightly to one another while Sidney was in Germany and with that bond he felt in his heart that she was a girl he could spend his life with, even if he didn't make it back from the war alive.

"EEEEEEK" Sidney jolted his eyes awake to Shayla shrieking and then straightening her arms upwards. Instantly forgetting the small size of their sleeping area Shayla nearly fell backwards off of Sidney's rack, sending her hands jerking upwards and connecting with his face as he reached forward to keep them both from falling to the floor. The sharp prongs of the ring scoured up the side if Sidney's face, immediately drawing blood. The gash in the side of Sidney's' face wasn't deep and in all of the frantic commotion in the morning he forgot to actually ask her to marry him.Once they got the cut bandaged and they were able to sit and laugh about the shrieking and nearly falling out of the bunk they began to laugh.

Shayla was excited to wake up to find a ring on her finger,she was so tired from the long journey back to Sidney's arms that she was unaware of his imperceptible actions in her sleep. With a large gauze pad on his face and a girl chuckling about her reaction to waking, Sidney made his way down to one knee to officially request her hand in marriage. The start to the day was clumsy in a romantic attempt and even with Sidney bandaged while looking up from bended knee Shayla was more than overexcited to accept Sidney as her lifelong husband. Sidney suggested that finding a Chaplain to wed them just days before he was scheduled to deploy would take a few hours to secure but he was grateful to make it happen, Shayla was too excited to think clearly and was too busy wiping tears from her eyes to pay much attention to what else was going on, she wanted to call home and share her great news; they both did.

Shayla was frantic with excitement, Sidney was doing his best to avoid counting down the last two days before he was to have everything he needed packed, and the rest in a box to go into storage until he returned, the clock was his shadow and even with Shayla by his side, there was no escaping the countdown. Sidney and Shayla spent most of the first day of their engagement in hugs and happy embrace, the world around them silenced and went to the wayside as all they could only see was each other. Sidney called Delores and Isaiah as soon as the hour was a kind one to call while Shayla continued to call aunts and cousin's back home, the news was good and it was spreading wildly. The first day was long, it was filled with emotion and excitement but Sidney knew that if there was to be time to be wed before he would have to box up his life and report, that there was no more time to wait before they would have to stand before a chaplain and exchange their vows.

Shayla calmed down enough and gave her new fiancé enough time to speak his mind about a quick marriage, he was bright eyed and ready to make her a bride but it wasn't what either of them truly wanted. Circumstances change, arrangements can often fall apart and promises get broken but Shayla dreamt about being in a flowing white dress in front of her loved ones so she had to come clean with her admission. "I can't marry you like this" Shayla began. With heart wrenching tears Shayla explained her dreams of her wedding, she loved Sidney and was elated to become his fiancé but she couldn't cheat herself just because there was a small fear deep inside about the pending war. Sidney felt ill, he wanted to be good and married before he shipped off and even though it meant forgoing a fancy expensive formal affair as well as a honeymoon filled with romance, he still felt the pending urgency of time.

Time is the master of all men. Time is only known to the human world and yet we are controlled by it, obsessed with it and imprisoned by it. A dog wakes up, hopes to eat or get to see familiar faces and when it's dark they try to sleep again. There is no day that a dog worries about what time it is, most of the time "dinnertime" is dictated by their human and the actions of arriving home or some habit that can be learned. People have no true concept of time until long after they are born and in that time we just do as we're told, eat when we're told and go to bed also when we're told. When we realize what time is in our lives we become enslaved to it, always trying to beat the clock before time runs out and we expire.

Shayla wanted to be married to Sidney, she wanted to spend the rest of her life with such a good man and even though it ripped her heart out having to say "not today" she still held him and did her best to assure him it was because she wanted it done right. Sidney was in fact hurt, they returned to his bunk to begin packing for his year and a half long deployment into the desert with no certainty that he'd return at all but they did it together to keep talking. The gloomy weather only compounded on the emotion, the feeling of rejections that Shayla didn't want to jump into getting married was a hard blow to deal with and even though she begged and pleaded for him to understand, he still needed his time to heal.

When Sidney returned to his bunk mail had been delivered. Sidney snatched the clump of mail addressed to his bunk-mates and threw the pile on his small table in order to get started on packing away his life, Shayla silently followed close behind. Shayla didn't like the ugly feeling between her and Sidney, he was quiet and moody and she didn't know how to help him get to a point of understanding so she gave him some quiet time for a bit. Sidney huffed and puffed to vent a little as he tossed around his clothes and belongings he planned to store, it was a hard task to sort through things and wonder if he'd ever make it back to see the things he was storing away, it made many of his band t-shirts and scrap books of concert tickets seem trivial. The room was shrouded in despair and vastly different than the freshly engaged excitement of just hours before, the reality of war was enough of a hardship and Sidney felt let down, Shayla didn't know how to make her fiancé feel better about anything so she sat quietly and sorted the mail into four piles, one for each bunk-mate,

"You've got one" Shayla interrupted Sidney as he was punching clothes into a long green seabag he was packing tightly. Sidney turned to make his way towards Shayla and tripped over a belongings bag on the floor near his feet, in his anger Sidney got his feet tangled and in the moment before he started to fall, he gave up. The energy spent being angry and the moments lost to silence were just that; lost. Sidney was tangled at the feet and unable to do anything but give in so he plummeted to the ground. Watching the ground come rushing upwards Sidney tilted his head back and did his best to take in a

139

large chest full of air and began letting it out to soften his sudden thud to the ground. With a thick smack Sidney landed hard onto the cement floor, the skin smack was nearly a clap and once his body came to rest he laid his cheek down onto the ground and again, he simply gave up.

Sidney was already tired, he knew that he was still lucky to have Shayla and that they loved each other, he felt let down that she didn't want a fast wedding but it was a nice distraction from the pending unknown that he was staring at for the next year or so of his life so he also knew he was rushing things rather than take a longer course of action.

Shayla couldn't help but to begin to chuckle, her blurted out snort wasn't at his expense but rather the face he made on his way to the floor. "You look like a baby that just bit into a lemon for the first time" Shayla quickly explained why she began to laugh. Sidney let his face contort in surprise and frustration as he fell, one eye opened and crossed while the other closed and sunk downward towards his unevenly twisted mouth that was just above a lowered pouting bottom lip. Shayla slid her chair back and went to lie down beside Sidney, she knew he was juggling high stress and pressure so rather than help him up, she joined him on the cold ground for a few minutes just to show that no matter where he was, she was by his side.

It was a small gesture but Shayla taking up a side position right next to Sidney did in fact make him feel better, although he remained quiet, a few small tears dripped from his eyes down onto the floor while he just watched Shayla smile at him. Shayla sat and smiled, she knew the strength it must take in order for Sidney to want so badly to stay and be with her and to avoid going to war but the honor to his fellow soldiers and to his military overweighed his own heart or his mind and she admired him for that. Shayla reached her right arm over to caress up and down Sidney's back to help comfort him, they were both scared but they were scared together. Sidney slowly let his eyes close, the internal struggle was exhausting and even though he was frightened about the next year or better, knowing that he still had Shayla by his side brought him some peace.

As Shayla rustled to get comfortable the sound of wrinkling paper crept out from beneath her, there was something half hard wadded up in the envelope she forgot she laid on top of when she joined Sidney on the floor for a few moments and the noise when she moved caught both of their attention. "Oh yeah" Shayla relaxed her concerned eyebrows once she realized what the sound was. Wriggling side to side Shayla pulled the envelope addressed to Sidney from beneath her and slid it to him to open. Sidney didn't bother to untangle his feet from his bag, one foot still propped up while the other wrapped around it and resting against the metal bar of his bunk, the resting position was by no means comfortable but he had

141

Shayla by his side so nothing else mattered for the time being.

Sidney worked his finger to slowly slide the tip under the flap to open it, the address was from his parents and with very little time left before he shipped out, he wanted the comfort of reading his parents' penmanship. From the side Sidney pulled at the letter tucked inside and as it was almost completely out, the small wax square fell to the ground. Before Sidney could make sense of what he had released from the envelope Shayla snatched it from the ground and began to twirl it around trying to make sense of what she had discovered. The letter was from his mom and as usual it was wishing him all the best and praying for his safety but the few dried water marks that distorted the ink on the lines gave clue that she was crying when she wrote the letter. Sidney felt bad that his mother cried but he also suspected that she kept her emotions off the letter by suggestion from his father, knowing how hard the sad feelings can make shipping out.

Sidney read through the letter expressing the pride his mother had in him, the days from his youth that she'll cherish for eternity and how it took one small child to turn her into a mother and that no matter what, that can never be taken away from her. Sidney did his best to keep his stoic look but by the sight of his reddening eyes Shayla knew that he had a heavy heart and she wanted to help in any way that she could, just as soon as she figured out what in the world the small square in her fingertips were.

"Hey buddy" Sidney spoke up once his vision lost focus on the papers he was reading and noticed what Shayla was playing with. "Meet Paper Paulie." "Paper who now" Shayla responded to the confusing introduction. As Sidney was putting down the paper he noticed his father's handwriting on the back: "Take care of each other, you both have to come back to me."

Isaiah was a man of very little writing, it was a struggle to learn to read and write growing up so when Sidney saw that his father wrote those words in his own handwriting he knew that he and Paulie both had to return to him and that was when the burning in his eyes let more tears stream to the floor. Isaiah was a man that preferred calling than writing, it was much easier and much faster to pick up a telephone and dial a phone number to get a point across, it was a hassle to sit down with a pen and paper, form the words, check the punctuation and then to make sure the address was affixed correctly and then wait weeks to get a response. Isaiah wasn't illiterate like his father but it was a struggle for him in his youth to learn to read and write. The older brother Clarence also struggled a little but with the help of Ronetta the boys learned to read at the most basic level to get them through school. The writing was hardly legible but it was clear enough to get the point across.

Shayla recognized the backward letters right away, she taught a little here and there so she identified that Sidney's father Isaiah was dyslexic and that must have been why he could read but struggled to write. The hand written note from Isaiah meant the world to Sidney, it showed that against all of his frustration and dislike for writing, it still meant something so dearly that he sat down to pen a small note for his son and seeing that squiggly misspelled message struck a strong sense of pride deep into Sidney. Isaiah hated writing, growing up his family was understanding and even once Ronnie's Radio's had opened, most things were put down with a register rather than hand written out by the owner. Isaiah hated feeling defeated, he hated that writing came so much easier to all the other boys in school, even Rocket Ricky who didn't even finish the high school could write early in grammar school.

"Paper Paulie was the one friend my pap had with him in Vietnam; he saved my dad's life over and over and was by his side the entire time." Sidney began telling Shayla about the small square.Shayla listened to the story while still looking for a fold or a crease in the now black dirtied square wondering if it was just a small address book or what this Paper Paulie was or how it worked, it was strange and it didn't make any sense. "Is Paulie a General or someone that can keep you from shipping out, is his phone number in here?" Shayla still didn't understand about Paulie, she thought the wax contained a way to contact the man; she didn't realize that the wax *was* the man.

Sidney reached over and took Paulie and showed Shayla the faint color below the dirt imbedded wax covering, he did his best to explain how Paper Paulie started out in one of the Dakotas from some little kid as a school project and how he sent it to his father while he was deployed. With blue pants and a red shirt Paulie emerged from a dirtied envelope where he remained crammed down into a side pocket for a long bloody muddy day, it wasn't until promises were made to read the letter if he returned to the base named Chicago that Isaiah finally got to read the letter that was sent to him by a stranger half way across the world hoping for his safety. "Awww" Shayla let out while Sidney continued to speak. Isaiah struggled to write clearly but with sloppy handwriting it made it easier to write to a child rather than another adult that might have had a hard time reading the penmanship. Sitting down to write when he could Isaiah forced himself to block out the sounds of men running or shouting, even the bombs exploding in the distance seemed to silence down when he took his time to correctly place each letter to write his pen-pal.

Taking the time to write to his pen-pal forced Isaiah to remove himself from the war, from the men dying all around him and the notion that at any moment a bullet can find its' mark on him and then he'd never have another tomorrow. The stress of battle can wear on anyone, the constant notion that a trip wire can rip apart your body, a bullet can take your life or that maybe the man fighting beside you would probably be gone before his next meal and it can mound up and give you headaches or keep you from sleeping. Isaiah found that writing to his pen-pal made him remember what it was like to be eight or nine, he had to think about what to write and how to write to a small child so as not to frighten him or pervert him to the vile world that waits for him to enter as an adult. Each time Isaiah wrote a response letter he made sure to include that "Paper Paulie said *hi*" and that made him smile.

Isaiah once explained some of the social and political goings on around the time he was growing up, it was still shaky in regard to social acceptance of many things. "Not more than a hundred years ago could women not vote, not fifty years ago a black man had to use a different drinking fountain than a white man, forgive passed grievances and free yourself from the ugliness that hatred can bring but always remember that if you vote to keep someone from doing something that yourself or others can do is doing the same ugly thing that had been done to your forefathers and that is wrong" Isaiah taught Sidney about understanding.

"There were churches growing up that wanted you to have blind faith that some man came back from the dead to command that a black man and white woman shouldn't marry, or that two men can't marry or even that women are property to a man, if a man really did come back from the dead he would have to prove it to more than one lowly cat wouldn't he? And wouldn't he bring a more peaceful path for mankind rather than leave them all for thousands of years to keep being hateful and misled?" Isaiah once poised the question.

"Grow up, keep your mind open and have love and understanding for all men around you" Isaiah warned Sidney about the dangers of being a closed minded person; the history books are full of them. Rulers took legions of followers to go and kill people that believed in different things, or in the name of peace, killing in the name of peace! Sidney took notice of all of his father's warnings and when he got his written orders that he would be deploying into battle he was conflicted but he also knew that he swore an oath and his honor would help him to uphold his vow and serve just like his father did.

Shayla sat and listened to Sidney talk more about the adventures Paper Paulie had been on, she asked if there was ever any contact with the little boy that created such a powerful piece of paper and that was when Sidney spoke about the last major offensive that Isaiah was in: *The Grinder*. Shayla was surprised to hear about Ronnie and it made sense that Isaiah named his store in honor of his younger brother, she was saddened to learn that all the notes were in a pocket and bled through but it seemed to fall into place in fate that Paper Paulie was wax coated and survived it all, and now he was in Sidney's possession for good luck while he was deployed into the Middle East to combat. The two squabbled a bit while on the floor, they had a great many things to still do but lying on the floor, together, took priority.

Sidney looked at Paulie, the hardened wad of wax had been hidden away in the bottom of an old jungle boot in the bottom of a closet for almost twenty years except for when he took him out, the same time he fell and narrowly missed cracking his skull open in his kitchen. Shayla agreed that it must have been lucky that Sidney lived through his fall, hardly needing any stitches rather than a major brain surgery to keep him alive, even now as an grown man the scar on the back of Sidney's head is small, just a small little line that doesn't grow hair that can only be seen when his hair is cut very short in the back. Sidney kept a smile on his face while observing the roughed up piece of twenty three year old waxed paper. "In all accounts I shouldn't have this." Sidney began to recall the battles, the blood and even the length of time that has passed, all were reasons the piece of paper should have washed away in the mud or slipped into the unknown or simply not exist, or even that his father Isaiah hardly let it out of his reach since getting it, all were reasons he shouldn't have possession of Paper Paulie, but he did.

Ch. 8

Sidney didn't mind the plane ride to Germany, it was long of course and it took a day or two to adjust to the time change but he acclimated quickly. The plane ride to the desert was starkly difference. The troops flew in a large carrier with equipment and trucks so it was hard not to notice the smell of the fuel or how stripped down the plane was on the inside, it made for a long shaky flight. Sidney knew that when he put his things in storage that he might not ever return for them so he added his parent's names and address on the box as well as Shayla's just in case anything went poorly for him someone could claim his things. Shayla flew back to Florida later in the day after Sidney's flight left, she hoped that leaving right away could put it out of her mind that he was flying into a conflict zone, she wanted to trick herself into thinking that he was just still in Germany but the whole flight home she spent dwelling on watching him and his gear march up the loading ramp to the large plane, his head hung low and his feet lightly dragging with each forced step away from her.

The first two days after leaving Germany (and Shayla) behind were tough, the main thought was about not getting to marry his sweetheart but it was for the better reasons, it just wasn't an easy reason to swallow initially. Sidney wanted to marry Shayla and she wanted to marry him but it was indeed smarter to wait until they could afford it and enjoy a proper engagement and honeymoon, not cram it all together in half a day with a chaplain presiding over the nuptials in a country where neither of their parents could attend. Keeping Paper Paulie close in his pocket kept reassuring Sidney that he had a friend with him in the sand and dirt. Paulie had spent two years in the humid jungles of Vietnam and now he was touching down in the arid sands of the Middle East, his purpose had been extended long passed what anyone may have thought *he* would have but he did still have a purpose.

The lines for the phones seemed endless and while waiting Sidney wrote both of his parents as well as Shayla, his phone call could go across in minutes while the letters could take weeks to hear a response but the ability to communicate was a major relief of the stress placed on you when you arrive into a hostile place. Sidney thought about how his father wrote to his pen-pal, he removed himself from the hell of gunfire and death and took himself to a much simpler time in his childhood and wrote as if there wasn't a war going on, Sidney decided he was going to do the same thing for Shayla. Sidney decided that he wouldn't mention the death or destruction; he was going to focus on the niceties of the area and as an anchor to keep him grounded rather than get stuck in the ugliness that was sure to follow.

Paper Paulie

The first rockets fired sometime early in the dark hours to officially start off the tactical offensive, there was silence in the communication bunker known as "The Boom Room" that Sidney was working in until the explosion echoed through the night sky. There was small chatter between the intelligence rooms that were keeping track of troops and vehicles all while establishing areas of safety to fend off future enemy attacks. Sidney kept his headphones on and performed his tasks but he also worried that being stuck in a communications command post might leave him vulnerable or blind to an attack coming from the hills in the near distance. The bunkers were hot and there wasn't a person that hadn't sweat through their uniforms in the first twenty minutes of their shift despite the measly fans but they all worked and kept coordinating attacks and lines of supplies.

The bunker was dim with the lights of all the screens and monitors, each member had a platoon under their watch to keep track of, how many engaged with insurgents, how many were moving along with convoys and how many men were being deployed each night and who was moving where to coincide with the orders and battle plans of the top Generals like Command Sergeant Harmon Belleaux making the hard decisions of sending men into combat. Sidney knew many of the men that were in infantry, one such man was a private Zacyz, a tall skinny guy with brunette hair and wire framed glasses,he had a frightfully crude lip smack when he chewed his gum and he happened to be from Washington. Zacyz was

151

on base with Sidney when he landed and leant a hand giving him a quick tour of the base before he packed up for another deployment to patrol the local mountains for bad guys.

Zacyz grew up a boy from a small town, so small that he commented that the military base was nearly the size of his town and he was in awe that it was mostly tents and sandbags as they walked passed row after row making up the bunks and barracks for all the soldiers. Some of the soldiers early on had been in close small engagements while patrolling, the closest Zacyz had seen was a few men hurling stones and threatening an oncoming jeep full of American soldiers with an assault rifle. Luckily when eight armored soldiers stepped to confront the irate man swinging his rifle it could have easily turned into a battle on the busy streets but they put on a formidable show by stepping out in cadence and the troublemakers dispersed. Zacyz admitted to feeling "mighty queasy" when he stepped out of the assumed protection of their jeep, "when you feel the breeze on your skin you can't pretend the jeep doors will keep you from getting shot and it makes your stomach knot up something bad."

Sidney listened to the suggestions of Isaiah when he was told to keep his head down and watch all around, the rows and rows of dirt paths running between the tents meant to house soldiers all looked the same, like mirrored images that represented the uniformity in the military, it was dizzying to absorb all the information coming at you while you are walking to your bunk, you are supposed to know where to be and when to be there within ten minutes of offloading the plane that brought you in, Sidney was fairly lost until Zacyz gave him half a run down. Sidney spent the first day too confused to be afraid and the sight of platoons of armed men weren't much different than back in Germany but to see them loaded up with rockets in the back or large trucks that were dirtied from the real streets definitely made it all very real.

Sidney was able to find a phone and his call to his parents which was the only call he was able to make when it was finally his turn that afternoon, Shayla was still on a flight home so it was too soon to call her. Delores sounded half asleep when he called, it was very early in the morning and he forgot about doing the new math for the difference in time zones. "Hey momma" Sidney started, it made his voice crack just enough for her to jolt further awake and begin to worry. Sidney explained that he was just a little concerned about everything but that he was alright; she peppered him for a few moments before he raised his voice enough for her to hear him ask her to calm down.

Sidney was healthy and safe but the surroundings required some time to adjust, he was missing being home and the sound of his moms voice took him back to being a young boy, he wished he could close his eyes and that she could just make everything all better for him, but that's not how things go. Delores and Isaiah were both pleased but slightly let down that Sidney didn't get married, he was really looking forward to it and they rooted for him but they were also both a little enlightened that they could still look forward to partaking in the wedding ceremony with their only child. Sidney nervously tapped at his pocket, the small hard piece in his pocket patted against his leg when he tapped, the motion was hardly a distraction but it continuously assured him that Paulie was right there with him.

Sidney and Isaiah spoke for a few minutes, the payphone prices were outrageous even with a calling card but Shayla helped to join Isaiah and Delores to keep money on it so that Sidney didn't have to worry about not being able to call and talk when he needed to. Isaiah understood more than what his son told him about, he knew when Sydney talked about the size of the compound that it was more about the troops and artillery filling it rather than just the shear acreage it took up. Isaiah reminded him over and over to be diligent and hardworking and very observant of his surroundings, there weren't dense jungles that enemies could dig into or long tunnel networks that the enemy dug to hide underground but there had been over twenty years passed and no limit to the new ways that people could use to kill one another.

When you look back over humanity the one thing you can't seem to find it just that: humanity. Mankind excels at killing themselves and each other, wars over anything and everything have coerced man to be a step up over and over to be the better killer and with victory comes the right to write the history books. Each period in time is stained with the blood of war, one side opposing another for blood and body counts, the entire world is shaped by war, one religion fights off another and kills many of those practitioners to become the dominant religion in the area, it indoctrinates the newborns so that they will grow up to be soldiers for that religion and the cycle goes on for thousands of years. If it isn't religion it's a dynasty, monarchy, democracy or fanatic trying to chase power, none of it is good no matter how you look at it and it mirrors organized crime, you pay for protection and are threatened with harm if you don't commit your one and only life to it.

Sidney knew that Isaiah knew what he was really saying when he said it was just busy; he knew it meant that there was a lot of troop movement and hustle around the base. When Sidney said he didn't get out much it meant there were ample reports of enemy movement and that they were confined to the base and when he said that he was staying busy it meant that there was enough action to keep him working that there was hardly time to sleep in between things going on. Sidney knew that he was in a better position by going into troop logistics and communications (thanks to his father's radio store and his own upbringing around it all) but also that now people like him had more options in the military than his fathers' time when they were pigeonholed to infantry. Isaiah knew that his son had a rough year ahead of him and that talking about it occasionally would help to ease the stress but there were also rules in place that prohibited sharing information just in case the phones were tapped or things like that so it was a delicate balance for both men.

The after effects of having been to combat were very real to Isaiah, there were many nights where he would frighten Delores while sleeping because he would shoot awake or lurch out of bed reflexively. Delores understood only a small sliver of what Isaiah had actually been through, he didn't think she could handle hearing the whole truth and when it came to the darker side of humanity, the side he lived in for nearly two years, he was ashamed that he had to be *that* person in order to survive and he was ashamed of what she would think of him if she ever found out so he just remained quiet (like so many others). Sidney was never allowed to play war or army growing up, at least not at home where his parents might find out. Sidney knew there were dark secrets locked behind his father's eyes when it came to his time served but like most men it was pushed deep down and ignored, but he understood much better now.

Sidney did his best to keep a stern look, even if his eyes watered he refused to wipe at his cheeks to make it obvious. Getting to speak to his father a little brought him back to his training, back to the grand view of doing what he had to do to get home and it restored his confidence in himself to make it home safely, plus he was instructed to bring Paulie back to him and he sure didn't want to disappoint his father. Back to the first overnight shift; Sidney knew how crucial his job was making sure that troops weren't encroaching on one another and barraging each other with gunfire in the darkness. It was important that each squad knew where their backup was if they got into a hot zone or where they were heading to in order to get there safely and it was a stressful time knowing that this was real life and not simulated training, there were lives on the line.

Lima Company was the infantry platoon run by a Commander Hawk, he was a man well versed in warfare and highly ranked at some college in North Carolina before joining an officer training academy. Hawk stood tall and proud and was often chewing on the butt of a cigar, you never actually found him smoking it and when asked why he never smokes the cigar but only chews on it his response was always "I like the option" meaning he'd smoke it if he felt like it and he'd be damned to let anyone take away his right to choose anything for himself. Zaycz was in the Lima Company under Commander Hawk's orders and their first mission was to clear the local mountain range for several days to separate the goat herders from enemy combatants that posed a threat with long range rockets from the distance.

Lima Company drove armored personnel carriers out as far as they could go until they reached an impasse that could only be maneuvered on foot. The second shift Sidney was at the helm of his monitors and radios, he was in charge of helping to navigate Lima Company through the dusty dried mountain range and valleys until check point One-seven–three. One-seven-three was a clustered divot where three mountains met; several hundred years ago geologists suggested that it was the meeting point of several mount streams that then ran down through many of the villages that still existed, except it was just dry rock bed now.

One-seven-three posed a major threat because it was inaccessible by truck from any angle and with the large rocks it would be easy to hide entrances to caves anywhere, plus being at the bottom of several mountains it was dangerous to fly a helicopter in near it to look around due to the high ridges that could mask large artillery fire so it was up to Lima Company to go and clear everything out, and it was up to Sidney to keep track of where they were and how they were going to get there.

Sidney was tasked with navigating the entire platoon; nearly ninety men were under his directions and one Command Major that like to chew butts (cigars to start). Sidney knew it was a tough job, the mountain range wasn't comparable to the Himalayas or even the Appalachians back home but it was still formidable enough to cause strategic hardships making sure to cover both sides of each mountain while converging on one-seven-three. When Sidney took the lead chair to begin coordinating the assault on one-seven-three he hadn't heard of much in regards to opposition in the mountain range, one of the other coordinators was in charge of a group called Golf-11 and they were converging on one-seven-three from the other side, the larger hope was that both groups would reach one-seven-three in the day light and be able to see one another and keep from shooting at each other while securing the area.

Sidney and a private named Mickelson were sitting at opposite desks giving commands and taking information from their platoons under their order. It took a few days of check-ins every twelve hours for updates at first, Sidney and Mickelson both slept at their computers or took very small breaks away to prevent any missed information, they took turns fetching food or ducking away for showers, it was an intense few days getting all the necessary and readied men to where they were supposed to be in order to secure a vital area deep in the mountains. Mickelson did his job to make sure his team was humping along the eastern ridge while Lima Company came in from the west.

There was very little resistance along the first few days the two teams slowly swept across the harsh landscape, the rocky terrain made for slow travel and the harsh heat depleted the troops of their energy faster than anticipated. The Battalion Command Post or "Boom Room" was a hot oven of a room, the computer fans were all pointed at the massive computers tracking large amounts of information and if the fans would have stopped running some of the large towers would have melted down so the room sat at twenty degrees higher than the scorching desert surrounding them, there was no real relief.

Keeping track of two separate platoons worth of men converging on a mountain range was stressful, the closer the mapping showed that they were getting to one another the hotter the boom room seemed to get.Reports were growing increasingly frequent and both Sidney and Mickelson kept updating the positions of the troops but worried that at any minute the troops would be embattled with each other if they weren't careful and the fates of the two platoons would solely rest on Sidney and Mickelson whom were guiding them through radio correspondence.

As Golf-11 was responding to their whereabouts and giving intel that they had a group of locals that seemed to be gathering together when a sudden "pop" rang out over the radio. Dread filled the room that fell silent, reports of small gunfire rumored in the days before but as the radio crackled it confirmed; "engaging in enemy fire from the other side of the ravine."

Sidney listened to Mickelson direct Golf-11 and reported back to Lima Company that their support platoon across the valley was taking on fire and to double time it to back them up. In hopes that they wouldn't fall into crossfire, Commander Hawk agreed keep his rifles up and his aim true and signed out. Sidney could only listen to

Mickelson's radioman and explain where they were taking fire from and from what angles the men were scattering around in order to take their enemy head-on on the mountainside.

Golf-11 was spread across the tops of the mountain and it took nearly four hours for the rest of their members to converge on the right side of the slope to join in the fighting. The opposition was fierce, men defending their home land had more to lose than the invading armies but the end ideology was the same, the issue was timing of the same vision. Golf-11 had nearly three dozen enemy fighters pinned in behind the rock strata, each man was firing in a quick engagement and the radio man called out as many positions as he could and as fast as he could in the early hours.

The *Boom Room* was alive like a beehive, each busy body was moving in an organized chaos that looked like a dance from above where the general sat and observed. Command Sergeant Harmon Belleaux was a man born and raised among the racial tensions of Mississippi in the late-fifties; he enlisted in the army to ship off to Vietnam figuring that he was a target to get killed regardless of what soil he lived on so he might as well fight for more rights back at home.

Belleaux was a broad chested man with a long military career behind him; he was nearing his twenty year mark when he was given orders to endure a tour in the desert. Belleaux didn't mind the heat, the man was
161

from a long line of people born and raised in the hot southern sun and when the heat didn't make him sweat, he'd toss enough hot sauce on his plate to eat through the table. Most of the Generals eat at a few selected tables in the mess hall reserved for higher ranking officers, Belleaux often found himself without anyone to either side of him while he ate because the smell of all the hot sauce was so intense just being near him could cause a Cajun's eyes to water and nose to run.

Belleaux pointed and snapped his fingers from a small platform that gave him eyes to watch several computer screens all at once. Belleaux kept his hands moving like an orchestra conductor and if he had been playing chess he would have been a master playing a dozen games at once, many men kept a side eye towards Belleaux and moved supplies and lines of armed men according to the subtle flicks of his fingers, the man hardly spoke while running the entire *Boom Room* but his orders were clear.

Sidney waited to hear from his platoon but watched as Mickelson moved lines of men according to checkpoint positions on the charted geography of the land. The radio man was level toned as he reported, only a few men of Golf-11 sustained injuries and it didn't sound like any would look to be fatal but until the area was cleared the men would have to wait because it was too risky for an air evac by the choppers.

"Engaging" Hawks' muffled voice broke through the radio; his clarity was impeded by the fact that he never took his cigar from his mouth but the excitement in his voice made him sound giddy.Hawk didn't even bother to ask permission to join in the fire fight, he had fellow soldiers having fun and he wanted his fair share also. While Golf-11 was hunkered down and returning fire to the few dozen men scattered down the hillside Hawk led his men at a brisk speed into the battle field; he didn't believe in strolling.

Lima Company had rushed and pushed for several hours to ensure support for Golf-11, even in the heat and uneven terrain Hawk pushed his men to support their brothers in battle. The radio man of Golf-11 queued in and said they could see Lima Company charging down the hill behind the tucked in enemies, leading him to call out a reassuring; "nap time guys, wake me for lunch."

Commander Hawk led his already weary men into the valley, the small group of enemy fighters were no longer a threat from behind many of the large boulders that sat in the now dried up river bed. Men knelt down to aim but didn't stop moving for long as they shuffled down the loose gravel and sand, there were a few plants that held firmly below footsteps but the heavy soldiers mostly sank into the loose top gravel as they jumped and jostled towards the enemies down below.

Golf-11 watched and kept suppressing fire on the enemies while Lima Company made their way down the mountainside, the firing kept most of the enemies distracted long enough that a majority of Lima Company made it half way down the far side before one of the men shooting down below turned; causing Lima Company to open fire. Lima Company exchanged gunfire and within a few minutes of the surprise flank attack, the river valley was secured.

Sidney and Mickelson were relieved that their decisive plan to duel sweep the mountains worked, it was risky separating both sets of troops and starting them at different points but the phrase "divide and conquer" held true, Belleaux just nodded to get most of the men picked up by helicopter once they had everything secured, then he about faced and went to lay down after nearly thirty straight hours of work.

Sidney was breathing heavy still after the on and off communications with a platoon embroiled in gunfire, the unknown made it scary to have to wait and he wanted to help more but he knew his place was at his desk in the *Boom Room* where he was expected. The entire room was musky from everyone sweating, the air outside was dry and parched your lips within minutes of standing in the sun but inside the small metal bunker it was as hot and humid as a sauna and it was taking on a funky locker room smell from everyone cheering and panting while the fight was being called out and responded to.

The room had over a dozen people all with technical and electrical backgrounds, mostly men although some women were also in that small bunker fighting for elbow room. Everyone was in their military fatigues but each shirt was drenched in sweat and brows remains beaded with sweat no matter how often they were wiped. One of the girls that was coordinating another platoon was standing and swaying her hips to try to keep from fainting from the heat while fanning herself lightly with a folder was named Marissa Shields. Marissa was from the northern states and wasn't all that thrilled to be standing in a puddle of her own sweat but there wasn't anything short of a rocket that could make her leave her post or her men in the field. Marissa kept her hair short and in a small bun at the back of her head just like protocol dictated, she was a confident girl with a gorgeous smile and a steadfast eye on everything around her.

Marissa reminded Sidney of Shayla and each time he caught a glimpse of her big bright toothy smile he missed Shayla that much more. Marissa was a strong girl, her hair was dark blonde and she had a light dusting of freckles across her cheeks. Marissa was able to type on two different keyboards at once(one per hand) and it was as baffling to watch as it was entertaining. Sidney was impressed with Marissa's skills as a coordinator, she was a fit young girl and she performed her job diligently. Belleaux was a stern officer that hardly spoke unless he had to but he did call out to Marissa to give her a thumbs-up when it was her turn to watch over the whole *Boom Room*. Marissa had a higher rank and within a week of her taking second in command in the *Boom Room* she had shaved a few inches under her hair at the lower hairline at the back of her head for heat relief, the extra hair only made the heat worse anyways.

Seeing the shaved back of the head around Marissa's hat was a fad in the heat, the few girls around there all had the sides and backs of their heads taken down in order to remain cool while in the sweltering heat, Marissa remained in a wide stance and vigilant like an eagle when she was in command, when she was off duty she was often seen jogging around the base with some of her platoon members but she was always an astute soldier. Marissa and Sidney worked close together, more often than when he worked with Mickelson because he and Mickelson would trade off shifts. Marissa was an onist, an onist is someone that wishes to be everywhere and experience all things all at once so standing in the *Boom Room* was as close as she could get, each radio call in to report made her feel like she was there while being at different places all at the same time.

Back home Isaiah and Delores were still running the bakery and the radio shop, holding dearly onto Ronnie's Radios was growing harder with the constantly changing electronics and fast paced boom-boxes the kids were listening to were growing more and more intricate with lights and tape decks and now CD's were merging onto the market. Isaiah wanted to keep cherishing the memory of his late brother but the notion of selling his store to one of those big companies was growing more

and more enticing. Isaiah and Delores worked long and
hard for a long time and if they sold the radio store and
focused on the bakery, they could expand it a little and
add in some more space for a lunch eatery rather than just
make sub-sandwiches, they could do a little more cooking
and baking, and do it together. Delores loved the bakery
and now that Sidney had moved away she just cooked for
herself and Isaiah when he was home, she enjoyed being
able to whip up meals with sides but there wasn't as many
to feed anymore so when she first started offering
sandwiches at the bakery she felt there was so much more
potential for her store.

It's funny how things in life twist and turn to get
from one point to another, Ronetta and Eddie Venney had
four boys that they raised up, Ronnie passed away in
Vietnam and Isaiah started out a barely functioning radio
store in his name where he met Delores. Delores was
working for the Vassilles at the small bakery they started
nearly twenty years before, and now Isaiah and Delores
had been long married, both owning their own stores
while their son Sidney Hendrix Venney was coordinating
troop movements half way across the world in the
military while they were looking at another change in life.
Isaiah didn't feel old enough to retire but when Delores
asked him to consider giving up the extremely long hours
and consider cutting back he felt lost. Building up
Ronnie's Radios was a long process, Isaiah lived in the
small backroom for a long time while working at the train
yard overnight so he could be present in the shop for the

business for the days, here it was twenty-something years later and the thought of moving along was frightening.

Isaiah did his best to keep from worrying endlessly about Sidney, he knew what sorts of horrors took place in war and spending days reviewing electronic manuals helped to fill in his time. Isaiah prayed that his son would remain safe, he knew that Paper Paulie was with him and that even though the little paper figure may not have been the reason he made it home from Vietnam, he sure hoped that the little luck charm would hold up and bring Sidney back to him. Delores was excited that Isaiah might reduce his work hours to under sixty a week, her husband had always worked hard and they both knew that the only way to get anywhere in life was by working hard but she also knew that as he aged the long hours would wear him down further and further so she was glad to see that he considered taking more time for himself. Delores also worked hard, she spent many early hours at the bakery and once she had adequate staff trained she still spent hours and hours on the books and the day to day running behind the scenes and after all it was still her role to be the caretaker of her family.

With Delores as the caretaker and Isaiah as the protector the Venney family was very close; which made it difficult when Sidney signed up for the military. Having their son in the military in Europe was hard for Delores and Isaiah; they were often finding themselves reminiscing about Sidney which often brought about tears and fond memories. Delores didn't like thinking about what her husband went through and what her son might be dealing with, they raised a strong boy that knew when to sit down and shut up and when it was time for action, she sensed that he would be much more like his daddy and enlist to serve but she still didn't have to like it.

Delores and Shayla had insisted on exchanging phone numbers through Sidney, if they were going to be family it was essential that they got to know each other. Sidney was leery about his mom and fiancé interacting but he knew there was no fighting it so he agreed. Once Shayla was back in Florida she was the first to call Delores, she was polite in introducing herself and then the two ladies spent the first of many hours speaking back and forth. Shayla and Delores became pals, there were ample stories shared and information passed back and forth about potential wedding arrangements as well as family histories. Delores loved that Shayla was a cooking sort of girl; it's always a mother's job to make sure her son is fed and happy. Shayla came from a family that grew together in the kitchen so she loved to cook *with* Sidney, not just *for* him and even if it was the simplest things like washing dishes together, she saw it as valuable time they got to spend together; Delores adored Shayla.

Delores was speaking with Shayla on the phone when an alert came over the news channel Delores was watching. Shayla had ample news of the front while on base because there was information constantly streaming back and forth since their base also had reserves readying to ship out in the coming months anyways. Troop activity on the base was easy to read, when there were swells of supplies and soldiers then there was going to be a large shipment going out somewhere, everyday large planes were flying in empty but going out full and it just reinforced to Shayla that Sidney was going to be away for a while.

The alert spoke about a major military offensive to sweep a mountain range near a forward base, they were referring to one-seven-three, Shayla knew about it but Delores was kept in the dark for security reasons. Delores caught on that Shayla knew about some of the things but only from rumors on the base, Sidney knew he wasn't allowed to share sensitive information with anyone that wasn't in the *Boom Room* but there was still enough intel going to and from bases back in the states that nothing stayed quiet for long.

"Bombing of American base" was all that rang out as the two ladies were discussing family Jerk chicken recipes and both gals went quiet. Shayla dropped the phone in her rush to get to a television to find a station reporting what had happened, Delores just froze. Channel after Channel was brightly lit with family shows or commercials selling things, none of which were what Shayla was frantically searching for.

There was no time to wait as Shayla began to panic, she had all the faith imaginable that Sidney was alright over on base but the second word rang out that a base had been attacked everything changed. Shayla was in her small dorm, on bases they were bunked 4 to a room so she didn't have to crawl very far on her hands and knees as she fell towards the TV before she began fighting to find a more information. Shayla forgot she dropped her phone but it didn't matter, Delores was silent on the other end anyways.Time came to a halt and each motion seemed to blur as she pushed button after button waiting for an image to come across the screen, an image of what the attacked base may have looked like or even some suited reporter ready to share relieving information of any sort.

The image of a desert colored base with a large section of the most eastern part of a wall burned and billowed smoke upwards into the air flashed on screen, there was no way of telling where the base was except out in the desert. Shayla clasped her hands and waited to hear the name of the base, knowing that they wouldn't actually release it for some time due to security risks and so on. Shayla remained on her knees, rocking back and forth with clasped hands while some reporter tried to shout into a microphone against the background noise of wailing sirens and helicopters buzzing around overhead. Sometime in the early hours a truck with some makeshift bombs had rammed into a sparsely manned wall and crashed halfway through it. The images from the news camera showed a base with armed jeeps moving all about, medical ambulances crisscrossing and soldiers moving back and forth searching the rubble for anyone hurt. Large brick walls were constructed and then reinforced with sandbags to offer a barricade against any gunfire or attack but a truck running through with several bombs was sure enough to take out a large portion of the perimeter, injuring many on the other side.

The attack was fairly well coordinated, it hit near an area where there were many tents and small buildings established on the base, it happened early enough that there were plenty of people sleeping within and it was set up for maximum destruction. At the break of day troop rotations were at their lowest as the night patrols were wearing down and the day patrols weren't up and running yet, the truck had several propane tank explosives loaded in the back so when the front breached the brick the bombs were launched forward and then exploded. The reporter continued to talk about the amount of destruction, which increased the dread and worry across the viewing area; including Shayla and Delores. In the background behind the reporter the soldiers climbing through massive piles of wreckage looked like ants, Shayla was nose to screen trying to make out any of her friends that were over in the desert with Sidney but you couldn't make out much of the small black specks.

Shayla remained knelt on the floor with her hands in her lap, she was on the verge of making herself something to eat after her day of work when Delores called, the topic of foods and recipes was a favored one between the two of them, it was much more settling than talking about the war so far away and the unknown waiting to hear from Sidney every few days. The night settled in and the same report looped over and over, scans of the rubble wall and jeeps hooking up to large chunks of twisted metal that used to be a truck being pulled out into the open sand to investigate while others hauled bricks out of the way to recover things or people from underneath. Shayla's roommates came and sat with her while also watching the same news reports and they did their best to support their roommate but they also worried on their own for their friends too.

Delores was stricken with fear; the notion of her dear son caught up in such a place was enough to make breathing difficult and when Isaiah returned home he found his wife clenching the telephone in her hands while her eyes remained locked on the television. Isaiah had heard the news on the radio and watched a little of the coverage on the television in his store, he hoped that his wife was ignorant to the goings on because he knew she worried so much.

Isaiah reached the handle on his front door and heard the television, as he entered he recognized the reporter talking about the destruction and chaos caused by the bomb that destroyed a large portion of the military base as they were gearing up for heavier and heavier fighting. The look on Delores' face as she grasped the phone scared Isaiah, she had the same look on her face when he ran to her in the hospital when Sidney was much younger, and now the notion of his son possibly hurt or killed just punched him in the stomach.

Shayla sat knelt down in front of her television until it was late, one of her roommates hung up the phone in hopes that some of them would get reassuring phone calls but Shayla was locked and determined to sit until she heard something on the screen. A roommate named Lea spent a few moments holding Shayla's hand before convincing her that everything would be alright and suggesting strongly that she get into bed, there was still work to be done in the morning and the only reason Sidney hadn't called yet was because it wasn't his night to call and that he was probably so far from the base that got attacked that he didn't even know about it yet, he was almost certain to call in a few more days like his normal routine, Shayla nodded off the attempts from Lea but her mind was too panicked to focus or keep it from wandering to allow any real sleep.

Isaiah spent a long afternoon comforting Delores also, she was worried sick about Sidney as any good mother would be and it took a bit of time to convince her that Sidney was a good smart boy and that he'd call when he was able to, it may have been a motherly intuition or just worry but she held out for a bit longer before giving in and going to bed like Isaiah suggested. That night Isaiah had bad dreams about being back in the jungle, the feeling that he was being watched even after he woke up had caused him to lurch forward a little to scan the room several times before laying back and trying to sleep again, it was a night of uneasy sleep for all of Sidney's family back in the states.

Paper Paulie

Ch. 9

Sidney was on his way to his post in the *Boom Room* when a ground shaking blast sent smoke and dust a hundred yards into the sky and rock particles wafting across the rest of the base. The morning pre-sun air was crisp as Sidney arose before the daybreak, when the night covers the land the temperature drops and offers a brief night of relief from the days' blistering heat and it was an ideal time of day for many of the soldiers to run or jog around the base.

Close to the *Boom Room* quarters Sidney passed SFC Shields, she was jogging while she could in order to run off her anxiety or aggression that builds up during the trying days of tasking each member under her command with specific details in order to make sure the soldiers on patrol or out in combat have the supplies and backup they need. Sidney was admiring the quiet of the morning, the air was still and even with some light hustle around the base, it was still relatively peaceful compared to that of the later morning when trucks and helicopters began moving in hoards.

Shields was in her issued dark green shorts and a light tan shirt tied up at the midsection, her socks were rolled down to cover her laces to keep some sand from falling within the lace holes. Shields nodded as she passed and as Sidney lowered his arm from his brief salute the world around them exploded and all the sand below their feet became airborne. Sidney stumbled back and to the side of a small bulkhead as a wall of sand rose up from below and rushed passed, after the initial blast everything was silent. Sidney scrambled to cover his face once things began to register in his mind what to do, there was no sense as to what happened and it all blurred for long moments, all Sidney could do was just stay fetal and keep his face covered as grit and pebbles rained down from above. The dark of night was momentarily lit up with an orange hue in the very near distance for a moment and once he pieced it together with the large boom and the earth shaking him off his feet, he realized he had been near an explosion.

Sidney was trying to shake off his arms and begin to blow sand from his face when he felt a hand slam into his chest and begin to jerk him up from the ground. With the disorientation and the sand cloud covering over any ability to see anything Sidney tried to shove off the hand that frantically grabbed at him, he feared he was being kidnapped or abducted. Sidney struggled, he had sand in his eyes, his nose and his mouth, coughing and sneezing wasn't doing enough to clear him of his burden while a mighty hand still pulled and tugged at him. Sidney swung his left arm to free himself of the pest nagging him then he felt a sharp sting of a hand slap his face.Sidney stopped and began brushing his face clear of sand globs and once he could see, he faced Shields; also brushing sand from her face. "We gotta go" the petite gal shouted. Shields was bracing herself up with her hands on her knees and her sweaty shirt hiked up over most of her face to keep from inhaling more sand.

Sidney tried his best to follow Shields as she worked towards the chaos, she was insistent to help and find out what had happened just moments after she had jogged passed the *Boom Room* and outer perimeter. The sand cloud smelled of burnt metal, similar to hot batteries and melted wires.Shields had globs of sand caked onto her where she had been sweating, each time she tried to wipe her forearm across her face to wipe off some sand she just ended up moving more back towards her mouth.

With a few jogged steps and the turning of a corner around a metal corrugated building Sidney and Shields raced to find out where the blast took place in order to help in any way that they could. As the dust began to settle it became more and more obvious what had happened, there was a large gap blown into the outer wall that was built to secure everyone within, the brick and mortar used had been blown all over the base and sent ripping through tents, and soldiers.

The confusion only grew, there were men shouting and groaning while others scurried about trying to gather their gear or prepare for a second assault. A siren bellowed out from the warning speakers overhead drowning out any shouts or verbal commands, the sounds of everyone were already muffled and now with a deafening siren giving out warning only meant that hearing was certainly not going to happen. Sidney stumbled as he got closer and closer to the pile of rubble and twisted metal that once made one of the buildings on base, each step became a challenge as the rocks slipped and gave way underfoot.

Shields ran into the thick blowing smoke filled sand and quickly out of sight as Sidney fumbled to help anyone that he could come across in the haze. Sidney helped two or three men to their feet and as he kept inching further and further towards the large gap in the outer wall, he came across more twisted metal and piles of bricks. There was no telling who was who, the dark cloud made identifying anyone impossible, it didn't really matter who was dragged from the ground; they needed the help.

A shadow emerged from the thick of the smoky dirt, it was hard to tell until they nearly collided and knocked Sidney back a few steps when it was clear that Shields had been helping someone to walk and to make their way out of the densest part of the grog (grimy blowing dirty smoky fog). Sidney wasn't sure how to help, there were so many people moving around and in and out of the smoky haze but he followed his gut anyways. On her way back to the thicket of smoke Shields shouted to Sidney; "Venney, clear it" to a still confused man who felt he was spinning around in circles.

Shields was still moving with a brisk pace when she grabbed onto Sidney's left arm and lead him further into the thicket, everything was still muffled under the suppression of the air raid siren. "The Boom Room" it clicked that Sidney was only steps from his command, and that it was half mangled and twisted around the large computers and monitors inside.

Sidney realized that half of the steel corrugated building that was the *Boom Room* an hour before was now ripped apart and full of rubble. When it suddenly hit Sidney where he was standing the shock tore through him like the blast did through the wall. Shields rushed around trying to clear smoke in order to see what was going on and the yelling and flashes of light from search lights was all dizzying and overloading Sidney's senses. Sidney closed his eyes to focus, in all of his training he couldn't remember how to even breathe but he closed his eyes anyways to try and think, or picture where things were laid out before the disaster.

Sidney tried to imagine his lovely Shayla, he wanted to picture his soon to be bride and let her beauty and bright smile warm his heart and bring him peace among the chaos but his mind was blank. In the horror of reality Sidney couldn't picture Shayla, her long curly hair or smooth skin, he couldn't picture the shape of her body

181

or the sway of her hips that just melted him, it had all been blown from his mind and he was grasping to find a small moment of peace to center himself in order to get back to working efficiently.

A bump from behind brought Sidney's eyes wide open, everything was still dark and smoky but turning a little Sidney began to see Shields again out of the corner of his eye, she was higher in rank but saluting was put on hold as they both tried to figure out how to best help the hurt or wounded soldiers as well as secure the area until more help arrived. As Sidney turned he felt a vice on his leg, something grabbed onto him so he reached out and grabbed Shields' arm to brace himself and as they both turned they looked down among the rubble as the fog cleared for a moment, there was Belleaux, lying under a bit of bubble and against one of the tables that had been overturned in the debris.

Shields and Sidney both dropped to their knees to begin to help their Command Sergeant and as each of them reached out for an arm to pick him up by he saluted. "Permission to leave my post?" Shields and Sidney looked at one another through the haze as they tried to unscramble what the wounded man was asking among all of the confusion. "Am I relieved of duty now? I'd like to turn in" Belleaux struggled over the loud noise in the distance. There was a sinking pit in Sidney's gut instantly, Shields began to raise her arm in salute and as Sidney followed in the honorable tradition of respect, Belleaux went lifeless and limp.

Even to the end Belleaux wasn't going to abandon his post until he was properly relieved, in the trauma of it all there may have been some confusion or even delusions of himself back in his younger years but he remained a military man to the absolute end, a tough and unwavering man that had fought long and hard for his title and rank and when life left his body, Belleaux was finally at peace. Shields dropped her head, she had worked under the Command Sergeant for several months of the deployment and now he was gone, and she was in charge... all of the sudden. Sidney did what he could to heave himself up from the ground, he was a soldier and it was no time to be confused and whirl-winded by the blast; there was people to help and a mess to clean up.

"Gotta make a command" Sidney insisted to Shields as he bumped into her while standing back up. Shields was getting a handle on the gravity of their surroundings and was starting to get caught up in the chaos herself, especially with the blow of losing Belleaux. Shields wielded her power in the *Boom Room*, her strength was maintaining discipline and coordinating troop movements and convoys to support a war, but with the dusty wind settling on her skin and goops of mud sticking to sweaty spots on her face and body she was losing her fortitude.

Sidney knew that Shields was a leader, he wasn't sure of what else to do so he shouted that they needed to rebuild the *Boom Room* to stay in contact with all of the platoons out on patrol and waiting for supplies. In the midst of the settling dust and the visions of rubble becoming more defined the urgency of reestablishing links to the troops out in the country was essential and had to be a priority. Sidney knew that Shields was dealt an upset losing her Command Sergeant and if she was given too long to consider everything then she might lose her grip on herself so he pushed that command had to be rebuilt and that she was the perfect soldier for it: she had to.SFC Shields knew the ins and outs and what it would take, and Sidney was at the ready to take her orders. Sidney turned Shields to face him and he raised a salute; "Your orders... Ma'am."

Swarms of soldiers rushed on the scene, more and more bodies came in waves to clear rubble and begin treating the wounded while hand carting them to a hospital tent. The rebuilding of the wall had begun within minutes of clearing out the last of the injured or deceased and all the while there was still heavy dust and the smell of chemical in the air. The sun began warming up the desert sands and Sidney and SFC Shields already had moved a majority of the intact electronics into a small storage container and began establishing another command post for the wayward troops. Sidney kept Shields moving anytime she looked like she was about to stop or sit down he would shout at her, her first tired response was "you know I'll have you peel potatoes right? to which Sidney replied; can it wait a day?

Sidney knew that in the rush of chaos she was
polished steel but he didn't want her to become still and
begin to fall apart. Sidney knew his role, he was support
and with Shields waving her arms like an orchestra
conductor to men running power lines or moving
computers she looked like a hummingbird at a feeder and
Sidney helped to facilitate in any way he could.

With the help of a few other electronic engineers
the new *Boom Room* was half functional, there were half
of the monitors and the bundles of cables were rerouted or
spliced and elongated and there was enough to make due
until further notice. The communications with the *Boom
Room* were only interrupted for less than three hours
before function was restored and with the bee-swarm like
intensity of each soldier performing their duties, the
precise robotic like coordination of the *Boom Room*
Belleaux required was back on track. Shields kept putting
her hands towards her head to rub her eyes, the adrenaline
was fading and in so her once rhythmic arm oscillating
turned to more of a stammer. Sidney tried to see the larger
picture, how he would set up a command if he had the
chance(which now he did) and he tried to keep it
functional from the beginning but was continuously
tripped up while men had to remove computer cases to
dump out sand that landed on the delicate hardware.

The functionality of the first *Boom Room* was iffy,
the concave row of monitors made for a good perch from
Belleaux's crow's nest but the engineers were nearly

elbow to elbow and breathing in each others air. The new Boom Room was a bit smaller and with some loss of personnel and equipment they still had to find the best way to establish not only room for the operators but also for all of the equipment within. The computer towers couldn't be touching anything on the sides due to the excessive heat and you couldn't prop them against walls so Sidney tried his best to make sense of where to stack the towers and to use wood platforms to help dissipate the heat as they stacked upwards. Using the surviving desks and chairs meant that there wasn't enough for all but there were also a few soldiers that were injured along with the loss of Belleaux so the entire unit was condensed on the fly.

Sidney tried to see things from Shields' vision, her set up wasn't vastly different than it was originally but the computers weren't arranged side to side but rather in a horseshoe shape around the outer wall of the bunker, it gave way to better visibility from the elevated position for her to see each of her logistical coordinators while they correlated troops and supplies that were out in the thick of combat. Shields knelt down to use her ankle knife to cut a small portion of the band of her sock off to use as a head band, her midriff was still bare but coated in muddy sand and the stream of sweat that ran down the middle of her shirt shed sand each time she twisted or turned, she needed her short hair up to keep her cool.

The new *Boom Room* was alive like a beehive, there were men lying under tables running mazes of wiring while others' were booting up the computers to begin running diagnostics. The air was heavy in mourning for what had happened and also hung stagnant with each others breaths in the enclosed area, but there were men in the field awaiting their support and it was crucial they were back in business a.s.a.p.

Shields began to wobble, her legs crossed as she turned a little and as she rotated her body, her feet forgot to follow suit. Sidney darted to her side and began to reach out to catch Shields, he was concerned that in her fall she might knock over someone or something and he wanted to prevent any further injuries. The first thing to flash through Sidney's mind was that perhaps Shields had a concussion from the blast or a head injury. As Sidney grabbed hold of Shields he tried to brace his legs out to ease them both to the ground. Sidney lost his footing and slid roughly on some sand and the two crashed together onto the floor of the new bunker they were still installing all of their electronics into.

Sidneys' outstretched legs each turned in different directions as he fell, the sand on the metal flooring acted as ball-bearings and there was nothing he could do but accept his fate and submit to gravity while hoping to keep from landing on Shields. The shipping container Bunker that was being filled with computer equipment still echoed when Sidney and Shields fell, there were tables and chairs being scooted around to position everything in a way that soldiers could work efficiently and get back to work promptly.

The few moving people stopped when Sidney let out a bit of a wail from scraping his leg on the sharp corner of a desk as he dove trying to help Shields; that leg ended up in the air while the rest of his body contorted. Shields and Sidney collided and both let out groans and huffs, Shields had a whimper in her big exhale as she asked Sidney; "you know I can have you peel potatoes right?" while Sidney had a sigh of relief and responded "can it wait a day?" Sidney managed to cradle Shields' neck and roll enough to soften most of his comrades fall, the concern was focused on keeping his superior officer from a head injury, she needed to run the new *Boom Room*, her strength inspired that of others' and it was still needed.

"I miss my husband, I miss my dog Walt and I miss morning coffee with my friends, how about you?" Shields piped up. Sidney let out another huff and grabbed at his thigh, it had scraped against the corner of a table, the side pocket was half torn off but the rest of the fabric but the skin was intact to his relief. The sharp pain jolted up his leg causing him to wince a little but it was comforting that the leg was there and not spilling his blood into the sand.

Sidney responded to his superior; "I miss my fiancé, I miss air conditioning, and I miss my mom's prime rib, oh and not being blown up." With a slight chuckle Shields began to curl herself upwards before standing up, she put her hand down on some of the material that had ripped from Sidney's pocket on the ground and turned to look. "What is that" she asked while pointing down to a hardened wad of something next to him. Sidney didn't even look; he patted his hand around in a circle for a moment before knowing exactly what Shields was referring to. "That's my guardian angel Paper Paulie and everything will be alright. Shields took in a large breath and reached her hands behind her to stretch out her shoulders before letting her arms fling back to the front of her, she then swung her hand at Sidney to encourage him to get up and get moving again, Sidney brought Paulie up to his mouth and kissed it before returning it to the safety of his pocket, this time a different pocket.

Before helping Sidney stand Shields spoke up again; "you know I'm going to want to hear about that right?" Sidney crossed his legs and rolled forward to stand up, with a small smirk he looked down to his pocket and nodded in acknowledgment as he pulled on her hand to rise up, "can it wait a day?". Paper Paulie had been in Sidney's pocket the entire time he had been in the desert, the hardened wax that once kept him dry from the rainy jungles of Vietnam some twenty years before hadn't even softened in the heat and he remained close with Sidney.

Sidney understood ever so much more now the value of the small paper doll to his father, it now meant the same to him. Sidney worked through the day, he ran cables with many of the other engineers and tested equipment for shorts or damage to get the room running to as close to pre-blast condition as possible, they were the main intelligence and communications hub for the base and lives were on the line if they failed.

The base Commander took due notice of the diligence and hard work of Shields and also of Sidney in their work to reestablish their post quickly, their efforts to keeping the military moving was top notch and impressed many far up the chain of command. Sidney and Marissa Shields worked through the day and into the night before they could rest or call their families to assure them of their safety. The electrical engineers and other assorted soldiers began hauling out the gear stored in the large metal shipping container once anyone that needed treatment was attended to, the scorching heat had the "tin-bin" warming up quickly so one soldier named Takacs used a rough saw to make vent ports in the top for outward air flow and other decisive cuts for openings to run needed wiring. The old *Boom Room* was always hot like an oven but it was essential to keep the machines cool so the engineer named John Takacs devised plan.

Takacs knew the military protocols for changing things, it was a long process and full of red tape. Shields was focused on getting the command center up and running and at nearly any cost so he took the initiative to put his engineering skills to better use; functionality. Takacs knew his capabilities but he also had his hands tied under Belleaux's command so he was forced to bite his tongue rather than put his skills to use. As the new command post was being put together in such a rush he used the distracted attention of Shields to put together cooling units for a more productive room. Sidney nodded a little as Takacs just sort of told him he had to make a cut, Sidney suspected he maybe should have asked for a reason but who was he to question a man with a skill-set he wouldn't have understood.

With enough metal tubing and cardboard from the piles of boxes waiting to be returned John used a small pump and one of the fans to create water cooling across the top of the metal roof, it took a few hours to work but he knew the cooling demands of the computers (and fellow soldiers) beneath him in the room. The cardboard helped to insulate the roof from the abusive sun above and the water tracing back and forth through the pipes and discarded truck radiators carried away most of the heat that was caught rising from the room below. John earned his engineering degree while a reservist and used most of the government money for his education but once there was rumor of war, he was called up just before graduation. John was quick on his feet and a fast thinker, a keen mind he attributed to his mother, with scraps of tubes and a steady welding hand there were long lines of pipe tracing back and forth across the room to maximize

191

the efficiency of his water cooling all the while also using a small radiator leading outside and deep into the sand to relieve the brunt of the abusive heat, within an hour of John finishing his welding and pipe-fitting the room was nearly twenty degrees cooler than the ambient temperatures and much cooler than the old *Boom Room*.

Some of the *Boom Room* operators were injured in the blast, and with the loss of Command Sergeant Belleaux the powers that be put Shields in charge immediately to resume organizing the war supplies, to her right hand she appointed Sidney to help with all of the logistics. John Takacs remained on hand to continue improving on what the military had started, he found ways to use the corrugated siding of the shipping containers to weld a second layer over top with small gaps and with a minimal fan in conjunction with some baffles the new *Boom Room* was now feeling almost air-conditioned for those inside. With the local sand as an insulator against the outside heat as well there were three layers of sheet metal on the outside of the new *Boom Room* so they decided to rename it, to carry on using the old name of the old building it was time for a new call name.

"*The Woofer*" was built in a day; it was more compact but more efficiently cooled. With Shields in control, it didn't matter if the Alpha dog was male or female, it was all about how the pack was lead and all of the controllers in the *Woofer* made up Shields' pack.

Marissa Shields was given higher ranks in the field but her bravery and quick thinking to begin helping people moments after the blast was what she was credited for the most, she and Sidney were both given high honors and medals for their actions that morning. The night ended with Marissa still in her running clothes, her hair still tied up above the small fuzzy strip of shaved hair at the back of her head for heat relief and all of her body still covered in either dirt or someone's blood. Sidney was also honored for his bravery in battle and it meant the world to him but that day was a haze; he followed orders until Shields stopped running long enough to realize what had happened, and it was adrenaline fueling her until that point. Shields wrapped up the night swaying her hips as she did when she worked, she had her rhythm back as she shouted out orders to the call controllers and she was back into her groove as an operator.

The long day had passed after the explosion ripped apart the *Boom Room*, Sidney was able to call Shayla the morning after *The Woofer* was operational, she was so excited and relieved to hear from him she wasn't angered by the lack of information that he gave about what had happened, it was all supposed to remain confidential anyways and she was getting used to it. The five minute phone call Sidney got with Shayla was too quick, they were hardly able to speak it seemed before the timer dinged into the phone in the background alerting them that their time had been reached.

Shayla was enjoying Florida as she had been but without him it all seemed to have lost its luster. "The sand is no longer smooth, the ocean no longer shiny or vast and the sky just isn't the same blue without you" Shayla began to speak. Sidney needed to continue to hear her voice, he would have dumped an entire paychecks' worth of quarters into the machine for just a few more moments of her comforting tone. The rush of the blast and the days after were still in fast forward and it was all numbing until he got to hear the soothing voice of his love over the phone, and without effort; the emotions came forth.

Sidney knew he was lucky to be alive, had he been in the *Boom Room* just a few minutes earlier he might have been caught in the blast or ripped apart by the flying metal debris but he couldn't tell the girl he loved, he couldn't really tell her anything about it. It was amazing to have such a wonderful women back home hoping for the best for Sidney, he truly missed her and it was a burden to have to keep such a wild day from her, but he had orders to follow. Shayla agreed to call Isaiah and Delores for Sidney since he was out of call time and Sidney let the handset hang up on the receiver.

The air still smelled of chemicals with an undertone of gunpowder, there was always a grain of sand in his mouth and no matter what his eyes were always irritated by the heat and dryness of the desert, Sidney was miserable. The newness and bewilderment of the new desert ended shortly after it began, the burned marks around the base were a constant reminder that outside the tall barriers were a hostile group of people that saw them as foreign intruders and threats and acted just as hostile as possible, there were moments he wished he could curse all of the men with a spell that turned all of their drinking water into sour milk and their hands all turned to feet, both were serious offenses in the area and he was raised better than to wish poorly upon someone and he knew it.

Speaking with Shields was relieving, they both asked discretely if the other was doing ok as they were nearly together when their base was attacked and then worked side by side to clear debris and injured soldiers from the rubble of their old command post. Sidney suspected that Shields was such a strong woman she may not admit to feeling dizzy which is why he exercised extreme decorum to keep from undermining her strength, especially in an already masculine atmosphere. Shields always nodded and smiled when Sidney gave her the thumbs up checking on her discretely and she appreciated his concern. The higher ranks were often lonely as you became known to give orders rather than defy them as the younger ranks sometimes did. Shields loved her work; she was momentarily offset once the explosion hit but her training kicked in and it carried her through the chaos until late in the day.

It was a Thursday when Sidney returned to the Woofer. After a day to roam the base and speak with Shayla he heard news that things were returning to secure and that was a major reassurance, it was often hard to know what was happening outside the walls of their command post because everyone had headphones on and were jammed into a small dark container talking with troops hundreds or thousands of miles away, all while oblivious as to what was going on ten yards out their front door.

The seclusion from the surrounding base was both a blessing and curse. The benefit of being in an office was that you could picture being anywhere; well, anywhere sandy like Arizona. The unknowns that can go on while you are working in a blacked out bunker are that you can't tell if there are troops running to one urgency or another just outside your door because you are wrapped up talking with other people and you are completely unaware.

Sidney took longer routes to the Woofer to work, his stalling before the blast saved his life but also it was a bit comforting to look around the base and get a feel for the ambiance before enclosing himself in for a twelve hour shift. On the first Thursday since the bombing Sidney and Shields were both working in the Woofer, since she had become the in charge officer and he had become her number two they had been alternating working days or shifts while still getting everything back in order as well as new recruits trained in order to fill the slots emptied when injured soldiers transitioned home or to one of the hospitals nearby. Sidney pulled the heavy reinforced door open and followed the shadows inward, it was time to get to work and it was less of a chore now that Takacs had worked his engineering skills to use the earth around and under them to both insulate and also air-condition the metal building, it took a minute but Sidney did in fact stop sweating, something that didn't happen in the *Boom Room*.

Stepping in and taking a long pause to adjust to the dim lights Shields came into focus, she was standing at parade rest with her hands clasped behind her back and her feet shoulder width apart in her desert fatigues. Once in the building it was no longer strolling the base but back to business. Sidney glanced around to see all of his fellow coordinators sunken into their chairs with heavy headphones on while taking turns calling into microphones or telephones and using the computer controllers to change routes of supplies or personnel. Before Sidney could even address his superior officer; Shields swiveled to turn her body forty five degrees and her head ninety to watch him walk in a remove his cover (his cap). Sidney nodded in place of his salute because he was indoors and no longer wearing his hat, but also wanted to respect is superior in the chain of command, it was just respectful, as well as the way he was raised.

Sidney jerked his head left and right to loosen up some of the stiffness that hung with him since being half blown to the ground, it was just muscle stiffness that resided a little but was sure to dissipate in the next day or two. "Well then" Marissa prompted the conversation. Sidney was boggled, he let his eyebrows raise up and his eyes widened as he searched the corners of his memory for what at all she could possibly be digging at.

"Well how are you today ma'am" he responded.

"I'm well of course, just waiting on you"

"Waiting, ma'am? Am I not on time"

"Waiting for a story you owe me soldier" Marissa spoke up as her mouth cracked into an impatient smirk. In the fray Sidney had forgotten all about telling her about Paulie. "Then you'll have to tell me about Walt." Shields nodded with a light forward head bow in agreement and finished turning her body to face Sidney. "I thought I was due to peel those potatoes you warned me of" Sidney joked, Shields followed with, "it can wait a day."

Sidney began at the beginning, starting with Isaiah Dante Venney getting a letter while in the raining, humid muddy jungles of Vietnam and the day that took place before Isaiah could even open the envelope. Sidney recanted each detail about the fire fight, the river that he lost his platoon to as well as crawling among dead bodies and tall grass tufts trying to get back to his base overnight, each heart beating moment that could have been his last. Each minute that passed was one more behind him as he bargained with a folded envelope, each time he came closer to losing his life, he promised the envelope that he'd open it, just as long as he was delivered safely back to his barracks. Sidney recanted the story as it had been told to him time and time again, no exaggerated detail or missed nuance, and all with great clarity.

Shields was intrigued, as the choreographed soldiers worked in the background Marissa leaned back against the bulkhead and continued hanging on every word while Sidney retold the story he'd heard dozens of times. The first time Isaiah told his son about owing his life to a small folded dirtied square of wax and paper it just made Sidney want to play with the paper soldier, he was just being told a story, a fable or fairy-tale, it wasn't till later in life that the reality of the Vietnam war or what his father Isaiah survived lost its fictitious hue and became real. Hearing his father's story of war long after he left childhood behind still had a magical appeal to it until the bomb ripped into his own base. Sidney avoided confronting the realism that can't be truly comprehended unless you have experienced it personally like having had to pick up a detached arm or leg or give your commanding officer permission to die, things that shouldn't be taken lightly, or even joked about at all. Sidney knew that he was going to struggle with such details but that was expected when you land in foreign territory for war and like his fellow soldiers, he had a job to do and he'd deal with emotional things later, much later when he was home.

Paper Paulie

Sidney recanted each harrowing event that Paulie guided Isaiah through, there were long battles including *The Grinder* and the slaughter that occurred there. Shields remained silent as she listened in about the small paper guardian angel that Sidney carried with him through his entire deployment to date and even though she would have been skeptical in her pre-war days, now she was certainly a partaker in the mystique of lucky charms. Isaiah had many close calls, from bullets that whizzed past his head to shrapnel or bombs exploding eerily close but after each one, a quick pat down ensured that his body was without holes or damage and he was able to remain fighting; with Paulie in his pocket. Sidney's tone went somber when he spoke about the end of the battle on the Grinder, where his father found his own brother dying on the field and there wasn't anything he could do but make sure his body was carried down to be sent home and properly buried on his home soil, the down turn was indeed sad but Shields spoke up and asked what happened to Paulie when it was in Isaiah's shirt pocket.

Strangely enough, his paraffin wax coating that was meant to protect him from the brutal humidity and rain of the jungle had sealed him into a small wad of wax around his folded paper body and made him impervious to the soaking blood that Isaiah was drenched in after shouldering a body all the way down the large hill. Shields glanced down towards Sidney's pocket and let her right eye twitch at twice the speed of the other while she quickly performed some mental arithmetic and looked back up to Sidney; "yeah, that little hard wax wad is over twenty years old, hell, it's older than I am and the reason I'm here." Shield snarked and huffed with a smile realizing that the small black thing she saw flop out onto the floor had a grand story behind it, it was a little fun to comprehend.

"Walt huh, as in Disney?" Sidney responded in the silence. Marissa perked back up after the story of Ronnie and Isaiah finding one another in the midst of airborne debris and gunfire while clouded in the smoke from burning soldiers and explosions. Marissa cracked a smile; "not quite. Walt is a Vizsla and an active one, my husband and I are both avid joggers but that will come up a bit later. I used to practice run down a long stretch of road that was lined in pines and rarely traveled in the cooler hours of the morning, it was also evenly paved and not torn up from heavy traffic so it made for a pleasant run. So after a few weeks of running one day this lil pup came barreling out towards me, now mind you when I say wee pup I am talking like eight pounds, about as skinny as a salamander but determined to investigate me by seeing what I was doing."

Marissa shifted her weight and crossed her right leg over her left as she leaned back on her hands against a mid-wall railing to continue on with her story. "So this cute little dust colored critter with a hairy chin comes charging out like he's storming Normandy and stopped, just at the end of his driveway and sits back to tilt his head and watch me jog by, that's it, just sit there and watch. Every morning for a week I'd catch a glimpse of this little guy do the same thing, never barking, never so much as wagging his tail, just sitting with his head tilted and watching me jog by. After a few days I began to look forward to seeing him, he'd sit and poke his head out a bit to look down the road, I guess he probably heard my music blaring from my earbuds or maybe my footsteps pounding the pavement but either way, I began to imagine he was just rooting me on in his own way.

On day eight or nine I was keeping a good stride as usual when the little guy finally decided to be vocal, he was up on all fours and squeaked out a brand new half bark half howl, I guess he finally wanted to try to talk. So the house he belonged to had red wood sides and some ivy growing down around the base and this morning there was a work truck parked in along the far side with ladders and tool boxes stacked in the back. Just as I removed my one earbud and stopped to bend down to pet my small audience a man walked from around the side of the work truck. The man was already sweaty, but then again so was I, but he was dirty from working. The man was wearing a backwards ball cap, had a muscly sweaty chest and arms with dirty rough hands and a leather tool belt loaded to one side and jeans that had been worn through under his black knee pads.

My eyes scanned up the paint splattered legs, over the gritted and grated knee pads and up the slim fitting thighs to the toned bare midsection of a guy about my age. Here I am having jogged less than half of my five-mile morning and certain that the guy could see my shirt sticking to my sweaty body and my jogging capris weren't very flattering, I was gross. I watched the man's pecs flex as he reached his hand out; "I'm David." I stuttered to find my words, I felt like the small puppy trying out his voice. I hard swallowed and began to nod my head; no I wasn't talking, just nodding like an idiot. My hands were already sweaty, I still had one earbud blaring in my ear and I couldn't raise my eyes up any higher than his mouth. I watched as the man spoke again and I just couldn't stop. I was staring at beautiful white teeth tucked behind a soft delicate mouth that moved like the breeze through wild grass and he had one dimple, one small dimple on his right and finally, with a little yelp growl from the little guy sitting by my feet, I found my guts to speak.

I introduced myself and apologized for having stopped to pet his cute puppy, I tried to convince my body to turn from this man and leave back to my run before his wife came out or something. There wasn't anything wrong with a neighborly introduction but I was gearing up for a marathon in another month or so and didn't want any facial bruises for my finish line photo because some guys' wife pummeled me,ha-ha. David bent down and picked up the puppy in his workers' hands and I struggled to keep my knees from buckling as this man with tender lips and hard hands cradled this sweet little puppy in his hands.

"My brother Josh asked me to come roof for him for two days and was going to let me take one of his last two puppies home as a gift afterwards, he mentioned that all of them have been too afraid to go down the back deck steps to venture out into the yard except this one, this one tramples down each morning to investigate the end of the driveway and then returns, I guess he just really wanted to get to know you."

"Walt Whitman once said; "Curious, not judgmental" I guess that's what this guy is doing, just going to watch you jog by" David quipped. I am not the most well versed reader, I know that Whitman once said: "keep your face to the sun and the shadows will always fall behind you" (but only because it was on a running t-shirt I once got for a birthday gift) but this guy was very well educated, and it made him dreamy. David claimed his curious little pal (he held up); "this guy has good spirit, I think I'll keep this one." Seeing a hardworking intelligent man with a puppy in his hands was kryptonite, I was powerless and him calling dibs on that little fan that cheered me on sort of broke my heart, I had no claim to him but he claimed me, of all his litter he was the brave one to explore the outdoor world and he found me, each morning for over a week he came out for me and now his owners' brother *David* (in a snarky voice) was going to take him away, I felt a pit in my stomach.

Paper Paulie

I fumbled for my earbud and let the heartache lead the way back to the long lonely road I was jogging and as I began to slip the plastic speaker back into my ear and resume my run, little Walt spoke up again. "I told you he had good taste" at first I thought David was being gross by commenting on my butt from his view in spandex running pants behind me but as I whipped my head around David had already turned his back to me and Walt was trying to climb up over his shoulder to bark at me. David was turning back around: "I was about to let you go without asking you to dinner because I'm sweaty, smelly and dirty from roofing and actually rather shy, I guess this puppy wasn't ready to see you go, to be honest, neither was I." I once again lost my voice but I found a large smile and with it came fiery warm cheeks flush with delight. I felt myself get high-school giddy and begin to bounce on my toes a little as I jetted my eyes around to the banged up work truck and the roof covered with shingle bundles; anything to avoid eye-contact enough to be able to speak. "Dinner huh" I asked as I tried to keep from biting my lower lip with nervousness. "How about seven-thirty" David asked.

I stepped back slowly towards the road and playfully responded; "Seven it is then." I watched as a smile broke over those soft lips as they pulled back to flash a toothy smile, I totally knew he said seven-thirty but why does the guy always have to take charge and pick the time? I jogged down the road to round the fire-hydrant I deemed my halfway point when I clocked my run and

205

on my way back I found myself nearly sprinting just to get to see him again. On my way back I looked up the road and through the rather dense pines I could see the little puppy waiting for me again at the end of the driveway. My heartbeat raced more from excitement, except it was the running that had me out of breath. After a few minutes of running David was already up on the roof and working, I'm not going to lie and say that I wasn't checking him out hitting a hammer or glistening in the sun. "You said six-thirty right" I hollered up to him. David shouted back; "YEAH, see you at six."

Ch. 10

When is war justified? The solemn voiced pastor speaks up again after a moment of silence to continue on. Paper Paulie remained buttoned safely into a pocket for Sidney as he remained posted at the right hand of his commanding officer Marissa Shields as they worked to conduct supply shipments back and forth to the cities that troops were marching through like a swarm of locusts. It takes a lot of man power and man hours to keep the battle weary men and women of our armed services marching onward and under the command of field generals or other commanders that are following the grand schematics laid out before them. It was nice that Sidney and Marissa shared stories of their home life and knowing that even his superiors were human, many of the war worn higher ranking officers seemed to have distanced themselves from humanity in war and seemed cold, but not Marissa.

Long after Shields had told Sidney about the origin of Walt's namesake and having met the love of her life many conversations had revolved around the *Woofer*, stories from "worst Christmas present" to "most embarrassing trip to the emergency room." One topic arose time and time again: "how can this place be considered third world when they have so much potential to climb out of their own ignorance?" The main theme revolved around large oil fields that were constantly bombed by the local citizens, sabotaging by members of the same society and bombings among their own people and it was disturbing to witness time and time again. The radios in the *Woofer* were a nonstop chatter of radio squawks and men shouting orders or positions, the influx of noise was often hard to drown out and with such information streaming in it was sometimes hard to keep it all straight for the coordinators at the radios.

There was a soldier that many of the troops boasted about, he was a man with a Jamaican-American heritage and tune to his voice, he would carry a portable karaoke machine with him and climb up on top of a truck to perform. The young soldier entertained masses of troops on nights in the front of headlights to light up his small stage. It wasn't until years later that young musician released his first album and all of the soldiers that instantly recognized his almost nasal lyrics knew he made it into his calling. Sidney was lucky one night to catch a makeshift concert, the karaoke machine had flickering lights and a speaker that belted out a background beat while the hip-hop artist grooved along, all while giving his fellow soldiers an escape from their surroundings. Shields and some of the other gals on base were dancing while several of the other soldiers were rapping along.

Sidney was nearing the end of his deployment, after several months had passed since the bombing of the side garrison wall. The work was steady and every soldier knew what they were required to do, many men and women were acknowledged for their part in the steadfast clean up as well as search and rescue of injured soldiers. The land was rich with people using the ingenuity and skills to power their homes with what measly power the government could keep on when it wasn't being sabotaged. Women made the best of when to wash or visit the market at the safest times and many of the men bartered or traded for any of the necessities their families needed. Some night's music could be heard from the distance, some random notes from a wind instrument would carry on with the breeze and in the few lulls between engine roars or men shouting, sometimes something peaceful could be made out.

With his background Sidney was often being recruited to help wire up small radios or larger stereos, many soldiers talked about convincing Sidney to adapt one of their smaller personal radios with a higher frequency repeater and transformer to establish a small base radio-station but many of those same guys would just run long speaker wiring and all share the same compact disc player instead because they didn't really want to share if there was going to be some rule aboutequal music play across the genres. The days were hot and long and easily slipped into a dull rhythm. Sidney called home or Shayla as often as he could, with calling cards constantly needing a recharge it was easier to call once or twice a week rather than every day. Sidney asked dozens of questions each time he got Shayla on the phone; he wanted to close his eyes and picture being right with her rather than twenty-hours away by cargo plane.

Shayla loved hearing the story about Walt and that Sidney worked well with Marissa and was saddened to hear about Belleaux of course but relieved when Sidney called and explained that he was alright. Sidney being at war was hard, Isaiah knew first-hand the horrors that take place and the thoughts that his son must be facing, all he could do was keep him up on plenty of distractions by typing him letters and sending him pictures of things from around home that might remind him of what he's fighting for, pictures of the leaves changing or some of his favorite burgers or Delores's meals that he might miss. It was an collective effort of the Venney's and Shayla to keep Sidney flooded with letters, sometimes Delores would even just send recipe cards just in case he found himself in a position of getting to cook, he never was though.

Shayla continued to teach languages and consult with local businesses that dealt with foreign companies, she was very well educated and enjoyed it but she was dutifully near the phone each time she and Sidney had plans to talk. Shayla made a weekly call to Isaiah and Delores as well; she would check in on her future in-laws as well as report the latest from what she had heard from Sidney so Delores didn't feel left out. Shayla continued different cooking lessons to fill her time, she had once promised Sidney that she would wow him with meal after

meal and she looked forward to learning. Shayla's mother
Marlene learned to cook from her mother and her mother
from her mother and so on so when Shayla was a young
girl she was tasked with rolling out dough and stamping
out biscuits, childlike tasks that she saw as a chore(like
most young girls) but she saw the value in it all as she
grew.

Shayla had a well versed palette after having had
the opportunity to travel extensively during college.
Shayla loved the foods bright in color and texture, foods
from her native backgrounds but she also enjoyed foods
with an Asian appeal to them as well. Shayla grew up on
fruits and fishes, foods that her mother grew up on and
passed down. Shayla loved spending most of her
childhood in the kitchen, well she loved to taste and
sample rather than roll dough or have to scrub out pots
and pans but it was still bonding time with her mother and
grandmother. Shayla wanted to broaden her cooking, she
knew that Sidney was more of an American with a side of
soul cuisine kind of guy and she wanted to make sure she
had the best recipes for lasagna or collards she could
come up with, especially for the relief of her future
mother in-law Delores.

Shayla enjoyed getting to know Isaiah and Delores
over the phone, knowing that Delores owned and spent
most of her life baking in the little bakery that still stood
could have been a little intimidating but Shayla took it as
a sign to stick with cooking or grilling and to steer clear

from the baking so as not to step on any toes, besides; nobody can compete with a mothers' cooking. Having grown up in Cape Coral the beach was always in Shayla's life and as days passed and it grew closer to Sidney coming home she began to realize that he might want to move closer to his aging parents up the coast and that frightened her. Shayla loved being near the Gulf of Mexico, the warmer beaches were tucked in away from the larger Atlantic, the beaches were often covered in people grilling and partying nearly all year long, it was a big part of her life. Marlene loved to visit the market with young Shayla in tow and then meet up with plenty of neighborhood families at the beach for cookouts and good laughs and that culture was instilled deeply in Shayla so she was always sharing a bright smile with passersby.

Coming up Shayla followed the boys out into the ocean, the surfing wasn't grand by any means but body boarding and light surfing was a great excuse to stay in the water or near the beach. When the news would report of storms coming up from the Caribbean, Shayla and her pod of surfing buddies would get their bigger breaks and big waves and they would hit the surf until it was too nasty or too late to continue on before calling it a night. Shayla worked, cooked, and day dreamed about moving back closer to the ocean, she was only an hour from it as it were but that hour drive turns into a two hour round trip and it takes a few hours to make a trip worthwhile(realizations about adulthood that bum her out about growing up) but she had Sidney. Shayla saved her concerns; she knew that even though finding a place to live as a married couple would be a team effort, it wasn't a task Sidney should be bothered with until he returned safe and sound to her.

Shayla shared her excitement about finally getting to marry Sidney with Marlene and Delores in the audience but she also kept plenty to herself, both mothers' seemed to overwhelm her with their own ideas and influences of what they wanted and each time it seemed to quickly overshadow what she had dreamt of for herself. Delores wanted very traditional: the long flowing train as she glided down an aisle of a cathedral type church while Marlene wanted her daughter to have more native song and food at the reception, all the while with her youth spent at the beach she herself had visions of sandals beneath the dress and a shell necklace adorned across her collarbone and an airy light linen suit on Sidney. Every little girl has envisioned that one moment when the man that she chooses to spend her life with, lifts her veil and confirms his love to her, Shayla wanted a beach influence and if Delores had too much say in it, then it would just remain a dream.

Shayla kept her wedding plans to herself but noted many ideas and locations, of course they were all very dependent on Sidney and what he also wanted but it didn't mean she couldn't plot and plan in her moments of down time, it also kept her distracted from his absence anyways. Sidney fought his best to keep his head on straight and focus on that final plane ride home, too many soldiers took that flight in a box but he was secure enough that he would be able to walk off that plane and into the loving arms of Shayla and perhaps both of his parents to the tune of dozens of cheering family members instead of to a memorial unit carrying caskets. Separately Sidney and Shayla had their own dreams, their own visions for after the deployment ended and what was to become of them afterwards, but together, they envisioned themselves growing old together and finding out all the wonders that life had to offer them as a couple, a vision that would help to keep them bonded to one another.

The days drew out and the hours seemed like the doldrums of time where not even the second hand moved if you watched it. From inside the *Woofer* Sidney struggled to avoid a face to face stare down with the row of clocks on the walls, calls would come and go and routes changed but the clocks remained still. A dozen clocks each set to specific time zones labeled underneath all sat frozen on the wall until one single blink would nudge them in unison to the next second. The last few days that seemed to trickle down were mind numbing, a constant buzz of people came and went and even with an increasing amount of work to do, Sidney couldn't keep home out of his mind. Marissa relieved Sidney in command when his shift was over and they worked to help facilitate other junior officers to assist in the operations of the troops but it felt distant, almost clouded over and fake.

Paper Paulie

Sidney knew not to talk about transitioning home, he would have to spend a week in Germany debriefing and so on before going stateside but it was still a welcomed change. Talking about going home was rude, there were still troops landing and being welcomed in every other day while others' just didn't make it onto a roster anymore, the assumption was that they vanished from the base just like their name did from a clipboard of what soldiers you were responsible for for that day. Marissa still had several months left to go before she could return to her home life and her husband, Sidney felt heavy in his heart for her and wished she were leaving behind the hot sweaty nights and sand blistered knuckles at the same time but like waves breaking on the beach, each soldier had their own rhythm and purpose. The ship out orders arrived with less than forty-eight hours before he was to report to Al-Azur air base, it was once a small airstrip that the US had quadrupled in size while they were in the area and it made for a rough bit of terrain, to get to it, you had to travel what everybody called "Hell Highway."

The highway was pitted and pocked with large holes and craters, it started out a supply line that the US bombed clear and then they crudely paved it to get to and from the flat land of the airstrip but occasionally an explosion sends part of a convoy into ditches and soldiers scrambling for cover. With good trajectory several of the enemy soldiers knew where to hide and how to angle one of their rocket propelled grenades or bazookas to get an

215

explosive close enough to send a truck off the *Highway*, and they did it often. The *Highway* was an eerie calm stretch of road, even when you could see other cars or trucks sound seemed dampened, quieter, almost inaudible, even the normal speaking voice of the man you were sitting next to seemed muted when you tried to speak, as if the ghosts of the explosives took away any bit of sound as your body shook and jostled down the long two lane minefield.

Sidney couldn't tell Shayla when he was leaving, any inside information of travel outside the base was deemed confidential and the powers in charge didn't want any chance of their soldiers being targets to anyone outside the base, or there to be any sort of planning for an ambush. Sidney knew that talking about the highway would only worry his lady back home so he swallowed his concerns and triple checked all of his stowed gear before his final shift at *The Woofer*. Focus was waning for Sidney on that last shift, for anybody on the cusp of going home there is a tension of mirage about it, that uneasy feeling that something could go wrong at the last moment and only when your feet set out firmly on friendly soil can you breathe easy and let your shoulders relax. Sidney blinked often to keep his eyes from drifting to the row of clocks on the wall and tuned in on his coordinators at their computers, each moving and changing route and supply line ensured the men in the field had any and everything they could ever need to do their job.

Paper Paulie

Marissa had an inkling when she showed up to relieve Sidney for the last time, she already had the next day's role call roster and he wasn't on it but she didn't really want to know for sure. Once the official duty relief was sealed with a snap salute, this time, Sidney let his hand linger at his brow for his commanding officer that shared her heart and her character to help him through his time during his deployment. Sidney strained to fend off that stinging that started in the corner of his eye, that burn that precedes a tear but the harder he clenched his jaw, the faster the tear welled up and rolled down his face. Marissa stood rigid and firm in mirrored salute, she was dutiful and even as soldiers come and go, there aren't always fellow members you share such trying times with and bond with, and she knew she'd miss that in Sidney as she returned his salute.

The background noise began to crackle through the murmur, one voice stuck out and then another and like a dam breaking, the noise that was just soft background clutter came back to full volume and it broke the moment of pure respect and admiration Sidney and Marissa were exchanging. "Can it wait a day" Shields asked with a quivering lower lip and clenching eyebrows. With a sharp about face Sidney turned himself, even as both eyes welled up and his jaw muscles bulged, Sidney remained respectful and diligent while in uniform and wanted to show is commanding officer Marissa Shields the utmost respect he felt she deserved. Sidney stepped past a few long tables that held up flak vests and helmets and grabbed his gear before stepping outside one last time, letting the heavy metal bunker door slam behind him.

The stars were still overhead and fighting to shine bright instead of fading away into the light of day when Sidney looked up. The smell of dry desert air filled his nose again, the same air that chapped his nostrils when he first stepped into the loose sand of the desert many months before; an air that he swore he'd never miss was now going to be a memory. Growing up, Sidney never heard many stories of his fathers' time in Vietnam but the occasional family Thanksgiving brought the remaining brothers around and Isaiah would make mention of that putrid humid air of the jungle or the chemical burning smell that seemed imprinted into his sinuses, comments that never held much meaning until now. He well enough remembered the burning tire and hot electricity smell of the explosion and if he ever smelled burning diesel and paint fumes again it would be too soon, but now, as his time in the desert was already becoming a memory of the past, the air was less vile in his lungs. Sidney took a large step to his right and let his boot heels rock him back in the soft sand as he rested back against the corrugated siding of the bunker and he kept his eyes looking upward as he sniffled to clear his nose.

The orange streaks of the sun were beginning to shoot upwards into the sky, chasing away the small white flecks of stars into the night, already the days' heat was making its' way across the sandy blanket of ground.

Sidney half hoped that Marissa would step out for one last goodbye so that he could voice his gratitude for being strong when he wasn't during that explosion, or for being the model of how to soldier when he wasn't sure himself. He admired his father for being a good man and he wanted to follow that lead his whole life but out there, out in that desert where men were losing their lives and men were dying for a country they believed in, where his parents and fiancé Shayla believed in him, he had Marissa to believe in.

Emotions are a luxury, they are also a danger and when you let yourself feel, you allow yourself to be hurt. The risk of getting injured while at war is very real and when you hear or see someone that survived an injury and make it home with their life you know they should be forever grateful that they survived and you tell yourself you'll worry about it later and you keep working. You try to avoid really getting to know people because it hurts to lose fellow soldiers, but it's an eternal pain when you lose a friend. Marissa was a solid soldier and even when she lost her friend and commander Belleaux, she remained a human and wept for him but she also performed as an outstanding soldier and did her job, she exemplified the juxtaposition of both sides and did it gracefully. There wasn't much longer before Sidney was due to have his seabag stuffed and his person ready to haul out, he knew the time it would take and how long he had to do it but right there, in that one moment where he wanted to remain for just a minute longer, he kept staring up.

At night at the base you can see the stars, you just glance up and there they are, the same ones you've seen millions of times, the same ones you talked to as a kid and pondered about god, of life on other planets or prayed to when your dog was sick, but in the grandness of the universe, in all the heavens and entirety that could never possibly be discovered or known, there he was, Sidney Hendrix Venney, the product of two loving and hard working parents Delores and Isaiah Venney and he was going home. Sidney was safe, each time he woke up in the desert there was a small spark of worry in the back of his mind of what if today was the last day? Each day Sidney wondered if he told his parents enough that he loved them, did he thank them enough for loving him like they had, did he do enough to deserve them as parents, did Shayla know how special she was or did she wonder about his love sometimes? Each morning was heavy with millions of doubts and questions, but each one was silenced when he laced up his boots and went back to work.

He made it; Sidney stood half bent leaning against the bulkhead and let the sun overtake the tranquility of the night, a constant struggle each and every day. The night brings peace and slumber while the day sun brings activity and chaos with it. The daylight breaks into the night and rouses a vast number of things such as birds and other critters that scurry about with work to do; it also brings with it the conducted noise and movements of a military base as well as the rest of the world beyond the reinforced walls. Trucks vroom, and squeak, and honk,and roar, men holler and shout, even jets above seem amplified as they fly high above the clouds with just a loud fizzing noise to prove that they had been anywhere at all. Sidney never realized he didn't know what real silence was until he got out into the middle of nowhere, life in the big city coming up was so noisy, you just grew used to it, the first time he heard his own thoughts or even his own heartbeat, he learned what quiet was.

It was surreal, the noise and the constant bustle of a living base was all but behind him, the long haul and exhaustion seemed to anchor him to that bulkhead and even with a few deep breathes of dry desert air, he couldn't quite muster the energy to heave himself upright and onward. Heavy shoulders and shallow breaths of relief coerced Sidney to slump more and more, his uniform warmed with the wall he leaned on and the sand beneath his boots gave way, the desert was slowly trying to absorb him as it has done to the majority of life and humanity in the surrounding cities, and there was just no energy left to fight. A tingling started in the pinched toes and then shot through the tightly laced ankles and upwards towards the now bending knees, Sidney leaned forward to begin to set his hands on his hips but rather than place them at his bending hips, he let his hanging hands slap past his legs and slunk to the wall behind him in a last ditch effort to avoid being consumed by the land. With a hearty breath and a sluggish heave, Sidney was leaning forward over his balance point and dragging his feet from their imprints and off he was.

Sidney used the momentum of his pace back to his rack to pack like he was orchestrating his coordinators back in *The Woofer*; each arm movement was precise with action. As his arms swung to and fro he was pulling pictures from his wall, his clothes from their shelf and everything was almost neatly going into his bags; packed safely to join him in going home. The nostalgia of being out on base was still very real, he thought and wondered if perhaps in a year, or five or ten, if he'd look back and think of this final farewell moment. Everyone thinks that each moment is significant, that each goodbye hug or high-five or longing goodbye kiss is one to be cherished, but like each and every forgotten moment, its' importance is finite and falls to the back of the mind like so many others. How many moments had he forgotten? How many moments that meant so much at the time have faded from memory? How many moments have we forgotten despite swearing to ourselves that it was the most important moment in our lives at that time?

There were many memories of the time Sidney spent in the Persian Gulf, like there were for his father in Vietnam, but time is a trickster in that it can fade even the most precious of memories if they aren't visited often. There is no clear recollection how many pairs of pants were packed or if there were two or three hats that ended up in that duty bag, even the time it took to pack can't be recollected by now, but Hell Highway is still pretty clear for Sidney these some years later. As Sidney shouldered his gear and headed out of his rack for the last time there were already incoming soldiers already looking for their assigned sleeping quarter, his bed was still warm with his body heat and the dust hadn't even settled where he kept his clothes and already they had a new tenant, there was no time for turnaround, the incoming were there to replace the outgoing before the outgoing had gone, a precise machine in tune with the vibrations of the world within it and Sidney was about to become just a part time vibration.

We all have that small spark of curiosity in our hearts, that yearning to know what lies in store for us but it's also coupled with a crippling fear of finding out, do we grow old and pass on surrounded by loved ones? Belleaux did, he had a family back home of one sort or another but his life was in the military and he passed away being a soldier, doing what he loved and surrounded by his peers. There's a loneliness paired with the fear of the unknown when it comes to dying, people need a comfort to go forth with courage, soldiers leave behind a legacy even if they live long into their lives, the funeral for military members are an honorable send off for those that served and it is a way to serve them once again, ensuring that they are never alone and that there is no need to fear.

Standing on the exit line Sidney looked down the row of other soldiers, all sorts in all sorts of wear and tear from their tour. There were a few members with slings or bandaging suggesting they suffered more than a sunburn or blister. Sidney took a deep sigh of relief to see many of his brothers joining him on his flight home, each one of them had a longing stare in the distance, hoping that they were staring in the direction of their home. The sun was already warm as some trucks pulled from a hangar and circled the blacktop and formed a small convoy for them to begin to load themselves into and get one step closer to that final flight home. Sidney was still tense, he suspected that it would take some time to relearn to let his shoulders relax and to be able to let himself breath regularly but he was excited to try, especially with help from Shayla.

Each man fell from their straight line like domino's, man after man hurried to throw their large bag into the back of the truck before climbing in after it, the hustle and bustle seemed orchestrated and with the uniformity of the service, probably in some grand vision of things but in a micro view, everyone just wanted to go home. Finally, three other men were setting their bags up between their legs as Sidney hoisted himself up and over the tailgate, it was warmer under the canvas than in the sun just a minute before but there was hope that the drive would give them enough of a breeze to offset it soon. With a total of five other men situated in the back of the supply truck the engines growled to life and in an instant they were winding through the base and on their way to Hell Highway.

Tension grew with the shaking of knees and clunking gear as the road below the tires grew more rugged, from the back of the truck Sidney watched the main cargo doors to the base close behind them and it hit him that he was no longer in the safety of the base but rather an open roaming target for someone with a rocket and a mission. Each man was loaded up in their helmets and flak jackets but they were also blind to the outside while hidden within the canvas tarp, there wasn't any situation that could have been better or worse to ride down the highway with. Due to the amount of other cargo being flown out the military decided to add a few dozen men to an already loaded cargo plane too big for the base runway to get them home faster, the obstacle standing in the way was *Hell Highway*.

Each man sat silently and jostled uneasily in the back of the truck, road dust enclosed around the back of the truck, sealing them off from any vision of the world around them. The asphalt that once paved the way had been bombed and broken down so badly that it now resembled what was left of the Oregon Trail. After the long bumpy road and everyone sitting on edge waiting for yet another rocket or bomb to further disrupt travel along the lone road, they began to slow. The sides of the road were cluttered with twisted retched metal and burned out garbage along the entire route making a garrison of clutter that barricaded the travelers in between ensuring them easy targets for any ambush an enemy may set. Each man was unsettled as they held tightly onto their gear and trusted the two man driving teams to maneuver away from any dangers that might impede their safe arrival to the airstrip.

Each deep hole in the road seemed to upend the soldiers in the back and toss them into the air like popping corn before they would land back down on one another. Each bump was joined with an orchestra of squeaky springs and jarring metal on metal of the rear axle slamming into the bottom of the truck bed. Sidney looked back and thought about how quickly his months of tour seemed to go but in stark comparison to how dreadfully long this last leg of his homeward trip was. Worry can make the easiest of drives into the most dreadful. The concern of an explosive taking out any of the lead trucks was very apparent by the distances the trucks kept, their space ensured there wouldn't be some wild snare set to entrap them all but the distance also left room for concern when the trucks could hardly see each other through the dusty smog that trailed in the air, if the last truck were to have any problems, they would be left behind by the lead trucks that would be unable to turn around or come back for them, essentially leaving them behind to an unknown fate.

Sidney was joined by several other soldiers, war weary men that were anxious to get home and shed any number of pounds worth of sand and gear. One man had his thick framed glasses taped at the bridge of his nose, a clear sign that his glasses had been broken many times and each field fix left more and more glue residue on the frames, which then layered with sand making them look rough and dirty. Another man had purple bruising to the left side of his face and frayed holes along the left side of his jacket, any number of damages sustained in his time here. All the men in the back remained silent with exception to grunts or sighs with each deep pothole the truck hit or the muttered apology when one man landed onto another before righting himself back into his seated position. Any real words spoken would probably have been snuffed out by the groaning of the tires below them and the growling exhaust of the truck as it snaked its way down Hell Highway anyways.

*SSSSCCCCCRRRRRCHSSSHHHH** The truck came to a grinding halt with the screaming brakes sliding on the sand covered road sending all the men in the back hurtling towards the front leaving them toppled up onto one another. Inaudible shouting began to erupt from the front, the noise and commotion of the men in the back checking on one another made it hard to hear what was being said from the front but the two man driving team was shouting and hollering. Sidney pushed and jerked himself from the middle of the dog-pile to keep his legs from getting crushed as men tried to stand back up and pull themselves clean from the mess. Sidney rose up to a knee towards the back of the truck when in the cloud of drifting sand a figure stood up.

Thwap Without any thought or even a moment to process the shape of the silhouette Sidney cocked his hand back and for his life, delivered his hardest fist to the head of the person trying to climb into the back of the truck. The slap packing sound of flesh to flesh impact quieted some of the men in the truck still trying to stand up as the struck man let out a curdling holler. *Thump Thump* "yall ready" one of the drivers called out from the other side of a metal partition. The struck man grabbed onto the bed rail and began to slowly hoist himself up again, this time with one hand on the truck and the other on his face. Sidney could now see through the wafting sand that the man he punched was a man he recognized from his call line, a fellow soldier. "If I was enemy my English wouldn't be this good, and if I wasn't Army I wouldn't be getting up from that punch, move over" the man mumbled through his hand as he slung his leg over to pull his body into the truck. "You English ain't good" one of the other men from the back of the truck hollered out to let up some of the tension as Sidney reached out to help the man into the truck bed with the rest.

"Man I'm sorry, I didn't know nothing" Sidney began to apologize. One of the men rushed to help the fellow soldier into the back while another banged his fist on the partition to signal that everyone was ready to go.

There was no slow throttling and once again the men were bouncing in the bed of the truck like popping popcorn and Sidney lurched forward and nearly onto the man he socked in the face. Sidney tried to brace himself to keep from kneeling onto the man still grasping his face lying on the bed of the truck. The man looked up at the faces looking at him wondering what he was doing wandering around on Hell Highway. With a nasal voice the man shouted out that he was in the truck just ahead and got tossed out when they hit *Thump* the truck bounced and all the men spent a long, life contemplating moment airborne. The newest rider in the back spread out as wide as he could to keep from being tossed out the back hatch for the second time and all the rest pin-balled off of each other and the canvas canopy that covered them in the back. *Thunk-kerchunk* the truck bounced as the back tires danced across broken asphalt, the drivers zigging and zagging to keep from ripping apart their truck to get to the airstrip safely. Soldiers collided off one another as well as off the sides of the truck; each up-ended soldier didn't get much of a chance to right themselves before the back axle moved around beneath them again.

The soldiers in the back of the truck all slammed into a pile again as the back of the truck skidded to a halt. The barricade wall let out a few thundering booms as the driver and passenger slammed their fists to let the soldiers know that they made their destination. The trip was riddled with nerves and anxiety and when they came to a final stop, each man let out a tightly held breath and each began to let themselves smile; they had arrived. Each soldier took a moment to figure out which end of their world was up and which big duty bag was theirs that was jumbled in the fray.

Ch. 11

The flight and transition home was daunting; layover flights and stop overs' made the trip feel nearly as long as the deployment itself for Sidney. Sidney was able to call to Shayla when he reached Germany but the out-processing was rigorous, there was debriefing, a few days to wind down which they meet up for the majority of the day and march and drill between large grass fields in which they slowly perform basic calisthenics, each soldier laughed and loosened up during the juvenile exercises but that was the point, it gave them the duty of routine but also the reassurance that the grass beneath them was clean and safe. Some of the men grunted out hard push-ups while others put forth as minimal effort as could be allowed, knowing that they already put in their time and energy back in the battle.

Sidney took the initial instructions as he had in the rest of his tour, as clear and concise but after the second day he looked at the larger task that each man was performing, they were easing back from the high stressed life of their deployment and the routines were still adhered to their military but it was also slowly allowing each soldier to feel a bit more civilian, either way it didn't matter; the grass was luscious and soft. The first call

Shayla got from her beloved when he arrived in Germany was nearly 5 in the morning, her hand jerked the phone from the receiver and to her head before her feet were firmly on the ground and in the commotion of answering, some of her desktop affects crashed to the ground.Sidney had to wait for the clashing noise to settle before he was sure that it was Shayla answering the phone and that she was alright. Shayla was yawning through her greeting and even though her heart shot her awake wildly, her eyes and coordination was slow to catch up.

Shayla knew not to dote on how much she missed Sidney while he was deployed, she read studies that it was ideal to be supportive and reassuring as a spouse of a deployed serviceman but she couldn't help talking to Marlene or even Delores about her concerns. Delores didn't know Isaiah before he served in the military and she didn't have to worry every day he was out in a war supporting our great nation so she couldn't pretend to imagine Shayla's position but she was still missing and worrying about her son being gone and being able to talk to Shayla about it brought them closer to one another. Isaiah was reassuring to his wife and she was grateful but she also knew that as her husband his role was to be strong for her, even though his many restless nights told her that he was riddled with worry even if he'd never admit it to her. Isaiah knew first-hand the terrors that one can cross while at war, Isaiah crossed atrocity after atrocity and even after having found his own dying brother on the battlefield, it didn't end there.

Delores still worked her bakery but she had reduced her hours a great deal once Sidney was deployed, she thought about working more to keep distracted but she also wanted to help both her son and soon to be daughter-in-law by diving in with helping with wedding plans, even if not officially invited. Shayla wanted to make most of her plans with Marlene, it wasn't to exclude Delores but she wanted to make sure she included much of her island heritage as she could because it meant so much to her. Delores still sought out grand churches and hosting venues in both Florida and also Brooklyn, options for either place for Sidney and Shayla to decide when he returned home to them. Shayla still worked more than her share and the added help from both of her mothers' was truly a blessing in the end, even if it seemed a little overwhelming in the beginning. Delores wanted all of the best for her son, it was heartbreaking to hear that he was going to be deployed but she also knew that it was his time in the service that made Isaiah such a prosperous and stand up man and she also wanted that for her son, even if it meant she'd pace the halls of her now quiet home for days on end until his next letter reached her for reassuring comfort.

Shayla tried to fill long afternoons with trips to the surf, in her youth she felt the seas call to her from generations past and even into adulthood, she kept her wet-suit in her car and her hair was always lighter from the sun and saltwater. Shayla found the small pockets of time very empty, she used to love the silence and even just sitting on her board and listening to gulls in the air or the waves racing one another to the shore helped to bring her peace, but even within the stagnant five minute moments when the world seemed to pause, she missed Sidney each time. The five a.m. phone call changed everything, even with an opening in her calendar or an afternoon off, she felt the world begin spinning faster and faster around her, there was so much she wanted to have done and to be ready for when the love of her life came back home.

Sidney finally received his instructions near the end of his first week in Germany. Shayla wanted to make the long flight to him but they both agreed there were better ways to spend her time and money, plus they were both hoping that he wouldn't be there that long before returning stateside. Shayla was a busy bee after her five a.m. wake up call from Sidney, she suddenly felt the bomb ticking in her chest to rush and run amok to get things in order, she wanted to hurry to work-out twice a day to look her absolute best for him when he stepped back onto home soil, she wanted to have an apartment chosen for the two of them to share rather than living on base or in her small contractors dorm like room, she was also trying to coordinate with Marlene about wedding traditions, menus and places to have their ceremonies, all the while still keeping in touch with Delores and Isaiah, after all she couldn't be selfish and keep him all to herself.

Paper Paulie

Sidney got his papers, he was not only being sent home to the comforts of the states, he was also being granted an honorable discharge for his loyal support and bravery for the bombing that included a bronze star. Sidney got word that Marissa was honored with a bronze star for bravery and also a silver star for her valor under pressure, an award she had truly deserved. Sidney was bewildered with everything on his last day, there was so much going on and he wanted to wait and tell Shayla and his parents in person. The time difference was a nuisance to juggle for the two for the week in Germany, Sidney felt bad for the early morning callings to talk to Shayla, most nights she just slept with her phone rather than crash into whatever was in her way but he still knew he was waking her early. Sidney couldn't really call in his morning because it meant it was late for her, the opposing time zones were just a small obstacle and they both kept visiting the notion that in a few years they'd laugh about it or reminisce about how they go through such things to stay side by side.

The flight back to Florida where Sidney flew out from was like any other flight, a whole bunch of people stuck in cramped quarters, some watched movies while some slept, with the high tension life Sidney was leaving behind he found it a chore to try to sleep the entire way. There was that small spark of hyper awareness that nestled into his brain and he would pop awake to check his surroundings before laying his head back to just relax. Watching the dark clouds under the moon drift below the plane gave him an infinite feeling and even in a plane loaded with people, he felt as if for a few minutes, he was the only one drifting way up in the endless sky. The cabin lights were dim in the plane but out the windows the moon illuminated clouds seemed to blanket out below him and there was a tranquility that eased him deep inside of his chest.

The sun followed the plane, small strands began to pierce the blanket of clouds as the plane began to descend, when land began to become visible on the landing it looked like the light was chasing the dark across the land to open up a whole new world below him, a new life awaited him. The plane came to life with the cabin lights, the small blue hues turned into daylight bright radiating bulbs and people began to stretch and rustle as the plane continued to get closer and closer to landing. The sounds of the engines changed from the dull roar to a louder whistling of the wind as the plane tilted and banked to align itself with the receiving runway. The speed even seemed to increase as the plane rushed to the ground.

The crowds waiting for passengers to deplane seemed to be a large wave of people, the noise erupted with the first passenger stepping off the plane and the noise melted to become an indecipherable hum. Sidney and Shayla didn't think to discuss if she'd be waiting for him at the airport, he knew he'd love to see her but with such a mess of people and traffic it would be easier to catch the bus back to the base and for him to come find her after that, except little to his awareness, he had a small group of his own waiting for him to return. There were long lines of people awaiting the return of their loved ones, some women held babies, some kids held up banners awaiting the safe return of their daddies while some young teens held out streamers or spun noisemakers to celebrate the return of one loved one or another. Person after person was passed as Sidney small stepped on his way down the terminal, there were so many people and to see such outpouring support for the men he served beside filled his heart with the love and support from the great nation he was proud to serve.

Towards the back of the long line of people "*SIDNEY*" came blaring out of the already noisy crowd. Sidney looked up to see Shayla and her mother Marlene, a surprise that lifted away any heavy burden from his heart immediately, clouding over the last several months without her. His heavy pack seemed to disappear, the heavy boots that kept him grounded seemed to vanish and without any recollection of stepping even once, Sidney seemed to float towards his fiancé. Marlene and Shayla both stood up tall and they both began to turn away from Sidney and each other causing Sidney to stop in his momentum on his way to scoop Shayla up, from behind them stepped Isaiah, he was wearing a blue and yellow plaid shirt and pressed khaki pants with his Vietnam service cap squared up on his head. Isaiah stood tall and proud, he snapped his sharpest salute to his son that he

237

had ever performed in his life, he had no other way to express his deepest admiration and no words would be fitting enough for the young man he loved so much.

Sidney stopped dead in his tracks, his father wasn't the emotional sort of parent but he was willing to share how impressed he was with Sidney, his eyes were soft, his hand held firm to his brow and his posture astute. Sidney slapped his heels together and stood tall, he honored each of the members of his family before him and each of his service members behind him, there aren't many ways to be any more proud of yourself than at moments like that. Neither Venney man wanted to break their salute, Sidney stared deep into his fathers' eyes as his own began to water, his nose began to wet and he fought the urge to sniffle as long as he could. Isaiah couldn't swallow the lump in his throat, his eyes were already watery just watching his son walk towards him in uniform and when his soft eyes let the first tear drop; Sidney dropped his salute and lunged forward to stretch his arms as far around his mother, father and fiancé as he could reach, Marlene completed the family circle by patting her soon to be son-in-law on the back in congratulatory affection.

Shayla wanted Delores and Isaiah with her to welcome Sidney, Marlene was thankful for the invitation as well but knowing the importance of the day she offered to borrow a friends van and chauffeur. It was certainly an emotional day, the little boy that vroomed cars up and down the stairwell railing or used to park his cars in his fathers' shoes to keep him from having to leave him behind and go to work had returned from war; safely.

Delores was filled with emotion, she did her best to keep her eyes from leaking tear after tear down her face as they rode in the van and shared story after story of the last several months but her puffy eyes gave way that she couldn't stop tearing up. Upon arriving at the base to check in and get a small reprieve for the rest of the afternoon a Master Sergeant suggested Sidney get into his dress uniform and be ready for parade (march) within the hour before saluting Isaiah and thanking the senior Venney for his service then excusing himself.

Shayla and Delores weren't sure why Sidney couldn't join them for an afternoon of catching up back at their hotel, Marlene offered to host the family but her home was a bit of a drive so they agreed to go back to the hotel that Isaiah and Delores stayed at for the evening. Sidney promised to explain everything after the gathering and asked Shayla to escort everyone to the pavilion across the base as he rushed to change out his fatigues. Sidney was instructed to leave his dress clothes in a small locker with his affects before he shipped so he knew he would have what he needed and he was in a hurry to rush across the base to make his appointment. The Venney family stayed behind and followed Shayla's instructions as to where to go to get the parade pavilion, nobody was sure what the big to-do was all about but their focus was to spend time with Sidney and this was just a bit of a delay.

Shayla escorted her guests to the pavilion she was instructed to, there were many family members corralling into two lines to enter the building while it grew increasingly busy. Isaiah did his best to keep up while Delores held his hand tightly to make sure he didn't get easily winded in the sun and crowd, Shayla held the other. The crowd entering the building seemed rushed, it was a rather impromptu ceremony for returning soldiers.Marlene did her best to help Shayla carry punch and lemonade for the guests while they fought to get into seats.

The seats filled quickly, little children ran up and down the open aisles and then the lights went out. The stage lights came to life in three large lit up circles on the stage when an esteemed General marched out. With spit polished shiny shoes and pressed green uniform the General asked everyone to have a seat in order to get things underway. With apologies for the quick progression of events it was important to make notes of a few of the returning soldiers before the day could progress.

The line of soldiers that arrived on the mornings' flight marched in cadence behind the general to form a line of firm soldiers standing shoulder to shoulder at the ready. The general wanted to thank each and every person in the audience and then he began to speak about the soldiers one at a time. One soldier; PFC Spade was a man with reddish hair and wrappings around one of his forearms was honored for pulling a fellow soldier from a burning jeep in the midst of a firefight while another had held an ambush at bay in order for his supply trucks to arrive to a forward base, each soldier in the line was being awarded and it made Shayla and Delores antsy; they didn't know much about what Sidney had been through..

"Private first class Venney gallantly ran into a bunker after an explosion and in the line of duty he returned several times in order to help recover fellow soldiers and then proceeded to assist his commanding officer to quickly rebuild the communications bunker that had been destroyed to ensure that troops out in the field were still in contact with the base he was working in." Shayla nearly jumped from her seat hearing Sidney's name, she didn't know much about the explosion other than it had happened, she wasn't told that Sidney was near it, let alone running into it. Delores burst into tears at the notion that Sidney could have been so close to being hurt.

Isaiah slumped into his chair, his heavy head fell forward into the palms of his hands for a moment, Isaiah was overwhelmingly relieved that his son was fine but for that split second his woes and worries made an appearance into his mind. Shayla wanted to jump up out of her seat when she watched the General pin the bronze start onto Sidney but Marlene put her hand on her lap and push her back down to her seat to keep from being too disruptive. Shayla clapped a few times but the silence in the room quickly gave her realization that she should stay quiet until the end just like everyone else, even while her feet tap-danced back and forth with glee.

The program was relatively short, each member was awarded one metal or another for bravery, courage or acting in a way that went above and beyond expectations and job description, each member was exemplary in their actions and a model of the military training they had received. "I conclude with a salute to each and every one of you" the General began ending his sincere speech. "It is my honor to represent the United States Army when I say that I am honored to be represented by each one of you, our great nation commends you." The General turned and saluted the line of soldiers, they in turn snapped a salute and let out a collective "Oooh" as they all raised and then stomped down their right foot before turning to the door they entered from and they marched in cadence of the stage, the General held his salute the entire time.

Most of the attendees were wiping away tears of pride and joy as they rose from their seats and began to make their way back out with loud roaring clapping. Delores leaned over and hugged Isaiah, the pride that filled them both as parents was coming out in streams oftears; they hugged and held in relief that their one son came home safely, and like his father, Sidney returned a hero. Isaiah never really spoke much of his time in

Vietnam, there were many sights, sounds and smells that you can't ever really forget, there are some groups that have come a long way to help people who have been through those situations but those that have not have a hard time truly understanding what each soldier goes through. Isaiah felt heavy hearted when he knew his son was heading to war, in all the progress mankind has made, mankind itself is still a very young, and stupid, and a very violent animal and he feared his son may have to live his life with the things that he had had to but with the love and support of an amazing person, he has still managed to love, be loved, and live a full life.

When Shayla lead Isaiah and crew back out onto the vast blacktop Sidney was speaking with an older man in a uniform and wearing a silk sash around his neck. The man wore his sharp cap adorned with a few pins and insignia over very white hair. The man was a little heavier than most men in their military dress uniforms and as they stepped up the man stood firm, took in a deep breath and saluted Isaiah for his service to their country. Isaiah saluted in return as Sidney returned to speaking to them. With her time spent around the base Shayla knew exactly who the man was, Chaplin Tuttle. The Chaplin found his calling as a soldier and knew he'd spend his life serving his country then later on found a closer way to serve his fellow countrymen by serving their emotional needs.

Chaplin Tuttle greeted each member of Sidney's family one at a time and pieced it together who Venney was when he saw Shayla, she had spoken of him once or twice in their crossings and it all made sense now. Shayla excused herself and spoke to Tuttle for a moment on the side; they passed a few hand gestures back and forth and then nodded together. When she returned she looked at Sidney and warned him "you should tell us about all this, but first, want to get married?" Sidney opened his eyes for a moment "do you have any doubts" and with his retort, Shayla looked over at Tuttle. The jolly Chaplin Tuttle spread his hands out and asked; "what do I get to eat?"

The news was sudden; the day was already nearing the noon hour and suddenly there was a lot to do. Marlene just stared at her daughter, Shayla had often been impetuous but this seemed to top it all. Delores went wide eyed and was lost for words, there was so much that rattled through her mind that needed to be done and she didn't know where to begin. Shayla looked up at Sidney, he smiled knowing that he was going to marry her one way or the other and she made it happen to have his parents there so his wishes were fulfilled. Shayla put both of her hands up to calm everybody down before the chaos erupted. Shayla pointed to her mother and told her "call uncle Ruly, tell him to kick the caja-china, tell him full hog at Pompano bay at seven, then call cousin Lulu and tell him get my crew there at five." Shayla hadn't necessarily been planning such a wedding but it was her nature to want the beach and an intimate small group of her best loved ones involved and she also knew who to contact to make what she wanted to happen, happen.

Chaplin Tuttle piped up again, "hog huh? can I bring the missus?" Shayla flashed a smile and a nod to let the man excuse himself to go and get ready while Shayla approved of what Sidney was already wearing with a finger tracing him up and down the front, the rest were small details that could be handled on the way. The family scampered back into the van Marlene had borrowed for the day, her "girl how crazy are you?" was rhetorical and of course it went unanswered, but Delores chimed in anyways. The two matriarchs felt rushed to look their best but all that was really needed was to have them both tidy up a bit and put on their best summer dresses and then they'd all make their way to the beach where Shayla already had some cousins dressing up some tables and her uncle firing up plenty of food on his Cuban grill.

The small park had a few families playing Frisbee and laughing about while Ruly kept the charcoal hot on top of his metal box that had a pile of meat cooking inside, the cooking box is a familiar staple among Shayla's family and with a small trailer it was often hauled back behind a jeep for any size gathering they could muster up. The breeze was soothing and smelled of the ocean, a smell that Shayla loved almost as much as her soon to be husband. There was no need for shoes; she had a white flowy dress and a band of white flowers she twisted together in the van while they all drove to the park. The cousins had just about everything set up and when they heard uncle Ruly was coming they already knew there was going to be grub, they were also always

245

ready to go and meet Shayla to go surfing so that was what they planned for after the picnic anyways. Lulu isn't really a cousin, he's a best friend that also surfs, he's three-quarters Cuban and his wife Anyse is half Filipino and half Dominican, their little daughter Sandy is two and looks up to Shayla like an aunt.

The makeshift family of Shayla's got a little bigger that day, Delores closed her eyes and prayed when the van parked, she put forth so much effort to plan a big wedding back home and it wasn't that she was disappointed she just felt she wanted a large wedding for her son, especially with the Augie and the Vassilles in company. Isaiah knew how Delores felt without having to ask; he just sat beside her on the bench in the van and held her hand, this was Sidney and Shayla's day, and they were blessed to be a part of it.Isaiah didn't have to say anything to be comforting, they were both so overjoyed that they let a few long winded sighs out to let out more of their air from back home and take in the warm ocean air into their lungs.

Chaplin Tuttle pulled up with his wife Linda in their small station wagon and they were already ready to go. Linda carried a large glass dish and a basket full of dinner rolls to add to the table, she felt bad that she didn't have much more to offer on the rush but was grateful to get to attend.

Sidney and Shayla held hands almost non-stop since he landed back in Florida, it didn't stop through the

wedding or even during the meal where everyone
gathered around the circle of tables and shared in laughs
and stories from Marlene and Delores about the
newlyweds when the newlyweds were young. Sidney and
Shayla held hands tightly as Chaplin Tuttle spoke, he
knew the heart that was in Shayla and her love of people
and that it matched Sidney's honor to his country to
protect his family at home. Delores and Marlene let
themselves weep at the beautiful words that Tuttle spoke
unrehearsed and from the heart. The vows were
exchanged and with warm sand between her toes, Shayla
became the newest Mrs. Venney. The sun headed towards
the west when Uncle Ruly began to pull out piles of
steaming meat and other foods, everyone muddled around
and jeered one another.

Everyone grew closer after the wedding nuptials,
good wholesome family food will bridge any gap,
strangers become friends and friends become family.
Every glass raised time and time again in toast,
handshakes and hugs were as common as gulls on a beach
and shortly after the first few plates of food were passed,
Ruly, a short stocky man with colorful Hawaiian shirt
piped up; "I called *Mangon Acere*" as another station
wagon pulled up. Sidney looked to Shayla to explain but
it was too late and she stood up to swing her hand for a
high-five from Ruly. Three dark skinned guys and a girl
in Jamaican threads hauled some homemade steel drums
and bongos and string guitars with them and they made
themselves at home under the pavilion on the beach as

Ruly handed them plates of food. The band members ate and shared some laughs before they got to playing, the music was light and subtle at first while everyone ate.

Lulu was a younger guy and he dragged a large waste can over and did his best to clean up after everyone, each person did their part to contribute to the occasion, once everyone was done eating and a majority of the speeches were made Shayla asked Sidney to tell them what happened. The evening changed its tone for a moment while those who knew wondered and the guests sat in wonderment. Sidney didn't want to talk about Belleaux on his wedding day, he didn't want to talk about how scared he was and how lost he was but he also knew that his father never spoke about any of his events either and he didn't want his father to carry the shame and burden by himself anymore. Too many soldiers close themselves off, too many feel alone and too many go unsupported in their lives. Good men serve their nations and good men deserve to know that they can rely on people at home. There is no weakness in getting help, in fact that is where strength can be found; in the care of someone willing to open up. Sidney knew that a soldier will do anything to get the job done, even if the job is getting right again for your loved ones.

Sidney began by talking about lacing up and getting ready for his shift, he made it out into the dark night air and where he was headed. Sidney talked about his brazen leader Marissa Shields and having passed her on his way over to his station when a shower of blowing sand and debris tore holes in canvas tents just around from him, had he rounded the corner any sooner he would have been in pretty rough shape as a matter of fact. Sidney described how he tried to force himself up and forward and before he had the ability to make sense of things Marissa was already jerking him up by his collar and guiding him towards the blast before he has any idea of what happened. It was stunning to see his container building in shards and smoke and settling air blown sand filling the air, there were people here and there and each needed some form of help. Seeing Marissa rush in and out of sight Sidney started out just trying to keep up or make sense of things, each time he found someone he did his best to help move them out and towards help, it was Marissa that gave him the forward motion of what to do, he just followed suit, at first.

A few minutes after the blast Sidney was clearing away desks and trying to move debris off and away from some of the soldiers that were involved, it was then he came back across Marissa moving passed him as he was kneeling down towards Belleaux. Sidney hung his head when he repeated what Belleaux asked of him, it was the most somber moment of the evening and in (Shayla's makeshift family) family tradition; everyone there bowed their head for their fallen countrymen, everyone then raised up a glass in toast for a man they never met that gave his life to protect those back home and would never get to enjoy the company of his loved ones because he put his country first. Isaiah kept a long distance stare, he raised his head to see everyone around him bowing their heads but holding up their cups in support and solidarity, his son was the only other person around him that had served in that war but suddenly he wasn't alone anymore.

Isaiah let the small stinging in his eyes turn to tears, the military community is very supportive and caring but these strangers, they had just become family and even as mixed as it was they were all filled with respect, he knew he raised a good man that just married a good woman. The leader of the Magnon Acere group picked up a gourd covered with shells and cleared her throat, it was time for the guys to liven things up and begin playing at the request of Ruly. The music was a mix of steel drums and Caribbean vibes, reggae and jazz and everyone began to sway and tap along. The family danced back and forth while friends swayed and stepped and each member of the band contributed various talents or singing along. The girl with the band was named Renee, she had a soft voice and played a sweet flute when she wasn't lending her voice across the dancers, her curly hair bounced on her shoulders as she jibed. Delores loved to watch Sidney and Shayla laugh and sway with one another, their friends were vibrant and carried on with goofs and heckles and high-fives all while still eating endlessly.

The meal didn't really end; Ruly served the main plates and once the portable cooking box of his was done

and cooled off there was still a table covered with plastic
containers to choose from for more plates of food.
Chaplin Tuttle and his wife Linda stayed until the sun had
almost ducked down into the horizon before parting.
Tuttle and wife danced a little and made their rounds to
introduce themselves to everyone and also to thank
everyone for such a lovely time. Ruly stood stocky body
next to Tuttle's' stocky body and together they picked at
some of the juicier bits of the cooked meat, each time
they'd tilt their head back they'd savor the air, the music,
the food and the love that surrounded them. The band
didn't really ever change songs, they just took turns being
the focus of one tune or another and each one melted into
another as they played long into the evening.

After the first few official husband and wife
dances were behind them Shayla danced with her mother
and then with Isaiah, Sidney danced with his mother and
then with Marlene, everyone was laughing and having a
good time and it was a time that Sidney knew that what he
and his father fought for; was right. Sidney took the few
steps he needed to in order to take a seat perched on a
table top next to his father as he watched his wife, mother,
and mother-in-law all dance in and out of a circle with
Anyse and Linda while Sandy wandered around with a
handful of mushy cornbread.

Isaiah chuckled watching the little girl drop large
glops of mushed bread and then pick them up to eat them
again, it reminded him so much of young Sidney just

roaming around so long ago, it was hard to imagine how quickly the time had gone and how he was now sitting at that same sons' wedding and watching him dance with his new wife, it seemed just a day or so ago that he had just taken Delores as a bride and now it had come full circle and it all seemed to have gone in just a flash. Sidney lifted his left arm and rest it across his fathers' shoulders, something he was familiar with his father doing to him his whole life.

"You were right" Sidney spoke up while digging into his right pants pocket. Both Venney men enjoyed watching the commotion; their wives were enjoying themselves out on the cement dance floor and the waves were adorned with white caps in the distance as they sent ocean warmed breezes in over the dancing gatherers. The evening had been almost a dream come true; loved ones laughed and cheered and it didn't matter what race you came from, what your last name was or even who you rooted for during ballgames, you were family and you were loved.

Sidney pulled the small blackened wad of wax from his pocket; the wax had long been hardened and by this point probably become fossilized or even bulletproof. Sidney reached over and began to hand Paper Paulie back to its' rightful owner; Isaiah. Isaiah looked down and then back up and smiled while extending his hand in reception. "There you are my old friend, thank you for keeping my son safe" Isaiah spoke out loud as he brought it to his mouth for a thankful kiss and then to his forehead in deep prayer like sincerity. Paper Paulie had indeed done as he was asked, he kept Sidney safe through the war and brought him back home to his family and loved ones, he looked over at Sidney and together, they both made it back home. "Moment of honesty" Sidney muttered as me leaned in to whisper into his fathers' ear.

Isaiah turned his head and from under his eyebrows he responded; "always." "The only reason I hadn't rounded that corner that morning and been peppered with shards of metal or brick was because he dropped out of my pocket when I leaned down to tie my boots when I was getting ready to go to my post, it was truly the reason, I bent back down to pick him up and that four seconds…" Sidney paused to swallow down his trembling cracking voice, "is why I was four seconds late from rounding that corner and being within the blast radius of the explosion."

Isaiah nodded, there wasn't a doubt in his mind that his little gifted talisman brought him home from the jungles of Vietnam when so many weren't as fortunate and now, he was grateful and lucky again for Paper Paulie for saving his son and bringing his son home safely. Isaiah hugged Paper Paulie to his chest for a moment. Delores stopped for a moment and glanced to ensure that her dear love was alright and when they made eye contact, they exchanged a slight nod and a gracious smile.

Isaiah released his embrace on the small hard piece of paper, he had now had it for well over two decades and not only owed his life to it, but now also his sons again and now it was his sons turn to be the keeper of the lucky family charm.

Sidney tucked his chin back a little in disbelief, he thought back to being snarked at when he wanted to play with it as a child when he didn't know the significance of it, he remembered his close call that left an itty bitty nearly invisible scar on the back of his head and how the weird little thing was there and now; he carried it through a war. The once small paper doll that had been weather sealed in wax had made its' way halfway across the world and then back again had now also transcended a generation.The incredible little item was becoming unbelievable; the lucky little charm was becoming a marvel.

Isaiah and Sidney shared their views on how great the afternoon went, how long the flight was and of course how proud Sidney had made himself and his parents. Sidney had a long night before an even longer day but it just made sense to get married as soon as possible because he had waited long enough to have Shayla as his wife, and now he had her.

There hadn't been much discussion on where they were going in life or what the next step would be for them as a married couple, at that point all Sidney could think about was a "bed that didn't have someone sleeping six feet away" causing both men to chuckle, Isaiah nodded over to Shayla and reminded him "that'll never happen again."Sidney was focused on the night, there wasn't anywhere else in the whole world he'd prefer to be instead of right beside in father and a step away from his new wife, it was where he had dreamt of being for many long war worn months, it was truly a dream come true.

Shayla and Delores stepped toward their husbands, happy in the euphoria of light airy island music and surrounded with the love and laughter of friends both new and old. Shayla caught a glimpse of something that was being twirled in the hands of Sidney, in the shimmering lights above it wasn't very distinguishable. Before Shayla had to speak up to ask Sidney was in motion to stand up and tuck Paper Paulie back into his pocket where it was safe until further need for him. As Sidney stood and jammed his hand deep into his pocket he told his new bride that he'd be glad to tell her later about it then turned and thanked his father for ever so much more than the gift of Paulie then returned to take his bride for a spin around the dance floor, Delores took over the seated position next to Isaiah to survey all that their son had accomplished and how well he had come along.

The beautiful gathering lasted long into the evening; the song and dance lasted until most of the loved ones had exhausted themselves and just swayed while sitting on a picnic table. Ruly handed out platters for everyone to take home with them; hearty plates smothered in scrumptious food still smelling of a mild jerk rub and hints of smoky woods and tropical flavors. Marlene drove so her passengers were at her mercy and they all cleaned up to make sure the borrowed picnic area was as good if not better than when they found it and watched the attendees drive off one car at a time until there were no more.

Ch. 12

It was almost three years since that soft music filled night in a remote park in Florida when Sidney and Shayla exchanged their vows that they welcomed a little girl into their family, Ryker Mallery Venney. Ryker was a welcomed blessing and during her first few years before she settled in and began her educational career both Sidney and Shayla spent ample time bringing her to see his parents. Ryker was as ambitious and outgoing as any young child could be,she climbed on anything taller than she was, especially her grandpa Isaiah, she also played in the surf and loved the sand just like her momma. It was hard to foresee that such a girl would grow into a commendable soldier but she sure did.

Ryker followed her mothers' love of the surf while keeping up admirable grades and following her fathers' pursuit into the army. With a name that means "strong leader" that is exactly what she grew into. Ryker loved her life in North Carolina, especially when Isaiah and Delores decided to sell their businesses and home and retire closer to their son and grandbaby; she had everything she could ever need, especially the surf and close friends.Ryker also heard many stories of Brooklyn and living north while growing up so she followed her

257

heart to start school in New York. Ryker took a break from her degree in finance and arts just after the end of her second year when she enlisted. Times were tough over in the Middle-East and she felt a calling, Isaiah warned her and Sidney forbade her but neither had any luck in swaying her decision.Ryker had her familes' support and a few suggested tips to help with jungle rot on her feet or sand fleas in her bedding before she shipped out. Both father and grandfather had the same pit in their guts about her deploying, the tension was as nasty as the several thousand year old struggle for power had been over there and it worried the large family.

Ryker was certain of her destiny; she was to join the army(even though her country was already at war) like her father and grandfather, she was going to serve not only her country but her fellow countrymen fighting beside her. Ryker knew that there were dangers when she first shipped out, her letters home were short and stoic as she kept her head up and eyes focused. Being a medic fulfilled all of the aspirations Ryker had for herself and her pledge to serve her fellow soldiers. Each and every soldier she crossed was ready to follow her, her gait was steady, her brow was stern and there wasn't a situation she was afraid to charge into for the sake of doing her duty. Ryker had a large outpouring from her family through basic training, the love and support made the weeks of sleeping in the dirt and eating mushy meals only warmed by her own body heat not only tolerable, but an adventure for her.

Now, anyone that knew Ryker on the civilian side knew that Ryker didn't have any problems lounging around in flannel pajama pants and a hooded sweatshirt, she loved having her hair and nails done and she knew when to relax but once she put on her uniform she became all about the business. Ryker wore her uniform with generations of pride instilled in her, there was no shortage of patriotism coursing through her veins and when she was given her orders to head to the desert there wasn't an ounce of concern about going. Ryker set up a few care packages for Shayla to mail to her, lotions and polishes because even in the dirt, she still wanted to make sure she kept pretty and in good spirits. Sydney and Shayla sent more care packages over time with other fun treats or things to keep her in the now like magazines and soccer balls.

Sidney knew that as soon as her boots hit the dirt that it was time to send along Paper Paulie, and a long detailed story of what he had been through. It took an emotional few days to make sure that Sidney penned the story of Paper Paulie(many of the original details were vague now forty-five years later) who he came from, where he originated or why but he did know that the little paper guy had been through Vietnam and Desert Storm, it was her turn to be watched over by him in the latest conflict that required the presence of soldiers for security. Sidney lived in a semi-anxious state when Ryker shipped out, he knew what he had faced and how much worse it was now, there were many more factors and it interfered with his sleep until she received Paulie to keep her safe.

Stepping onto foreign soil was an awakening for Ryker; it surely wasn't the first time away from her parents nor the first time out of the country but being nearly half way around the world was a real testament to her inner strength and if she had the resolve to make her own destiny. At five-foot seven inches and one-hundred and twenty-eight pounds she wasn't very formidable in size. Ryker was almost named Emerald for the color of the ocean the day she was born but instead, her eyes took the green color. Shayla always told her the green eyes are because the ocean is in her blood. Ryker knew some of the lighter stories of her father and grandfathers' time in war, they discussed some stories a few times late at night at the back end of a family holiday and often when they were fairly certain she was in bed or out of earshot; she wasn't any of those times by the way.

Ryker knew she was prepared, there wasn't much that was going to back her down from anything and she figured sometime in the sun would be good for her. As a medic Ryker was needed in some of the bases that were in more dangerous areas, there were many times Ryker had to leave any form of safety and go and recover fellow soldiers that needed her skills or even locals that needed the help and each time she turned her foot to the problem, she did it with her head held high. Ryker knew she was there to help, she knew her role and she knew the family

history she had to back her up. Ryker liked being tough
enough to shoulder up any of the injured soldiers and hike
back with them, many of them outweighing her by over a
hundred pounds plus her gear and theirs. Ryker was
admired by her fellow soldiers and each of them knew she
meant business. There was never and hesitation on
Ryker's behalf when it meant saving someone; no matter
the cost she went forth full brazen and proved herself time
and time again.

When Ryker received a letter with a hardened wad
of what seemed like plastic she wasn't sure she got the
right thing so she hurried to investigate it. Sidney told her
on a few different occasions about Paper Paulie but since
he was stored away she never really made sense of it. The
small chunk of whatever it waswas so hard it wouldn't
even let her sink a fingernail into it to check it's material.
Ryker turned Paper Paulie in her hands in her down time,
it amused her to think off all the things and all the good
luck charms there were; she was holding some small
paper trinket that some kid some time ago made and sent
to... her grandfather something like forty something years
ago and it was now in her hands. To honor her father and
grandfather Ryker kept Paulie close, there was a small
knife pocket on the front of her uniform pants that she
opted to make just for him to keep him close and safe, she
even put a safety pin across the pocket as a reminder to
take him out if she changed her pants or laundered them.

Ryker wrote many letters home and of course she received many back after the long delay of mailing from each letter going through assorted channels and so on. The mail delays were a complaint among all the soldiers, everyone knew the reasons but if you were waiting on a soccer ball or something to do it seemed very long.For some of the guys waiting to get letters from loved ones, no answer made the wait maddening and everyone just tried to be supportive. Ryker had ample friends, some guys she had to stitch up from war injuries, others she treated blisters or heat stroke but she loved her job nonetheless. Each base or small camp Ryker went to often had people in need of her services, she saw some pretty bad wounds and as they progressed from blisters and scrapes in the beginning to severe cuts or bullet wounds or deep infections she thanked Paper Paulie more and more that he was there with her, it was also her way of keeping her dad and granddad with her when she was unsure of herself or things around her.

After a few months of being in the desert the hostility from the opposition mounted, there were more and more attacks on coalition troops and the radio near her was in constant noise from other troops and divisions that had been in gunfights or attacked. The troops' presence was obviously unwelcomed by small pockets of angry fighters but often greeted with smiles and cheers from the larger less aggressive groups of civilians that enjoyed the troops and some of the treats some of the brought. Ryker asked for bags of hard candy with every letter so that she could make many of the kids smile that she encountered as she traveled around. Even with the tension Ryker loved what she did. Ryker had a passion for people, like her mother she saw people as intricate and full of things that you can learn

One late night Ryker and her co-medic, a man named Kal got a call to help pull out some injured soldiers once a backup squadron came in to give them support. Ryker and Kal (a man with a Middle-Eastern heritage and ability to speak the language) didn't wait, they began to head towards the coordinates of the pinned down soldiers and ready themselves for anything that might come towards them. There were already four other trucks loaded with soldiers running hot ready to head for battle as they crossed the desert, the terrain was bumpy and Kal drove as straight as he could while Ryker loaded her issued weapons and strapped on her bullet proof vest and helmet, and then also helped to strap in Kal in his while following a caravan like a movie pursuit. The dark of night reminded Ryker of the stories that her father used to tell her, he mentioned how the lack of lights from local cities allowed the dimmest stars to shine brightly overhead and if you closed your ears and focused you could see for millions of light years, not something you could really find in the states due to all the light pollution.

It was hard to focus on the starry sky above as the snaps of gunfire sounded off in the far distance, it was muffled from the distance and the hum of the tires but the snapping sounds echoed louder as they grew closer. The medic truck that Kal and Ryker worked had racks for up to 4 injured soldiers on stretchers but they had enough supplies for eight to ten men if they needed them, they also had flares for air support if anyone is injured badly enough for a medvac chopper and so on. The anxiety mounted, Ryker had been parallel to a few firefights and Kal had exchanged fire a few times but going into a dark city late at night was unsettling for both of them. The four trucks veered off in different directions to get to their comrades as well as take up stronger positions so secure the small town, the shadows flickering on the walls made it hard to tell who was who and unless someone fired on you, you didn't dare to fire on anyone else for fear of hitting a friendly.

Kal shouted into a megaphone that anyone that can hear him should return home, his ability to speak the local language came in handy almost every day of his deployment, he was a commodity and was often requested to join multiple patrols every day, usually he and his partner Ryker would go everywhere together because they had a tight bond and wouldn't leave the other person behind no matter what. The first bullet cracked the windshield and Kal stood on the brakes to bring them to a halt, the crack was towards the top and the center of the glass and it more infuriated the driver rather than scare him, Ryker laughed it off because it startled her at first. There was no sign of where the bullet came from so they turned in order to find one of their own trucks to stick with for added safety. The unknown in the dark made it dangerous, there weren't any street signs and in the dark it was hard to tell where to turn to keep from getting blocked in. Each turn seemed to get them even more lost or jammed up in areas and it made the anxiety wreak havoc in both medics.

The village streets were dark, most of them were crowded with clutter or discarded garbage and they knew that under any of the random things on the ground could be an IED so they backed down a few streets to avoid any mess they might get tangled into. Ryker knew hiding behind the reinforced glass or armor of the truck wasn't an option, she climbed into the back of the truck to better watch behind them so Kal could focus on getting them to safety, even if it only meant going back to the outskirt of the city and waiting until they were needed. Two or three streets away the call came out, followed by an eruption of gunfire within earshot. "Flare out" Ryker called out for anyone that needed them to send up one of the signal flares so they knew where to go, the problem was, a flare would also let any enemy fighters know where the soldiers were so it was a hard gamble, one of the other trucks joined in and agreed that they should send up a flare and they'd join in to help clean up the area while the fight was still warming up.

Kal sped off while Ryker tightened down his vest for him, as partners they had to watch out for one another no matter what, even if it meant gearing up the other person so they could drive or work. One time before when Kal and Ryker were first starting out they were headed into a hot area and they knew that they'd be out for a while so they tried to eat on their way out. The vegetarian meal tasted edible but the problem was that the road was so choppy that every time Kal tried to feed a bite to Ryker it either ended up up her nose or being smeared up her chin, leaving them both to laugh hysterically. Kal had a wife and child back home and he wanted two more, but because of his skills and knowledge of the language he knew he could make good money for his family by going out in the military and he was signed for a long tour away from them. Kal called his wife often when there was down time, he always laughed and listened and never admitted to her that he was ever in any danger no matter what.

As soon as the bright flare rose above the homes and buildings the streets lit up like daylight under the red burning flare, they followed the trail backwards and began to head to the northwest corner of town. Ryker cocked and loaded all the guns available and she and Kal fist-bumped for good luck and knew that as soon as they could locate a reasonably safe place to park, they'd have to go and retrieve anyone that needed them on foot and try to stay out of the way. The tactics involved changed with each and every situation, the flare lit up enough of the enemies hunkered down that the back-up truck that arrived ahead of Ryker and Kal was able to find them. The back-up truck had many members of Hotel Company, guys that knew how to get things done and move along. The Tango platoon was just that, the infantry that headed into hot areas and either made them hotter or cooled them off, and they always bragged that they love to *tango*.

There were men hunkered down in many of the corners and a few of them pinned down behind the remnants of a wall, six men lying down and trying to cover themselves as best they could by compressing themselves together to be real small and really still. In the flashes of gunfire it was hard to see who needed what medical attention so Kal kept the headlights out and parked a few buildings away once he navigated what he was doing.Both medics slipped out of their truck and agreed to head as close to the pinned down soldiers as they could and then pull them out. The snaps of gunfire sent bullets whizzing passed them, it made the medics stay hunched down because they both knew all it took was one to catch them there in the dark and then their life was over. Kal took the lead; Ryker kept her left hand on the back of his belt and tucked her fingers into the waist of his pants so they could stay close together as they moved while she kept her tight right hand on a cover weapon aimed ahead of them.

Near the corner of a building Ryker called over to a friendly firing from within, the man introduced himself and leaned out the window, asking how he may take her order. The men pinned down had two good and four wounded with some holes in them, he told her that he'd

give them a fifteen count and give them enough cover fire
with the other soldiers that they should be able to haul the
wounded men out, the problem was there was no telling
how bad they were, they couldn't get a good enough
angle to get them out themselves until the other truck just
arrived, and luckily, they had medics in tow. Ryker
responded with; "*with* them? We're not *their* medics,
they're *our* cleanup crew." Kal laid flat on the ground to
inch closer to see how their patients were laid out, Ryker
laid right on top of him for the same reason, they stayed
close and tried to become one shadow as they peaked
around edges, the gunfire from the other side was close
and hard to determine its' origin, which made it more
nerve racking.

These were the moments that Ryker signed up for
and the ones that got her blood pumping so she was ready
to go. Kal slid out from underneath Ryker and she eased
to his left so they were lying side by side getting ready to
get back to counting; "I love our intimate time, just don't
tell the wife" Kal joked as he and Ryker were both lying
on their sides peering around the edge of a bullet riddled
corner. Sure enough four of the windows in the building
they were spooning had a few bright bursts of gun fire
from the same side of the street came to life to take
offense against the fighters bunked up in a dark building
across the alley, it was their queue. Ryker stayed
crouched while Kal lunged to take cover near the injured
men as fast as possible. Kal grabbed two of the wounded

men by their uniforms and shouted to the uninjured guys that it was time to go before dragging the men backwards.

Ryker staggered on purpose to avoid colliding into Kal and his patients, there were two other men left, one was injured pretty badly, the other "not threatening" according to him. There was a man with a bandage wrapped around his fist, which was still holding tightly onto his issued assault rifle while his free hand was still pushing down on a man lying on his side bleeding. "Orville" the kneeling man offered up his name as Ryker slid towards him on her knees, she in return shouted her name as she snapped off a few rounds into the offending building across the way.

"How are you boys" Ryker asked to find out who was injured and how. "He's hit in the chest, just below the collarbone, started bleeding pretty bad." Ryker asked what was next and what about him. The man began shouting back: "bullet took my pinky, went through my hand and into him, I'm wrapped and good to go, he needs the pressure, I half made a quick plug (referring to plugging the man's bullet wound) but don't lose it." Ryker asked if he was ready to go and they readied for a three count to get back towards the safety of the corner. Orville began shooting. Ryker grabbed a handful of uniform and with her right hand she popped off a few rounds while walking backwards and dragging the wounded man. Orville followed while trying to keep his hand over the bullet wound in his friend he plugged and he held pressure on as the three of them moved together.

Kal was hurrying to load his crew of men into their truck when Ryker was addressing the injured soldier, she was pushing and pulling and once she had an actual wound plug ready to load, she readied Orville to move his hand as they came to a halt near her recovery truck. "Hold on, don't hurry" Orville warned Ryker, she remembered he was hurt too and asked if he had his finger, "there might be a chance for reattachment with any luck" Ryker shouted to the man helping her. "What do you think I plugged his wound with" Orville asked. Ryker stuttered for a moment; "wait, you plugged *his* bullet wound, with *your* finger?" Orville didn't even look at Ryker, his eyes were trained on the houses across the way while he answered;" they told us to put a finger in a bullet wound if we had to, I wanted a place for safe keeping."

Orville looked over his shoulder and smiled, he kept his gun aimed near the corner to make sure they weren't going to be followed as he knelt down. The random snaps of gun fire began to slow a little so Ryker decided it was time to move again. Ryker grabbed the man by his collar and hollered to Orville that she was falling back to the truck she came in, by this point Kal should be sorting guys out and ready to haul out. Ryker kept dragging the wounded man while Orville stepped backwards carefully to watch behind them, Ryker sidestepped to watch both the truck and keep her back to the building full of her fellow soldiers covering their escape. Once at the truck Ryker dragged the wounded man into the back, Orville helped to drag him into the back while still watching around over the sights of his weapon. Ryker scurried around to the passenger side while Orville climbed over a pile of wounded men in the back all moaning and groaning.

Kal was slumped over in the drivers' seat, he was not talking or moving, the slight open slit of his eyes glistened in the night, Ryker knew it wasn't good. "Orville, pull him" Ryker shouted back over her shoulder as she got back out. Ryker Pushed Kal over so that Orville could pull him into the back, two of the conscious soldiers in the back were set up and aiming out of the back hatch to cover their rear while Orville wasn't even near the passenger seat when Ryker started the truck and began her drive. Orville knelt into the front seat, nearly sitting on Rykers' shoulder as he wedged between the seats. Ryker shouted to Orville to help get her out of the city, it was a maze of blocked off streets and Kal usually helped to keep her bearings, but not this time. Ryker worried about getting all of her passengers to safety, she needed a safe enough place to triage the soldiers but nowhere in the city was safe with a truckload of wounded men so she just had to get out, all while worrying about Kal.

With adrenaline flowing like a river breaking through a dam Ryker swiveled her head left and right keeping track of what she saw to each side, she wanted to turn on all the off-road lights to turn the dark narrow streets into an artificial daytime but she also wanted to keep a low profile to her truck full of injured soldiers, including her partner Kal. Kal had a wife and daughter he adored, it was for them he joined the military and used his knowledge of the cultural and languages to help better protect his family back home, his duty to them kept him in danger but also in high spirits when it came to helping to rescue other soldiers, Ryker promised his wife Mhyli that she would do her best to return him to her family in a letter she once wrote for reassurance. Mhyli was nervous about her husband Kal being at war and even though she knew better, he often told her he was doing busy work safely out of the way of harm, he needn't worry her when she had their daughter to care for.

With over half a dozen soldiers in the back of the truck the rear end rode low, it felt heavy on the rough bouncing through the streets. Ryker had a panic guiding her, her hurry was to get the men in the back as much help as possible but also to get them to safety first, there's no use in starting IV's if there's a chance a bullet can still tag them and end their life, it's a waste of supplies and it's reckless to the medics. Frantic rights and cautious lefts had Ryker turn the wheel over and over like she was driving a rally course as Orville did his best to shout directions to help as he half hung out of the passenger window gun first. With two men covering them in the back and Orville manned up beside her she could focus on navigating to find an escape, all she could do was look through the dust covered windshield and do her best to keep headed south, even if she had to drive through some of the desert until coming across the dirt road she came up she'd find her way back and to a secure place to evac out some of the more wounded men by helicopter.

The outer perimeter of the city was met with a vast darkness that spread out like an ocean, the headlights hardly skimmed across the choppy mounds of dirt that settled wherever the wind set them. Ryker pulled hard to the lever that turned on the overhead off-road floodlights, it illuminated small reflective rodent eyes over fifty yards away and the small tufts of plant matter that made for small hills in the sand. Ryker shouted to Orville that it was his turn because she had to check Kal as he lowered his body back into the truck cab and set his weapon down onto the seat. Ryker reached over and slapped Orville on the back of his waist to grab his belt and pull him back into the truck, with all the noise below the tires and clunking of the truck it was hard for him to hear while leaning out far enough to shoot across the truck if he had to. Leaving the dark city behind gave some comfort to Ryker that she was far enough away from danger to get started on her job, it was urgent she check on Kal.

Orville straddled the center of the truck while holding onto the steering wheel, the truck hardly lost momentum as Ryker eased the seat back a little to slide out from under Orville as he slid over to take over driving. With the truck tires following the bright lights on the road the two soldiers traded positions and Ryker slid on her belly back towards Kal, the pile of bodies all jostled around under her as she tried to climb and crawl to inspect wounds. Ryker began triaging, she began to hang the first of a dozen IV bags and she began inserting IV's into forearms of men while stripping and cutting away jackets and shirts looking for bullet holes to plug. Some of the men held tightly onto areas they were hurt and she insisted they keep holding tight while she worked. Every time Ryker tried to wipe some sweat from her brow she soaked her pants with blood from her hands first and blood moved further and further up her arms or across her body. The motion of the truck made her tasks difficult and after eight IV's were hung from some of the safety hooks overhead, she had enough guys sitting up so she could reach Kal; her friend.

Getting attached in combat is often dangerous, it only takes one bad day to lose several people you admire or care about and if you aren't on your game when it comes to trying to give medical help, you can make a bad day worse. Ryker has had plenty of practice administering IV's or plugging wounds while bouncing around in the back of a truck, it was something she had plenty of practice of. While training Ryker and Kal would take a volunteer or two to receive IV sticks while in the back of a truck doing donuts in the desert sand to improve the skills of the medics, namely Ryker or Kal stabbing men with needles while the other person drove as crazy reckless as they could, leaving a few bouncing soldiers

pin-balling around in the back with an open needle just
sticking into clenched forearms mostly. Ryker blinked
away the tears as she searched Kal, his abdomen was
soaked in blood and it was hard to tell who's it was, she
was praying it wasn't his own but there was no way to tell
until she found a hole in him, he was silent the whole
time.

Ryker tore away Kals shirt, she ran her fingers in a
frantic circular pattern to search for that warm spot where
her finger would sink into the skin and feel for the inside
of him telling her she found a bullet entry hole. Ryker
kept Kal wedged between her knees and in the dark she
ran her hands up his sides and around his torso, hoping it
was as it should be.Ryker held onto his right shoulder and
she ran her right hand around his head looking for a wad
of blood soaked hair to tell her whether or not he was shot
in the head, again no such hole. Ryker changed her
position to begin feeling his legs, it was aggravating not
being able to quickly find where he was injured, not being
able to find what was wrong with her friend made the
panic worse, her heart beat and made her chest feel like it
was full of stampeding bulls as sweat poured down her
face, causing the blood on her face to streak down to her
shirt.

Ryker searched frantically, there was no room in
the packed truck bed as men slid beneath her or moved as
she knelt onto a random leg, some men moaned or
garbled something but her focus was on her friend. Ryker

owed it to Mhyli, she owed it to a man that stood next to her and helped to her to save others, she owed it to her father and grandfather for their honor to their country and family, mostly, she was afraid to lose a good friend. Ryker let the tears stream down her face as she shouted, she shouted with anger to Kal that he wasn't ok, she was mad that her friend was hurt and that she couldn't fix him, she was angry that in the truck bed full of soldiers, they were hurt and none of them should have been. Ryker turned and with some help she rolled Kal a little to continue straddling him between her knees so she could get close and run her free hand around the back of him, each time she swept her hands she couldn't find a bullet hole.

"Kerssshhh" the radio squawked causing Ryker to stop for a minute. "Get that, tell them where we are and to hurry the hell up" Ryker shouted to Orville as he was leaned forward over the steering wheel trying to keep the ride as smooth as possible. Orville kept himself pulled close to the steering wheel to peer through the thick layer of dirt on the windshield as he stared out into the night, he didn't have any idea where they were but he knew he had to get the truck to somewhere. Orville shouted into the radio and told the heli-medics to meet them a ways down so they'd be landed and ready to receive many of the wounded soldiers they were hauling, including Kal. As the truck bounced over chunks of rocks in the road Rykers' left thumb slipped down, and in, she found the entrance wound, nearly into Kal's armpit. Ryker pulled her thumb out and used her index finger to explore the wound, she felt collapsed lung and bone fragments, there was no way to figure out how injured he was but she had a start to work with.

Ryker pulled one of the tampon like bullet hole plugs and jammed it into his ribs and then began to hurry to snake a tube down his throat and begin pumping oxygen into his lungs before she started an IV and compression's. She was franticly trying to do everything at once and she did a few compression's on his chest as she scurried to her knees in a circle to keep working with one hand at a time. His chest was rigid and she didn't want to break more ribs but without any fluid in his body for the heart to pump it was no good, she had to get the IV started first, but only after the hole was closed so it didn't pour out any more blood. With one hand squeezing a bag of air into his lungs and the other hanging another bag of IV fluid from a hook knob on the wall Ryker began to compress down, hand over hand as fast as she could to get his lungs to fill and his body to start working.

There was no real way to tell how long Kal had been out of air or blood, there was no response when she first got to him and there was no real guarantee that the aid would help if he had already been dead long but she had to try, he was her friend. "There they are" Orville shouted from the front talking about the medic chopper they were racing towards. The chopper was already on the ground with three men ready to receive most of the most wounded from Ryker's truck before they hurried off to the hospital. Orville skidded and jerked the wheel sending a cloud of dust and dirt into the wafting air of the helicopter wash, he cranked the wheel so the back end of the truck was closer to the chopper for faster offload. Orville threw himself out of the drivers seat before the truck was completely stopped and jerked down the back hatch to help offload wounded with his weapon slung around his back. The two men that were covering the rear of the truck rolled out and helped to pull the least of the wounded out, there were nine men in total in that truck, Ryker, Kal, Orville and six others.

Once the helicopter was almost loaded it was time to pull Kal out and load him next, but Ryker was still straddled across him doing chest compression's, refusing to give up. Two of the medics pulled on Kal's legs to get him into the helicopter, Orville caught Ryker and with a bear hug around her waist he pulled her to him so the medics could take over and try to help him. In the blowing sands of the helicopter wash and flashing lights there was no way to hear anyone, Ryker tried to fight off Orville, her arms had no strength left after pushing down on Kals chest for who knows how long so they hung down, her legs tried to kick but they felt like cement after clutching Kal for so long so they hung too.Ryker was soaked in the blood of half a dozen soldiers, including her own and her head also hung down.

Paper Paulie

The blood on her face was crusty and streaked from her tears washing it down onto her shirt and yet, she tried to fight;she fought for Kal, she fought to bring Mhyli her husband and father to future children, she fought to keep her friend alive when she'd lost other patients and soldiers before, she found to keep alive her sense of self and reason for doing what she did, Ryker was out of energy to fight but she fought the notion of no longer fighting but she no longer had anything left in her. Orville just held her.

Paper Paulie

Ch. 13

After Orville felt Rykers' body stop fighting and begin to go limp he began to set her down, he knew why she was fighting and he kept his head leaned back so the back of her head didn't connect with his face, her body nearly dropped when he thought her feet would touch the ground so he turned her and hugged her to get a better hold as the helicopter rose high above them. Ryker sobbed, she couldn't lift her arms and as the sound of the helicopter faded her balling turned to a sob. A soldier named Wade climbed into the driver's seat and stood up to shout across the top, "Get her in, I got us." Orville dragged Ryker around to the back and fireman carried Ryker into the truck then set her down. Orville sat in one of the small benches and kept Ryker seated between her legs so she didn't jostle much or fall over, all she could do was keep his arms around her shoulders and rest her head on his forearm.

Orville had a firefight a few months before that left him in such shape so he knew exactly how the medic rescuer felt. Orville and his small squad were tasked with roaming down some streets looking for a main target when they were surprised by a young boy that reminded him of his nephew back home. The small boy had to have been maybe six, he held a piece of fruit in his hand and as he got near, one of the solders tried to instruct him to go back home but it was too late when the explosion went off. The little boy was strapped down with some homemade rigging and when the bomb went off, it immediately killed three of the six men that were in the alley. Orville was splattered with the remnants' of his bunk-mate that was in front of him, and that bunk-mate was the only reason he lived through the explosion. As soon as the body parts and dust began to hit the ground men began to charge down the alley way towards them.Enemy combatants loaded with automatic guns and grenades to hurl at the soldiers that were trapped in a gauntlet of tall walls charged towards the soldiers and all they could do was fight.

Orville knelt down and began to shoot; it was a matter of saving the last few men of his small squad in hopes of making it home on his own. The garb clad men poured down the street as the marksmanship of the soldiers kept them alive; wave after wave of enemies seemed to stand up after the row in front of them dropped, it seemed endless. Orville kept his body snugged close to a wall and each time a bullet kissed the wall just in front of him it peppered him with shards of cement and it gave him the surge of adrenaline that came with such a close call with death. Each new divot in the wall made his fingers truer with each shot knowing that at any moment a bullet could take his life. The last few men in the fire fight held out, they didn't know how long they had to last or how long they had until their ammo ran out but in the heat of the fight, all that they could focus on what their target and the next shot they were going to make.

When the firefight was over a rescue truck came and with a full load of men, Orville and two other men were pulled out of the heart of a nasty ambush.In all, three soldiers died immediately from the blast while another died later of gunshot wounds leaving Orville and one other to take stock of how close they really were to dying right there on that dirty street that day, there were also twenty seven enemy fighters expired at the end of the fight, proving to Orville that it was his skill as a soldier that was the only reason he'd even see another sunrise. When the fight was over Orville and his comrade Strasburg hugged in gratitude and relief. The emotion that suddenly poured out of the two men that survived was suddenly onset and overwhelming. Orville didn't know how to handle the draining sort of crying that flooded him after the firefight was over, he hugged Strasburg who was another built man with arms as big around as his head and in a tight grip, they just hugged. Some of the rescue soldiers walked passed and knew how fortunate they were, congratulatory back pats happened as the rescue soldiers were pleased to get some of their men back safely and alive, they also paid their respects to the fallen.

Orville held onto Rykers' hands in the back of that truck, she kept her head down and let the moment of safety come over her, she was out of the danger but there was no word on Kal and all she had for that drive was the comfort of another human being to be there with her for a few bleak moments. Orville was proud to be able to thank the soldier that helped to save his crew and fellow soldiers, he knew firsthand the relief it is to see rescue, and medics, when you need them, he was thankful for Ryker and Kal and he also prayed that Kal was going to be alright, as well as his crewmen that fell back on the streets. Ryker was all but limp, she was braced upright between Orville's legs; he was holding her up just as much as he was trying to hold her for comfort.Ryker worked hard and risked her life for others'; she deserved some peace for a moment. The rest of the drive was just to the hum of the tires on the sand below; the driver reached up and turned the radio off to give his two passengers some quiet, everyone needed it.

The truck came to a halt; the security of the base was a welcome sight through the dust laden windshield with a spider web looking crack in it. Ryker hardly moved when Orville moved them both to the back. Ryker let her head hang and when she looked down at all of her bloodied clothes she began to pull at her shirt, the clotting blood made her shirt stick to her and it started to make her feel like she was being choked. Orville tried to calm Ryker, she lost her best friend and after such an exhausting ride trying to juggle the lives in a truck full of soldiers she was depleted of anything that made sense anymore. Ryker pulled and tugged at her shirt, she cursed and cried while fighting to stay standing up but weaving and wavering. *"Shhh"* Orville tried to calm the medic as she pulled at her own shirt trying to get all of the blood off of her. Ryker was half spinning circles trying to fight her own shirt and gravity while stumbling, Orville just tried to figure out how he could help his rescuer.

Ryker stood and yanked at her shirt, she didn't care about her surroundings but for the sake of discretion Orville was glad it was still dark out. Orville looked away from the medic standing in a blood soaked bra and dried blood all over her whole body, the half dried clots shimmered a little in the squint lights. Orville hurried to pull his shirt up and over his head; in doing so he pulled it down over Ryker and covered her in a dry shirt before hoisting her up onto his shoulder again and picking up his own gear in his free hand. Ryker couldn't do anything but weep as she swayed with the cadence of Orville and his walking. Orville knew he should have checked in with his platoon leader but he owed this soldier a little more appreciation, the truck was a disaster and the driver was already on his way to check in so he shouted; "Wade, tell sarge I'm taking a break, I'll be over at midday after nap time to head back out.

Orville headed to the showers, he knew that he might risk getting in trouble for what he planned to do but the girl needed to be showered off of the blood to begin to find some peace so that was what he was going to do. "Do you have a phone or anything that can't get wet?" Orville asked as he pulled the door open on the showers, each stall was small but Orville planned to just set her in the water to soak and rinse clothes and all before walking her to her bunk to sleep. Orville reached up to turn the water on while Ryker stayed slung over his shoulder, she was quiet and didn't respond when he asked her. Orville waited for the water to warm and eased Ryker down, there was nothing she could do she was so tired and the blood that washed off of her left dark circles on the tile below her. Orville squatted down and tried to run his wet hands down her face as they both sat in the warming streams of water. Each time Orville ran his thumbs down her face he held her gently and tried to clean the blood off of her, the shirt of his she wore suctioned to her body but some of his own blood that had gotten on the shirt began to lessen with the water as they both sat there; soaking wet.

The warm water gave some life to Ryker, her short hair had to keep being wiped to the side by Orville as he continued to try to ask her questions, he needed to know where her bunk was so that he could get her to her home safely and to dry clothes and to her rack so she could get some much needed sleep, he too was exhausted but this soldier needed his help first, she spent so long helping everyone else, including him that he wanted to return the favor. Ryker began to squirm, she tried to kick her feet a little and Orville jumped back a little, he apologized over and over, he wasn't trying to be forceful or anything, just trying to help clean her up of all the blood. Concern filled Orville, he couldn't tell if the medic was freaking out because she was realizing that he took her to the showers despite the fact she was fully clothed or perhaps she was frantic because she didn't realize who he was, he did his best to be reassuring but her kicking and sloshing in the water rendered his attempts useless.

Ryker fought to get her hand into her pocket while rocking back and forth, her wet pants made it hard so she turned frantically from side to side to wedge her hand into her pocket as Orville just stood there and watched, trying to figure out how to help the soldier. Ryker let the water stream down her as she pulled up a small black something from her pocket and she began to smile. The smile was mixed with a little bit of sobbing and a little bit of laughter, a tired sort of laughter that could only come after such a night. Orville squatted back down and wrapped his hands around hers and asked her what was so funny. "Paulie" she said barely louder that the noise of the running shower as water dripped down the hair hanging in front of her face with her head leaning forward. Orville let his hands run down her forearms to finish wiping off the smudges of blood as he tried to smile enough to fake that he had any sort of idea what she was talking about.

The half laugh returned to a whimper but a relieved sort of crying, no longer the painful and scared crying as she began to tell Orville about what Paper

Paulie was and everything she could remember. Orville let Ryker keep talking as she stared at the small square she held so tightly onto, he turned the water off and eased her back up and over his shoulder after he tried to stand her up and she refused. Orville interrupted a few times until he got an answer to his question about where her bunk was, he wanted to make sure she got home to warm dry clothes then he had to check on his fellow soldiers and then get back to work himself. Orville carried Ryker halfway across the base, his own wet pants made the trek laborious and his shouldered cargo dripped down on him was rubbing his shoulder raw also. Ryker's boots rubbed together while Orville kept his arm wrapped over the backs of her knees to keep her in one place so he could walk, Ryker quieted down after she thanked Paulie over and over again for keeping her safe.

Orville reached his destination, he carried Ryker into her small barracks and set her down onto her cot, she let her head fall onto her hands in her depleted state, her mumbling slurred with exhaustion. Orville stood closely and hugged her in thanks again for saving him and some of his men, he left her a deep and sincere apology and well wishes for her friend Kal and his hopes for the medics' recovery. As Orville stepped towards the door Ryker stood up and began to change out of her wet clothes, because of this Orville didn't even look back when he said his goodbye and he pulled the door shut behind him. Ryker struggled to get out of her wet gear, her boots were full of water, the shirt was way too large for her and it felt like a wet blanket to try and fight to get out of and her legs were red and raw as she slid her pants down, a mix of blood and redness from the wet pants rubbing back and forth. Ryker hardly made sense of things; everything was blurry and was a mix of numbness and had a dreary haze before just crashing into her cot.

Ryker crawled into her bunk, the comfort of a place to sleep nearly attacked her, she held onto Paulie tightly and in an instant, her eyelids met and she was asleep. Ryker couldn't recall sleeping, she couldn't recall hearing anything or anybody, not even the morning reveille and it was midday before she could figure out her senses and realized that she had slept away most of her day. Ryker sat up to find that her legs ached, trying to raise her arms up to pull back her covers enlightened her to how bad her arms hurt also. The pain of her arms only equaled the pain in her head, she knew she felt dehydrated and began to look around for any number of water bottles she normally kept at hand, her arms throbbed from her wrists all the way up to her neck, her body was tight from her head to her midsection and it made breathing a chore, she realized she was in rough shape by her third conscious breath. Looking down for water brought Ryker to look at Paulie; sitting on her pillow where he fell when she did and it immediately brought all of the previous nights' events back to her, right to the memory of passing out, which caused Ryker to pause before letting her eyes dart around the room.

Ryker set her feet down onto a pile of bloodied and still soaking wet clothes, the sight of the messy pile was grotesque and bloodied water oozed out under her weight. The commotion outside brought her realization to where she was, as soon as she could reach a few bottles of water she chugged two in a row and grabbed a third for a traveler as she stepped towards her shelves. Her clothes were ruined with blood, the clotted and stained underthings were not salvageable so she traded them out for new and clean and redressed for the day. Ryker dug out some aspirin from one of her first aid kits and put two more water bottles in her pockets and after kissing Paulie in thanks she put him in his rightful place and stepped out. The base was as it always was; people with thing to do and keep moving on, the normal routines and day to day activities, she felt a little behind so she needed to get back to work. Ryker felt every tense muscle in her body and even though she hadn't had anything alcoholic to drink she still felt hung-over with the pounding headache and full body of aches and pains.

Ryker went to begin cleaning out her wrecked truck, the large amount of blood dripped from it when she got out the night before and there was garbage strewn all over and even though it was a common sight after multiple traumas and casualties (and now without Kal) she knew she was in for some hearty cleaning before it was ready to get going again. Ryker stepped into the truck yard and to her surprise she found that her truck had been scrubbed and squeegeed. Ryker was in awe; the back had been washed out and there were no sign of wrappers or any of the cut and shredded bloodied rags or shirts or jackets or nothing. She looked for the dents she or Kal put in the fenders to ensure that it was indeed her truck and sure enough there was no mistaken that it was her assigned medic truck, she just couldn't make sense of things. Ryker found her higher commander Haaseth and sat down to rundown how everything happened, reports that all had to be filed and as they waited for news of Kal, she asked who cleaned her truck.

The commander Haaseth had no idea; her truck was back and in such order when she was in in the morning so she didn't question it. Ryker was astounded; the only thing that made sense was that Orville must have done it after he left her, that soldier must have cleaned her up and even after such a night, he must have returned and cleaned up her truck for her, absolutely amazing. Ryker looked around the post and she struggled to ask if anyone knew who Orville was, the problem was, there was no such person. Ryker searched for Orville during the rest of her tour, there were only a few short weeks before she was supposed to transition out and it was essential to find the soldier that saved her and she grew desperate. Post operators only had one Orville listed in the entire list of troops in the desert but he was a fifty-eight year old general and definitely not the man she had to thank in person. Ryker searched all over in her free time for Orville, the man didn't know her and was gallant in not trying to cop a feel or be a crude person, he was a soldier and a gentleman and she wanted to thank him in person for helping her when she really needed it but she couldn't find him.

[Back to the preacher talking] I had the pleasure of meeting Isaiah before he passed, he was filled with a profound pride in his family, in himself as a soldier and in the communities that he leant himself to, up in Brooklyn, Scranton, and here in North Carolina. In the care of hospice Isaiah had no fears, he lived a long life that anyone would be proud of, he had Sydney; a son that built an amazing life for himself with Shayla and their daughter Ryker; a strong leader that lived up to her name. Isaiah told me all about Paper Paulie and that is why I had to tell this story, an intricate design the universe spun and twisted that awed me. Isaiah passed on on a Tuesday and was surrounded by his loved ones, his dear wife Delores that was beside him for many decades and the center of his universe, Sydney and Shayla and the love that bonded them together for life and Ryker, such a strong beautiful soldier that is the epitome of what a soldier should be.

For all of you gathered today, thank you for listening to me go on and on and I'm almost done if you'll just hang on with me a little longer. Isaiah told me before he passed that he wanted me to thank Paulie for everything; for a long life overflowing with love, for the adventure of marriage and children and grandchildren and even growing old, every single day since he received Paulie, Paper Paulie was there for it. Isaiah knew that his time was limited; he and Delores moved here to North Carolina when they finally decided to retire and they built up another great group of loved ones, they enjoyed their community and when Ryker received Paper Paulie, he knew that she was in safe hands. Paper Paulie was by his side when Isaiah let out his last "I love you" to his beloved wife and family, he held Paper Paulie one last time and handed him back to Ryker, his newest keeper and then his life left him.

Many of you here have never even heard of small Paper Paulie (preacher holds him up) and that is why you had to hear about him and his legacy. I am moved to be able to finish my story for those of you here that don't know it, so for just a few more minutes and I will get back to the end of my story.

Ryker searched all over for Orville up until she was packing up to set out. It had only been a few weeks and she had her orders to go home. Now I stand before you and want to welcome Ms. Ryker Mallery Venney, daughter of Sidney and Shayla Venney and granddaughter of Delores and the late Isaiah Venney, also the fairy god-child of Paper Paulie. I would also like to introduce Kasten Earnest Harwell, a man of strong family name; originally heard by Ryker as "Orville" in the midst of the gunfire that night. As Ryker was packing her clothes an oversized shirt that had come back from the laundry with her stuff was out of place, she didn't have any reason for such a large shirt but in curiosity she looked at the name tag printed on the bottom to find the name: "Harwell, K.E." and in finding its' rightful owner, she found the man that unknowingly meant so much to her.

I would like to unite Ryker and Kasten in holy matrimony and with the witness of their best man, Armand Kal and may Paper Paulie preside over them as he has long before either of them were ever born (claps and cheers begin to roar) I have one more grand thanks, owed from years back, there is a gentleman in attendance, Kasten's grandfather George. Without much memory of the events, I'd like, on behalf of the Venneys' to thank him for his creation of Paper Paulie so many years ago when he was a young boy just following a writing assignment and mailing a simple paper doll to a lonely soldier fighting for our country. Through whatever the world may have thrown together, over forty years later, the grandchildren of the two strangers that became pen-pals for a brief time are now husband and wife. If Isaiah had not told me the name locked so deep inside the sealed Paper Paulie, I never would have made the connection of whom Kasten's grandfather was once the introductions were made this week preparing for the wedding.

Sometimes there are no answers, sometimes there is no real reason things happen and as much as Isaiah would have loved to hug the man that was once the young boy that mailed him Paper Paulie he passed on just weeks too soon. I stand before and unite two families that were tied together through Paper Paulie in the late sixties without any idea from either man. I am amazed and in awe of the workings of the universe and find myself truly inspired. May everyone here take in the amazement and without any prejudice, without any judgment or doubt, for what it is, just be amazed. The world can be amazing if you let yourself see such things. Forget about the things that taint your heart, forget about the small things that might knock you from your inner peace and just let yourself be truly amazed by the world around you.

With Paper Paulie as bearer and witness, Kasten Ernest Harwell, you may now take Ryker Mallery Venney as your lawfully wedded wife.